Flight Risk

Flight Risk

Nicole Helm

SAMHAIN PUBLISHING

Samhain Publishing, Ltd.
11821 Mason Montgomery Road, 4B
Cincinnati, OH 45249
www.samhainpublishing.com

Flight Risk
Copyright © 2013 by Nicole Helm
Print ISBN: 978-1-61921-952-6
Digital ISBN: 978-1-61921-618-1

Editing by Tera Kleinfelter
Cover by Angela Waters

First Samhain Publishing, Ltd. electronic publication: August 2013
First Samhain Publishing, Ltd. print publication: August 2014

Dedication

For my Grandpa Taylor, whose Antique Airfield is the inspiration for Antiques in Flight. In pursuing your passion, you inspired me to pursue mine.

And for my Grandma Taylor, for always being exactly what I needed. I miss you every day.

Chapter One

Trevor Steele loosened the tie around his neck. It had been choking him all day. He sank into a blue-and-white-striped couch and stared at the fireplace mantel. An orderly row of family pictures smiled back. Mom, Dad, Shelby and him, years ago, frozen in time.

Half the people in those pictures were dead and buried, and Trevor was left with the aftermath.

He glanced at his eighteen-year-old sister, hovering near the door. The black dress and heels should have made her look older, but with her dark blonde hair pulled into a ponytail and no makeup on, she looked like a little girl playing dress up.

What was he supposed to do with a kid graduating from high school in two months? A kid he'd barely been around the past four years and barely talked to in between undercover assignments. A kid who had just lost her mother. A kid who had nothing left.

Except him.

The choking feeling persisted, but there were no more articles of clothing to free from his neck.

"So..." His voice came out raspy. He'd been talking all day. Talking to people he'd known his whole life. Listening to Pilot's Point residents wax poetic about his mother's dedication to the town. Then people had gone on about his dad. The five years in between their deaths had disappeared, and it was as if he'd lost them both in the same day.

The pressure to be what Shelby needed and the town

expected felt like a noose. He wished for the anonymity of pretending to be someone else, but his undercover days were suddenly, irrevocably, painfully over. Even if he stayed with the FBI, he now had to be Trevor Steele all the time, for Shelby.

"I'm going to go upstairs." Her voice was little more than a whisper and she didn't look at him. In fact, Trevor hadn't seen her blue eyes angled toward him since he'd returned home from Seattle.

Too late.

His mother had still been breathing when he'd arrived, but barely. He'd said his good-byes to a quickly failing body. Not to Mom. There had been no miracle hand squeeze. She'd merely faded away and the words *too late* had haunted him ever since.

"Shelby." Trevor stood, at a loss. He wanted to comfort her, to make the pain go away, but all that came out was a lame apology. "I'm so sorry. I thought we had more time."

For the first time in a week, Shelby met his gaze. Identical blue eyes studied each other. "I think we all thought that. Even Mom."

Trevor crossed to her, guilt eating away any lingering uncertainty. He pulled her into his arms. It wasn't the first time he'd hugged her. The minute he'd walked into his mother's room at the hospice center, he had hugged Shelby exactly like this. Holding on while their mother slipped away.

"I love you." It wasn't something he said often, but as they were the only two people each other had left in terms of family, it seemed the right moment to say it.

She didn't respond, and he couldn't blame her. For the past five months of their mom's final battle with cancer, Trevor had been undercover. If Mom had pushed the envelope, he could have been pulled out, but Shelby was right. Even Mom thought she had more time.

"I love you too," Shelby replied, her slim frame shaking as she cried into his shoulder.

When the doorbell rang interrupting the moment, Trevor had to fight the urge to yell at the unfortunate visitor. Why couldn't the damn town let them alone with their grief?

Shelby pulled away, wiping her face with the back of her hand. "I'll get it."

But Trevor held her there, not ready to let the moment go without some reassurance. She looked so young despite the stress of the past six months. Her exhaustion was evident everywhere—the sagging shoulders, the black under her eyes. Yet she was taking the responsibility of parceling out flowers after the visitation, sending thank-you notes, answering the door.

Trevor worked up the courage to say the words he hoped she needed to hear. "It's never going to be okay that Mom's gone, but we'll find a way to get through it." *We.* A word that added weight to that noose.

She nodded and managed a wobbly smile as the doorbell rang again. "Welcome back to Pilot's Point where everyone pokes into your business." Her hand reached out to the doorknob, but she paused for a moment. "I'm so glad you're home. I don't know what I'd do without you here."

She didn't look at him, instead opened the door before he could formulate a response. His throat closed and it was hard to manage a breath. Shelby was under the impression he was staying inevitably. Trevor had taken a six-month leave of absence.

When Shelby opened the door, Trevor's guilt melted into relief. Callie Baker stood on the threshold. She'd changed from the black dress she'd worn to the funeral into jeans and a fitted black T-shirt. In each hand was a brown bag.

For the first time since he'd returned home, his mouth moved into the ghost of an honest smile.

"Calloway." Shelby scowled as she spat Callie's full name.

"Shelby," Callie returned. Callie's hands tightened on the bags, but she didn't snap at the use of her full name as Trevor expected. "I'm sorry about your mom."

Shelby's expression didn't change. If she was surprised by Callie's offered sympathy, it wasn't surprise enough to be polite.

"Shelby, don't be..." Trevor trailed off lamely. Under the circumstances, telling his sister not to be her usual bitchy self to Callie didn't seem right. "Don't be impolite."

Callie looked at him over Shelby's head, a smile tugging at the corner of her lips. She didn't have to speak for him to know what she was thinking. *Impolite? Seriously?*

"The polite thing to do would be to not show up where you know you're not wanted."

Callie's smile changed immediately from amused to the kind of sharp smile she usually flashed before offering a scathing comment. "I'm only half not wanted."

In terms of Callie's comebacks, it was tame, but Shelby turned on her heel and stomped past Trevor and up the stairs. At the sound of a door slamming above, Callie's smirk died.

"I'm sorry. I shouldn't have said anything. I wouldn't have come over, but I do owe you." She held up the two bags in her hand. "Vodka or tequila? Take your pick."

"You take the tequila, I'll take the vodka, and we'll work from there." All he could think was thank God she was here. Not just because of the alcohol, but because Callie was someone who would understand exactly what he needed right now.

"Fair enough." She stood in the doorway, not making a move to come in. They studied each other, silently assessing the changes over the past two years.

She was tall, lean and gorgeous as ever. The T-shirt she wore showed off the muscled arms she got from tinkering with antique airplanes. He'd never thought muscles on a woman were particularly sexy, but Callie had a way of making everything just that.

Her straight black hair was pulled into a long ponytail and brown eyes studied him from behind thick black lashes. She didn't wear makeup and rarely had in all the years he'd known her.

She had a little kewpie doll mouth that looked out of place on an otherwise angular face. Trevor knew that mouth could curse as creatively as any man he'd ever worked with, snap off the most sarcastic comebacks he'd ever heard, and kiss really, really well.

That's what happened the last time he'd seen Callie. She'd kissed him senseless before he'd pushed her away. He still kind of regretted that, but the kiss had stemmed from grief after her grandfather's funeral. So he'd pushed her away before she'd done any damage.

He hadn't seen her since, but they'd exchanged emails and texts when he wasn't undercover, as they always had since he'd left Pilot's Point. Over the course of the past two years, neither had acknowledged their one and only foray into more than friendship. Judging by her demeanor, that wasn't about to change now.

Callie hadn't stepped inside the Steele's brick ranch house in years. Little had changed, even if the man who stood in front of her had.

He'd been tall since freshman year when he'd shot up almost four inches over the summer, but all that teenage gawkiness was now filled in with lean, hard muscles, evident even under the layers of his suit. His dark hair was buzzed short, and those vivid blue eyes remained the focal point of his chiseled face. It was the kind of face that got a lot of female attention. Even though they'd always been *just* friends, it was no hardship looking at Trevor.

"The tequila is genius," he offered. Only then did Callie realize she was still hovering in front of the door, and they were studying each other in similar appraisal.

"We went through the vodka in about an hour after your..." He trailed off like he couldn't get the words out.

Two years and she struggled with it herself, not that she would show it. "After Gramps's funeral." Callie moved into the living room. "Funerals seem to be the only way we see each other anymore, Mr. Hot Shot FBI Agent."

He smiled a little, but it didn't last long and his mouth released into that tired, contemplative look people got after dealing with death. "Yeah, well, that's about to change."

"You're not staying permanently." Not a question, a statement. Callie knew as well as anyone Trevor had spent his adolescence waiting to escape Pilot's Point for the big world out there, just as much as Callie had always scoffed at the outside world in favor of home.

Trevor shrugged, unscrewed the top of the vodka and took a long swig right from the bottle. He winced as he swallowed the giant gulp. "For the foreseeable future. Six months leave of absence."

"I guess you can't leave Shelby here alone."

"She's going to UNI in the fall, but we've got to get through graduation and the summer first." His mouth was a grim line. "I figure six months gets me to September. Once she's settled in to college life, I go back." He gestured toward the couch, taking another big swig. "Make yourself comfortable."

Callie looked at the room. Trevor used to try and help her with her homework on that exact coffee table. Mrs. Steele always bringing them snacks and checking on their progress while Shelby complained she couldn't watch her cartoons. Callie always trying to convince Trevor they should do anything besides homework.

The Steeles were valedictorians, pillars of society, and Callie—aside from the last two years—had been the wild child of Pilot's Point. Taking a seat on the blue-striped couch was like stepping back in time, erasing all the changes she'd worked hard to make.

Because that old inadequacy surrounded her, some of the old defenses cropped up. "I've been on the straight and narrow for two years now. Your sister sure knows how to hold a grudge."

"Yeah, you wouldn't know anything about that. Would you?" He grinned and took a seat next to her.

Callie shrugged, but a smile tugged at the corners of her mouth. She'd always felt a little less in the shadow of Trevor's seemingly perfect life, but he'd never made her feel that way. Even when he was teasing her. Shelby was the one who made her feel like the loser from the wrong side of the tracks. "My grudges are fair though."

"Uh huh." Trevor took another long pull from his bottle, studied hers. "I'm not drinking alone, am I?"

Callie looked at the unopened bottle in her hand. She hadn't touched a drop of alcohol in two years. Two years of cleaning up her act in her best effort to keep Antiques in Flight afloat. What good had it done?

Thinking of her own problems, Callie unscrewed the top. Maybe a good drunk would be just what she needed. The liquid

13

burned its way down, a reminder of too many nights spent at the end of a bottle. What was one more? Besides, Trevor had offered her the same comfort two years ago. Her turn.

"Shelby thinks I'm staying. Permanently." He stared at the bottle in his hands, blinked.

"Then she doesn't know you very well." Of course, Callie knew Trevor well enough to know that added to the pain of losing his mother, he was now laying a heavy dose of guilt on himself.

"Why would she know me, Callie? We're eleven years apart and before last week I'd barely been home for four years. Why should I expect her to have any idea that me staying here is equal to a prison sentence?"

Callie looked at her own bottle. She'd never understood Trevor's need to always be moving, doing, getting out. In Callie's world, nothing was better than Pilot's Point. It was comfort, it was memory, it was *home*.

"Change," Trevor muttered, looking down at the bottle in his hands. He took another swig. "I'm supposed to be good at it." He shook his head, looking so beat down she wanted to soothe him. Unfortunately, Callie had never learned how to soothe away someone's hurt. She'd been too busy indulging in her own. She could offer a bottle of booze or a joke, but true comfort? Not Calloway Baker.

"It's not fair," he said, his voice scratchy and uneven. "She's eighteen. Two months away from graduating. Mom should be here. Hell, Dad should be here. It isn't right and it isn't fair and..." He shook his head again as he trailed off.

The words hurt because she remembered what it was like. Walking down that aisle wearing the cap and gown and knowing the people who were supposed to be there weren't. To have someone tell you those people were there in spirit or watching from heaven or whatever other bullshit excuses people used to try and help or soothe.

It wasn't true. Her parents hadn't been there in spirit, her grandma didn't have some special lens from heaven. They had been dead. Buried. Gone. At graduation the only people watching her flip that tassel with any vested interest were Gramps and Em. Now she only had Em left.

For the first time in her life, Callie felt a little empathy for Shelby Steele.

"I'm sorry, Cal," Trevor muttered, and his hand rested on her knee. "This must hit a little close to home."

Callie shrugged. "Been a long time." The memories would fade; some of the pain would too. Alcohol would help hurry the process along.

"It's not about me today. It's about Shelby. And you." She covered his hand with hers, and then carefully removed it from her knee. She took another sip, a little longer this time.

"I don't want to think about me," he muttered, leaning into the back of the couch. "Tell me about AIF."

From one depressing subject to another. Callie thought of the fly-in, the annual gathering of members of Antiques in Flight, where AIF made the majority of its money for the year. Antique enthusiasts flew or drove out to the airport and spent five days camping, eating, enjoying each other's planes, checking out the museum and library.

Last year, most people had attended to memorialize Gramps, but after so many problems, the donations had dropped significantly.

Callie opened her mouth to deflect the topic, but the truth tumbled out. "Em and I are holding on by a thread. If we don't recover from last year's disaster of a fly-in, we'll lose it all." She hadn't meant to be bleak about it, but in her head the fly-in in

15

six months would either make or break Antiques in Flight.

If Callie lost AIF along with everything else, she didn't think she'd make it.

Callie took another deep drink, willing the liquor to kick in. "Let's talk about something really stupid," she suggested before Trevor started to try and comfort her. He was the kind of guy who would offer comfort to someone else after his own mother's funeral. She was the type of woman who brought booze and bad news.

"I think the Cubs have a chance to go all the way this year."

"Yeah, right. This is really going to be their year." It was good to laugh. It had been a while since she'd had someone to laugh with. All she and Em ever talked about were bills, business and "what are we going to do"? There certainly wasn't much laughter when you faced losing your family's one and only legacy.

Trevor's smile faded quickly. "What would I do without you?"

Callie tried to keep the smile, keep some of the laughter, but it was slipping away again. "You do without me on a pretty regular basis."

"Not for the important stuff. You've always been there."

Callie sighed. She couldn't expect Trevor to focus on the happy. She knew how it felt to lose both your parents in such a short time. Of course, she'd been considerably younger. Still, it was important for Trevor to know he had people he could count on. That's what her grandparents had given her, until they'd passed away too. "You've always been there for me, Trev. This is payback." She'd buried her grief in the wrong guy, in alcohol, in bad behavior, and any time she'd needed to be bailed out, he'd been there.

Callie rested her hand on top of his. "It's hard, and with

Shelby it's even harder. I know you both pretty well, and you're the strongest, most together people I know. It's a lot to deal with, but you'll both deal. Eventually things get to a point where they're bearable. Besides, once Shelby's away at college she won't expect you to hang around Pilot's Point waiting for her to come home on break. She'll understand you have to go back to your life in Seattle."

Trevor seemed to consider this as he stared at her hand on top of his. He turned his so that they now touched palm to palm. There was a spark, some low humming sizzle of something. Just like when she'd kissed him two years ago. Had that spark always been there and she'd been so busy trying to drown out all her feelings she'd never noticed, or was it something newer, something born out of adulthood, of the people they'd become?

Frustrated, Callie broke the physical contact. Maybe old Callie would have been bold and foolish enough to try and find out, but this was the new Callie. Responsible, sensible, mature. Now was not the time to be thinking about attraction and sparks. If there were ever a time to do something that stupid. New Callie knew there were too many risks and too much outside stuff going on right now to worry about something so trivial.

Sometimes she really missed old Callie.

Trevor shifted so their knees brushed, and Callie looked up. He was staring at her, studying her face with a focused intensity that never failed to make her squirm. When his gaze dropped to her lips, his body moved slightly toward hers, even as her heartbeat increased, Callie knew she had to end the moment before it started. Too tired and scared to tiptoe around the subject, she went for straightforward.

"Don't even think about it," she muttered, staring down at the bottle. She was still embarrassed she'd thrown herself at him two years ago. Embarrassed at how easily Trevor had pushed her away and rationally explained she was acting out of grief.

No shit.

"Oh, I think about it," he returned, though his words were slightly slurred. He gestured his bottle toward her. "You don't kiss a guy like that and expect him to forget."

"It was a mistake." Maybe over the course of the past two years she'd found herself wondering if it had *just* been drunken grief, but she'd cleaned up her life enough to know exploring a romantic thing with Trevor would be the biggest mistake she could make. He was her oldest friend, her biggest champion. Mixing that up would mean potentially losing him.

"I know it was."

She refused to analyze why his agreement irritated her. "So let's not repeat it." It was best to forget she'd ever blurred the lines. Best to keep pretending that stupid kiss had been nothing, a little fluke of a mistake due to heartache and alcohol.

"You're right."

Time to change the subject, and create a little distance. Go back to the main reason for her coming by. Comfort. Help. "We need something to eat with all this liquor. I'll go rummage around for a snack. You see if you can find something to watch on TV."

At Trevor's terrible attempt to hide a wince, Callie stood. "I can make a sandwich or open a bag of chips."

"Are you sure about that? I've heard kitchens are known to spontaneously combust when you walk into them."

Just like that they were back on even ground. Exactly where they should be.

Chapter Two

Callie drove away from the Steele house, away from the epicenter of Pilot's Point, out into farmland and curving two-lane highway. The world around was greening up as April meandered its way toward warmer temperatures.

On another day, she might have enjoyed the beautiful morning scene. She might have rolled down the windows of her ancient Ford Taurus and smiled. This morning, a headache pounded behind her eyes and the contents of her stomach sloshed uneasily back and forth.

Monday morning with a hangover was no way to start the week. Monday morning waking up with Trevor's head cradled in her lap *and* a hangover was the worst way to start the week. She felt fuzzy, sick and confused.

She pulled into the gate of AIF and onto the gravel drive that led to the cluster of buildings. Gravel popped under her tires as she came to a slow stop. Instead of heading down past the office buildings, hangars and grass runway to the cabin she and Em shared, Callie parked in front of the library and stepped out.

She was already ten minutes late for Em's weekly Monday morning pep talk so there was no time for a shower and hangover breakfast. Instead of heading inside though, Callie stood for a moment. There was a cool breeze blowing in from the west with the faintest hint of spring's earthy scent. Dew sparkled on the grass around the buildings. Mowing would need to start soon. More work and they were already running themselves ragged. At this rate, she'd be mowing by moonlight most weeks.

Callie shaded her eyes and looked at the office, the Canteen and her shop. The sun's rays bounced off the gray metal buildings making them sparkle along with the dew. The blue and red trim would need to be repainted before September. More to-dos. They never ended. It could get frustrating or overwhelming at times, but it was better than the alternative. Losing it all. When Callie looked at all the beauty and memories around her, fear of losing it all grew exponentially.

Callie took a deep breath and allowed herself a moment— just a moment—to dwell on what might happen if they lost AIF. Without AIF Callie would have nothing, be nothing. Em would be able to get work in any library, no problem. Mary, AIF's longtime secretary, could get clerical work anywhere, or just retire. Without AIF, Callie was hopeless. She had no transferable skills and there weren't exactly a lot of jobs out there for an antique airplane mechanic who hadn't been able to finish community college.

But it went beyond her ability to earn a living. She could imagine Gramps sitting in his attic office, his dogs lying in varying positions around him, magazines and letters piled up everywhere. When she pictured her grandfather, it was always there. Always here.

Losing AIF meant she would have lost everything that had ever been home, and everything that had ever been family.

She crossed the gravel drive to the library. It was a repurposed house—her aunt and uncle's old house before they'd moved to Alaska. As kids, Callie, Em and Lawson had camped out in the backyard and snuck into the hangars late at night. The Baker grandkids, the future of AIF.

At the thought of her cousin, Callie's mood darkened. Lawson should have come home years ago, but his newly ex-wife's acting career in L.A. had kept him and his two sons far away.

If he would just come home, things would be so much easier. He would take over Gramps's role like he'd always wanted, and she and Em wouldn't be stretched so thin. The boys would be able to help out too.

But they wouldn't come, so it was a waste of time standing on the porch of the library wishing it could be. All Callie could do was control the here and now. Callie stepped into the library. What was once a TV room and bedroom separated by a wall was now a big, open room with shelves of colorful books on aviation lining three of the four walls. Five long tables stood on gleaming wood floors and sunlight streamed in through big picture windows. The wood-paneled walls not hidden by bookshelves were covered in prints of antique planes, watercolors of the airport itself, and other knick-knacks that gave nod to the overreaching purpose of AIF. *Keep the Antiques Flying.*

To the left, Em sat at a big, old desk looking over some paperwork. Mary sat stretched out in an armchair. For the past two years, it had been the three of them working their asses off to keep things going. Callie smiled a little. Maybe they hadn't always succeeded, and maybe they wouldn't always, but she had to be proud of what they'd accomplished since Gramps died.

"There you are," Em greeted with her perpetually sunny smile. "How are Trevor and Shelby holding up?"

"About as well as can be expected."

Mary held out a bagel and a bottle of water. "Lifesaver." Callie took a long gulping drink of the water. "What did I miss?"

"Well." Em and Mary exchanged looks Callie couldn't read, but she didn't need to know what the look was about to know what it meant. Something she wouldn't like.

"Well?"

"We were actually talking about..." Mary trailed off and stared down at her aging Metallica T-shirt. Most would look at Mary with her shaggy mop of graying brown hair, clear green eyes, and love of heavy metal and not pin her over sixty. Though Mary kept her exact age a secret, Callie knew she had to be pushing seventy-five.

"Trevor," Em finished, obviously working hard to keep her smile bright and innocent.

Callie looked from Mary to Em, frowned. "What about Trevor?"

Em stood behind the big desk. With her wavy blonde hair, big blue eyes and long, flowing skirts she looked like some kind of hippie angel. To Callie it was a constant marvel they shared any DNA at all.

"We were just talking about how he's probably staying in Pilot's Point for a little bit, right?"

"Yeah." Callie bit into the bagel, not sure why this topic was making her uncomfortable. "Until he gets Shelby off to college anyway," she added through a mouthful of food.

Mary perked up in her chair, looking at Em again. They were practically having a telepathic conversation, but Callie wasn't in the mood to decipher.

"That'd be August or even September, right?" Em asked, shuffling some papers on her desk.

"Yeah."

"And I assume since he's going back to Seattle in the fall he's not working while he's home?"

Callie closed her eyes. The food and drink were not helping at all and the headache drummed louder. "Would you two spit out whatever you're planning so I can decide whether or not I need to warn Trevor."

"Nothing to warn him about." Em gave a dismissive wave. "We thought maybe he could help out around AIF. As a volunteer."

Callie's shoulders hunched up to her ears. The idea was a good one, but she inexplicably felt weird about it. "Trevor is clueless when it comes to planes."

"Yeah, but he could run a mower, paint trim, and so on. All those little things we're always struggling to make time for."

All those things Callie had just been dreading. It would be nice to have someone around to take up the grunt work so they could focus on the important stuff. But Trevor? For some reason the idea of him underfoot day in and day out had her feeling a little unsure.

"Trevor's mom just died. He's trying to get Shelby graduated."

"Yes, but Shelby still has two months of school and Trevor's sitting around in that house by himself for most of the day." For the first time, Em's eyes met hers. As it always did, the bright blue depths reminded Callie of their father. A man Em could barely remember, and these days, it was getting harder and harder for Callie to remember clearly. But, she'd always remember those eyes.

Mary spoke into the silence. "We need help, Callie. And Lawson, well..." Mary trailed off again, sharing Callie's pessimism about the last Baker grandchild returning to his rightful place.

"Lawson will come home," Em interjected with a determined nod. "He's working on full custody right now, and then Sue can't keep him from moving back."

This time it was Callie and Mary who exchanged looks. Callie figured Mary was thinking the same thing she was. *I've heard that before.*

"In the meantime, though," Em continued, not meeting either skeptical look, "Trevor would be a tremendous help."

"What makes you think he'll agree to volunteer to be our grunt worker?"

"You." Em smiled sweetly. "You could convince Trevor to do just about anything."

Callie scoffed and shoved the rest of her bagel into her mouth.

"Oh, come on. That boy'd do anything for you, and you know it."

Callie swallowed, tried to ignore the way the unease was building, settling in her gut like a hard, tense rock. "Hardly."

"Remember in high school when he convinced Mr. Martin you weren't cheating on that test? Or when he broke Frank Winston's nose after..." Em trailed off, wisely choosing not to finish that thought.

Callie couldn't stop from finishing the thought in her head, though. Trevor had broken Frank Winston's nose after Frank had convinced her to have sex with him only days after her grandmother's funeral and then dumped her five minutes after he'd taken her virginity. And, like an idiot, she'd whined to Trevor about it and he'd had to get up on his white horse.

"What about when he was working for County and you got in that bar fight with Sheila Evans and he convinced everyone involved not to press charges?"

"Or—"

"I get the picture." Callie held up a hand in hopes they would stop rehashing the litany of ways Trevor had saved her ass over the years. "First of all, I want to point out that the fight with Sheila was in no way my fault. Second, don't all those events illustrate that maybe I shouldn't manipulate a guy who's done a lot for me into mowing our grass and hauling our trash?"

Em let out a lengthy sigh. "In another lifetime, maybe. In this lifetime, we need to manipulate anyone we can."

It wasn't often Em let enough realism in to admit that. Dejection infiltrated the room, weighing on all of their shoulders.

Callie looked from Em's sad expression to Mary's disconcerted frown and made a particular effort to smile and lighten the mood. "Adding a guy to this trio of female awesomeness might be a problem."

Buoyed, Em laughed. "True, it might upset the delicate balance of kick-butt estrogen, but I'm afraid we might need some testosterone around here."

Callie snorted. "Please. We do not need a man's help."

"Okay, it doesn't have to be testosterone," Em amended equitably. "But we definitely need help of any variety. I don't really care where Trevor falls in terms of gender. I just know we need his help."

"Fine. I'll ask him." Callie hunched her shoulders again at the thought of asking Trevor for yet another favor in a lifetime of favors. "But if he says no—"

"You'll have to find a way to make him say yes," Mary finished. "Maybe you could seduce him."

"Mary!"

"What?" She smiled, wiggling her graying eyebrows. "Might be a fun way to help out good old AIF."

"So much for girl power," Callie muttered. As if seducing Trevor would ever work. And if it would? Callie shook her head. She was losing her mind. "I've got to take a shower. I'd like to get my to-do list done before sundown so I can get some work done on the Stearman."

"You really think you'll have it ready by the fly-in?"

25

"I better. Best chance to sell it."

Em chewed her lip. "Callie, we don't have to sell it. You and Dad both soloed—"

Callie held up her hand. "Once I get it running again, we're selling it. Think what we could do with the money."

"But—"

"I'm going to grab a shower. I'll call Trevor this afternoon and see what he's up for. Later, ladies."

End of discussion. She'd already made her peace with selling a plane that held so much sentiment. One plane was no match for all of AIF.

Em followed her out onto the porch.

"Leave me alone, Em."

"This isn't about the plane." Em followed Callie's hurried stride away from the library. "It's about Billie's wedding."

"I don't give two shits about Billie's wedding. She's your friend. Not mine."

"I know, but I thought I'd warn you. Frank's a groomsman. The groomsman I'm paired up with."

Callie stopped short, her stomach pitching. "You can't be serious."

"I know Frank's a total jackass for what he did to you, but it was a long time ago. I don't want you to get all riled up about this. It's one night, one little walk down an aisle. No big deal, but I didn't want someone blabbing it around in town like it was, especially since it's three months away."

Frank Winston would not be putting his hands anywhere near her sister. In three months or in three years, but Callie had other things to focus on at the moment. She managed her best reassuring smile and patted Em on the arm. "No big deal, sis."

Em's worried frown deepened. "I know there's going to be

trouble whenever you call me sis."

Callie couldn't fight a wicked grin. "I guess we'll find out in three months. Right now, I have got to get in the shower."

Trevor pulled into the lot of AIF not quite sure what he was going to accomplish. He'd spent the entire day trying to maneuver around Shelby's unpredictable outbursts of tears. He didn't even have to say anything and she'd start crying.

It made sense a teenage girl would be prone to emotional outbursts after losing her mom. Trevor just wished he knew what to do about them. Especially when she would go on and on about how good it was to have him home. Where he belonged.

Why couldn't Shelby see he didn't belong in Pilot's Point? He belonged at work. Where women didn't cry all over him looking for comfort or expect him to know what to do when a boy called the house asking for his sister. He'd rather face a man with a gun.

He was grasping at straws by asking for Callie's help, but at least if she failed too he'd have someone to commiserate with.

He parked outside the metal building of Callie's shop, knowing she'd be there despite the workday being over. The sun was beginning to set and the air was beginning to cool. It was nice to be out of the house, to be outside, to be somewhere that didn't remind him of his parents.

The fields of green grass at AIF reminded him of summer as a kid. AIF would always remind him of those carefree days before life had gotten so complicated.

Trevor stepped up to the threshold of the shop. The door was open and he peeked inside. Callie was on a stepladder bent over a large, black engine of some sort. Though she faced him, her gaze was so intent on the plane, she didn't notice his presence.

She looked peaceful, which wasn't a common look for Callie. She'd looked so sad last night when she'd talked about AIF's possible future, and though he understood how much AIF meant to her, seeing her in a rare moment of peaceful fulfillment reminded him of exactly that and of how much she had already lost.

It didn't seem right to show up asking for a favor when she had so much on her hands already. Maybe he could figure out a way to deal with Shelby on his own.

He thought of Shelby's tears soaking the shoulder of his shirt over lunch. Okay, no, he couldn't do it on his own.

Em's sunny, soothing voice broke through Trevor's thoughts. She was standing off to the side with her back to him, talking to Callie. Callie's face was intent on the engine as she worked to screw something in. They didn't seem to realize he was in the doorway, and for some reason he didn't speak up. Instead he watched the two half-sisters talk.

They were a clichéd image of dark and light. Em with her blonde curls and blue eyes. She was shorter and rounder than Callie. A feminine contrast in a floral, floaty skirt and pink fussy top, to Callie who wore jeans and a black T-shirt liberally smudged with grease along with her forearms and face.

Then there was demeanor. Em was calm and elegant grace—kind, sweet, thoughtful. He'd never met anyone who didn't like Emerson Baker, or anyone who wasn't surprised over her and Callie sharing a father.

"I'm just saying my da—Tom could talk to Dana on our behalf," Em said, standing in the middle of the greasy chaos of the shop looking pristine and untouched.

Trevor watched Callie's face. The peace melted away into

resentment, presumably over the fact Em called her stepfather dad.

"I don't need Tom or anyone to intervene. I can handle it. I have another meeting with her tomorrow. I'll get it figured out."

"Callie, please don't be upset over this. I'm trying to do what's best. We have to get this permit."

Callie's mouth hardened into a thin line, her gaze glued to the engine in front of her. Her muscles tensed as she worked with something difficult. "I know."

Since Trevor didn't know what they were talking about, he tuned the rest of their conversation out and watched Callie. There was a kind of grim focus he found ridiculously appealing. As much as Em and Callie were contradictions, Callie was a contradiction herself. Those hard lines softened by round curves, masculine work somehow made alluring because she was doing it.

Either it was about ninety degrees hotter in the shop than it was outside or emotional distress was no match for his hormones.

He'd only been home for a week and already the next six months seemed like forever. And it wasn't just busybody neighbors, crying sisters and nothing to do that was getting to him.

It was new Callie. There had always been reasons to ignore his attraction to old Callie. She was too wild, too unpredictable, but mostly, Callie Baker had always scared him. All those repressed hurts and desperate attempts at masking pain. He'd never known what to do with it all except help when she got in trouble, or ride out the storm by her side as she tried to transform her grief into something else.

Getting closer always seemed too much of a risk, and he preferred to take his risks when he was legally authorized to carry an assault rifle and wear a bulletproof vest.

But new Callie wasn't quite as scary, and that was a problem. Because whether she had finally healed or not, getting mixed up in some fulfillment of teenage fantasy would only make things more complicated when he had to leave.

"Going to stand there staring all night?" Callie called out, not bothering to look up.

Em turned, her confusion quickly turning into a warm smile. "Trevor. We didn't see you there." She crossed over to him, resting her hand on his arm. "How are you doing?"

Trevor watched as Callie rolled her eyes. New Callie still wasn't perfect. Thank God for that.

"I'm doing all right. Thanks for asking. And thanks for the casseroles. Shelby mentioned you and your mom have been keeping her fed the past few weeks. It means a lot to us."

"No problem. How is Shelby?"

Trevor looked up at Callie, thought about the reason for his visit. "She's got a lot to deal with."

Em nodded sympathetically. "Of course. Let me know if I can help with more than just food. I'd be glad to."

Trevor looked down at his feet. "Sure thing." Em would be more understanding, definitely more of a nurturing help than Callie, but Em had never lost her mother. In Trevor's mind, the only option for honest to goodness help and understanding with Shelby was Callie.

"I'm going to head down to the cabin. Callie, we can talk about this tomorrow."

Callie didn't say anything, just nodded. On a sigh, Em left the shop.

"Before I came home I recall you mentioning you and Em were getting pretty close. That didn't look like sisterly devotion."

Callie tossed a tool into the box next to her, the clink of

metal on metal echoing through the shop. "Not seeing eye to eye at the moment. It happens when you work with family."

"I think it was more than that."

Callie shrugged, continued to work on the plane. Trevor maintained his silence. If he knew Callie the explanation would come tumbling out if he only gave her a few moments to mull over it silently.

One... Two... Three....

"I hate that she always does that." Callie gestured to where Em had disappeared. "Starts to say Dad then fixes it to Tom. Like I can't deal with her calling him Dad. So, she's completely forgotten our dad. So what? Her business."

"Yeah, you're dealing really well."

She pointed her new tool at him, scowling. "Okay, maybe it pisses me off she gets to pretend our dad never existed. Maybe I'm almost thirty and I still get a little jealous that she got some semblance of a family and I'm left with..." Callie tossed the tool into the box, jumped off the stepladder and began to pace. "What is wrong with me?" she demanded before sinking onto a bench and covering her face with her hands. "What the hell is wrong with me?"

Well, shit. He just seemed to attract female hysterics. What he'd done to deserve this punishment he didn't know, but it must have been bad to have Callie as the newest perpetrator.

"There's nothing wrong with you."

She looked up at him and scowled. "Don't give me that placating bullshit."

"Okay, so you're not perfect." Trevor sank onto the bench next to her. "Who the hell is?"

She shook her head, and Trevor was glad she wasn't crying. He'd only ever seen Callie cry at funerals and he was *so* not ready to deal with another female's tears tonight.

"Things were so much easier before this whole 'new leaf' crap. I didn't think about any of this. I drowned my sorrows in something else, and you know what? I liked it better. I liked it better than hurting all the time." She rested her elbows on her knees, stared at the ground. "And if I thought AIF would survive, I'd go back to being a complete fuck-up. It was so much easier."

Trevor draped his arm across her shoulders. "Personally, I like this new leaf a lot better than the old one."

She looked up at him and there was that something. That something he'd been ignoring with Callie since he'd been thirteen and realized girls weren't so gross after all. He'd kind of forgotten about that in the four years away, or maybe pushed it to the recesses of his mind. Now it was in the forefront again.

Trevor cleared his throat and looked at the doorway where the light was quickly disappearing. "You never thought back then. Now you're thinking, and it's probably harder, but I bet you come out the other side feeling a lot better. Maybe actually a little happier. Bad Girl Baker might have been easier, but she wasn't happy."

"Bad Girl Baker. Haven't heard that one in a while." He looked down at her and her lips were curved into a smile. "She wasn't happy, but she wasn't such a pansy ass. I miss feeling strong. I don't want to be this depressed, pathetic, whiny mess."

"There might be a happy medium between BGB and GGB."

She chuckled. "GGB? Good Girl Baker?"

Trevor grinned down at her. "Yeah. You take the strength of BGB and the maturity of GGB and then maybe you've got a decent human being who feels the way a woman almost turning thirty should."

"As ridiculous as that sounds, I think you might *actually* be on to something." She smiled up at him, then his eyes rested on that sexy mouth.

Shit. He really needed to be careful about where exactly he looked when it came to Callie. Eager to change the subject, or at least the subject in his head, he blurted out the reason for his visit. "I need your help with Shelby."

Trevor certainly knew how to pull the rug out from under her. Callie had forgotten that. Before he'd moved away how many times had she sat there thinking something was about to happen only to have him hammer her with something completely different?

Six months was going to feel like forever, but he just sat there trying to figure out her reaction, so Callie had to focus on this new topic. "You're joking, right?"

"You know what she's going through."

Callie stood, needing to get some space. Needing to get his arm off her shoulders. "Trevor, I don't remember my mom. And Dad died when I was eight. It's different."

"Maybe, but Callie..." He sat there looking so dejected and miserable she almost went back to sit next to him. "She just starts crying. We'll be talking and out of nowhere. Bam. And she wants to go back to school tomorrow. How am I supposed to know what to do with all this? I need help. I need you."

She turned to focus on the plane, sympathy making her uncomfortable and unsure. She didn't want to be drawn into this. Not only would getting through to Shelby be nearly impossible, but even if she succeeded it meant rehashing her own loss.

"I know Shelby isn't your biggest fan."

"She hates my guts. Let's not dance around that."

"No. It's not *hate*."

Callie snorted. She was pretty familiar with people hating

her, and Shelby was definitely on that long list.

"I was never a teenage girl without parents. You were. I need your help. I can't do this alone." He looked around the shop. "I know you're swamped here, and I hate to put another thing on your shoulders but..."

There weren't a whole lot of times in her life when she'd had the opportunity to help Trevor. Probably none where he'd ever come out and said he needed her. Mr. FBI Agent wasn't big on needing what he couldn't provide himself. Then there was the fact she still hadn't asked him about her own favor. If she agreed to this maybe him helping out at AIF would be more of a fair trade. Not that she didn't owe him already for a million past transgressions.

"Okay, fine, I'll help, but I don't know what you think I'll be able to do. Grief is a personal thing. You have to get over it on your own. Opening up to people might help, not that I'd know, but I doubt Shelby will open up to me."

"Hang out with us. She'll warm up to you and then maybe, I don't know. I'm playing this by ear, which you know I suck at."

"Yeah."

"Come over for dinner tomorrow night. We'll sit around and talk. I'm not hoping for miracles, just some advice on what to do. I don't know. I need help. You're the best person for the job."

What a joke. The only job she was best for was the one she'd been doing before Em and then Trevor had interrupted her. "Fine."

He stood, crossed over and gave her a quick, friendly hug. "Thanks, Cal. You're the best."

She didn't feel like the best. All that hope she'd gotten thinking maybe Trevor was right, maybe she could still be part of her old self, dissolved into feeling like a fake and a failure.

"Well, as long as you're feeling all warm and fuzzy, I've got a favor to ask you myself."

He was smiling, and it was a genuine one. Handsome and accommodating and, ugh, fucking perfect. So annoying.

"Before I ask, I want you to know this was Em and Mary's idea. I thought it was a terrible one, but they insisted."

"Spit it out."

Callie pulled out a screwdriver, ran it through her fingers and kept her eyes on the tool as she explained. "Since you're home for a few months and not working they thought maybe you'd be able to help out around here."

"Sure. I'm surprised you didn't think of it yourself."

Callie frowned up at him. He wasn't just genuinely smiling now, he was grinning. "You've got a lot going on."

Trevor shrugged. "What better way to take my mind off of it than getting out of that damn house most days?"

Of course he would be happy to help. It was her who was the ungrateful bitch who didn't ever feel comfortable doing anything for anyone else. "It'll be all the crappy grunt work we don't want to do or have time to do and we're not paying you."

His grin didn't falter. "Good. I think crappy grunt work will be exactly what my mind needs."

She turned to her plane. "That was a hell of a lot easier than having to seduce you," she grumbled.

"I'm sorry, what?"

"Never mind. Just mumbling." She reached up to examine the cowling, but Trevor's hand rested on her shoulder, turned her around.

"No, I think I want to hear this explanation."

"It was a joke." Callie rolled her eyes and flung her arms in the air so his hand fell off her shoulder. "Mary thought if you said no I should seduce you. Ha ha. Get it?" It felt completely un-joke-like at the moment. So much so a warm blush crept into her cheeks.

"Well, maybe I'm sorry I was such an easy yes."

"Oh, whatever." She refused to examine the low, melty way he spoke or the little fluttery feeling in her stomach as a response. "Go home, Trev. We'll see you tomorrow."

"Tomorrow." He chuckled to himself all the way out the shop door, which left Callie scowling after him.

She had a bad feeling about this.

Chapter Three

Wearing a pink shift dress wasn't why Callie was pissed off enough to punch something, though it was part of the reason. *Pink.* Even though the blazer she wore over it was black, the dress—borrowed from Em's mom—was pink. A disgustingly pale, girly *pink*.

Her hair was down instead of pulled back. She'd worn a little makeup and had tried really hard to project a together, professional appearance.

But makeup and the damn dress hadn't convinced Dana Caldwell that Callie was a responsible enough part owner of AIF and therefore worthy of the parking permit needed from the county for the fly-in. Dana was determined that if AIF was going to get anything, it would have to come through Callie begging on her hands and knees.

Not fucking likely.

Callie whipped her car into the AIF parking lot and slammed to a stop in front of the shop. She really needed to bang on something before she went to report to Em, because if she didn't get some of the aggression out she was going to explode all over Em's well-meaning concerns and questions.

Callie stomped all the way to the shop before remembering she was wearing borrowed clothes. A borrowed pink dress of all damn things. She couldn't do any work dressed like that.

When she turned on a heel to go back to the car, she collided right into a hard wall of muscle. Trevor. He was in grungy clothes streaked with dirt from whatever work Em had him doing that afternoon, but Callie was in no mood to deal with anyone right now.

Let alone someone who looked all rumpled and handyman sexy and took in her appearance with wide-eyed amusement. "Holy—"

Callie pushed past him, anger vibrating. "Don't say a word."

"Seriously, you have to indulge me in at least a few comments. You are wearing a pink dress."

"I know what I'm wearing." She kept walking toward her car, and Trevor followed her.

"It's cute. Who knew pink was your color? I might fall in love."

Even as she was doing it, she knew spinning around with her fist cocked was not the right reaction, but frustration eroded any sense of listening to that reasonable part of her brain. Luckily, before her fist could connect with his jaw as she'd irrationally intended, Trevor snatched her wrist and pulled her arm behind her back.

"What the fuck?"

She looked at the green grass in front of her and tried to even out her heavy breathing and blink away the idiotic tears stinging her eyes. Everything was piling up and all the little holes she'd plugged over the past two years seemed to be springing leaks again.

Why couldn't one damn thing go right?

It took a moment to realize Trevor was still holding her in place, his strong hand wrapped around her wrist. "You certainly got better at dodging a fist," Callie muttered, hoping the snide comment would take away the threat of tears.

"FBI agents know how to avoid a punch. Besides, a guy generally only lets a girl clock him once before he learns how to avoid it. You got your one and only success senior year."

Callie thought about that. Different reasoning but similar. Frustration at a boiling point. Trevor being there at the wrong time with the wrong comment. Didn't she have a lovely habit of going after the few people who cared about her? On a tired sigh, Callie tried to free her arm. "You can let go of me now."

"You sure about that?"

Callie drew in a breath and slowly let it out. "Yeah."

He let her hand go and moved so they were facing each other. She was glad to see he was angry despite his calm voice. She deserved for him to be really angry.

Arms folded across his chest, his blue eyes stared at her with what she imagined was a look he'd honed in the FBI. It was the kind of look you gave criminals or scumbags. "Want to explain that little outburst?" he asked, his voice a calm contrast to the look.

"I'm sorry."

Surprise softened the hard expression. "Well, that's more than I got when you actually connected." Then concern worked its way over his face and his arms dropped to his sides and Callie felt about an inch tall. "What's up, Cal?"

"Just..." She would not cry. Not in front of Trevor. Not at all. She was not a crier. "Bad day."

He cocked an eyebrow and she knew she wasn't getting away without an explanation.

"Dana Caldwell is in charge of one of the permits we need for the fly-in. I'm supposed to get this permit, but Dana keeps finding ways to put me off." Callie kicked a heel behind her and pulled off the stupid too-small shoe borrowed from Em. She repeated with the other foot until she stood in her bare feet on the grass.

"Wait a second. Dana Caldwell is Sheila Evans's older

sister."

"I know."

"The Sheila Evans who you—"

"I *know*. And I'm sure this is some sort of payback for all the horrible things I did to Sheila."

"You didn't do anything Sheila didn't deserve or start. Except maybe the flyer with Sheila's head on a cow's body you hung all over the town."

The laugh bubbled up past all the frustration and anger. Though the pit was still in her stomach, the edges around it were lighter. "I forgot about that one."

"One of your best." He grinned briefly before his expression turned serious. "It's not legal for Dana to hold that against you and keep you from getting a permit."

"Probably not, but she's got last year's disaster to use against me. We blocked a county road for upward of two hours. We've got a plan in place to fix the flow problem, but Dana's got the upper hand. I just have to keep..." Callie swallowed hard. "Groveling."

"Can I come the next time?" Trevor flashed another grin. "I've never seen you grovel."

"Bite me. I'm going to change. Aren't you supposed to be on your way home?"

Trevor glanced at his watch. "Shit. Yeah. Besides I can harass you about the dress tonight at dinner."

"Oh, right."

"In another situation I might feel sorry enough for you to let you off the hook, but you tried to throw a punch at me *and* I had to witness Shelby cry twice this morning before she left for school. I need reinforcements. Six o'clock. I'm cooking."

"*You're* cooking?"

"Yes. I discovered that if I make a really delicious meal for a woman, said woman will usually be impressed enough to sleep with me." He winked before turning toward his car. "Not that I'm trying to sleep with you," he called over his shoulder, still grinning. "Unless you wear that pink dress. Then I might consider it."

She hefted a shoe at him, but he easily dodged it so it landed with a thump on the grass in front of his car.

It made no sense that she stood there smiling as he drove off.

Whistling, Trevor shoved a key into the deadbolt only to realize the door was unlocked. Shelby must have beaten him home. Damn. He couldn't be the super-sensitive, great advice giver, but he wanted to at least be there when she got home from school.

It had been hard to leave AIF, though. For the first time in weeks he'd felt useful. He could forget about the dark shadows hanging around the Steele house, reminding him of things that would never be again. He'd smiled, sweated, enjoyed his day. Enjoyed it more when he got sight of Callie in the silly pink dress.

Trying to loosen his already-tensing shoulders, Trevor stepped into the living room. Shelby was standing by the ancient answering machine, her backpack still on her shoulders. When she looked over her shoulder at him, there wasn't that soul-crushing sadness in her eyes.

Nope. She looked downright pissed.

"Hey, sorry I'm late."

Shelby didn't say a word, just hit a button on the answering machine.

"*Steele.*" That was all it took for Trevor to recognize the voice of his boss, and realize whatever the man had to say Shelby had already heard, and whatever she'd heard meant he was in deep shit.

"This is Robbins. I've tried you on your cell a few times. No response. Probably no reception in the middle of nowhere. We need your signature on those LOA papers I emailed you two days ago. No Internet in Timbuk Nowheresville? Give me a call."

Trevor remained silent after the beep, but as much as he wanted to he didn't drop his gaze when Shelby turned to glare at him.

"I may not be up on all the FBI lingo, but I'm pretty sure LOA means leave of absence."

Trevor shoved his hands into his pockets, tried to come up with a decent response. "Yeah." It was the best he had.

"You told me you quit." Her voice went up a decibel, wobbled, but she wasn't crying. Yet.

"No." He was digging himself a bigger hole, but how else could he respond? "I never said that."

Shelby's mouth fell open in silent outrage.

"I never said I quit. You assumed—"

"Are you serious right now?" Her backpack fell to the floor with a hard thud. Anger was better than crying. Kind of.

"Shelby, come on. Let me explain."

She stomped over to the couch and sank into it, folding her arms over her chest. "This better be good." Her shoulders were back, those blue eyes a reflection of anger, and she looked so much like their mom in that moment his heart physically hurt.

Swallowing against memories of times his mother had uttered those exact words, Trevor sat down next to her. Did he have a good explanation? Not really. "I couldn't just quit."

"I don't see why not."

He rested his hand on her knee before she jerked it away.

"The bottom line is I have to figure out what I'm going to do. I can't live off of what Mom and Dad left. That's for you."

"But—"

"It's a leave of absence. I'm not expecting you to be on your own once I go back. I've got it all worked out. We can keep the house; it's paid off. You can come here whenever you want. On breaks and stuff, you'll come stay with me in Seattle. The apartment is kind of small, but I can get a bigger one."

"Seattle is half a country away. Pilot's Point is my home."

"I know." Trevor patted her knee. "I know. Like I said, you can come back whenever you want. We can even do Christmas here. You can't expect me to..." How did he say the rest without coming off the selfish older brother? Was it possible? Maybe that's just what he was.

"I'm already giving up six months of my life, and I'm not doing any more undercover work all so I can be around if you need me." Trevor shoved fingers through his hair, frustrated he couldn't get through to her. Why couldn't she see he had a life to lead that didn't involve being her guardian?

Trevor let out a long breath. Could he be more of a dick? Still, the bottom line remained. Pilot's Point had nothing for him. "I have a great job that I love. You won't be here nine months out of the year and if you want a decent job, you won't come back to Pilot's Point after you graduate college. You have to see this is the best choice for both of us."

When she was silent, he looked up. The anger on her face hadn't subsided. If anything, it intensified. "You let me believe you were staying for good."

Yes, he had. To .protect her. Or because it was easier that way. "I thought that's what you needed." Her fists were clenched in her lap and Trevor knew his explanation hadn't changed anything.

"I need the truth!" She jumped to her feet and stood in front of him, looking too young and vulnerable to be in his clumsy care. "I'm a mess right now, but I just lost my *mom.*" She fisted a hand at her heart, tears getting ready to fall. He couldn't face them as she continued. "I'm eighteen, prom is in three weeks, AP tests in a month, then graduation. My mom is *dead.* I deserve to be a mess without you trying to shelter me with lies."

"Shelby—"

"You're a terrible brother, you know that?" She wagged her finger in his face. "I used to make excuses for you because you were so much older and because you wanted to get out so bad, but..." She waved her arms wildly in the air. "It's you." With every *you* she shoved a finger into his face. "You've always cared more about yourself, everyone else, over your family. For as long as I can remember Callie Baker has meant more to you than any of your own flesh and blood. And I think that's horrible."

She stomped over to her backpack and hefted it onto her shoulder. On her way toward the stairs she fixed him with the meanest glare he'd ever seen Shelby muster, worse than anything she'd ever given Callie.

"I hate you," she said in a low, controlled voice, but the control quickly broke. "I hope you go back to Seattle tomorrow!" She stormed up the stairs, the rapid fire of her running footsteps soon punctuated by the loud slam of the door.

Trevor sat, not sure what to do. The words hurt. As much as he'd like to leave it at that, there was more to it. She was right.

Time passed and Trevor didn't move. Part of him thought—hoped—Shelby would come back down. He knew he should go up to her, but a heavy weight kept him locked on the couch.

He'd underestimated how hard this was going to be, and he'd known it would be one of the hardest things he'd ever done.

Prom, AP tests, graduation, college.

Honesty, tears, distance, inferiority to the task.

His mother was gone and more than grief, he felt resentment toward all she left behind. That knowledge only made the guilt stab deeper, sharper.

After an hour of staring at a wall, rendered immobile by the intensity and conflict of emotion, Trevor forced himself off the couch. His cell service was patchy, so he used the home line to call Robbins and explain that no, he hadn't checked his email, but yes Bumfuck, Iowa, did offer high speed Internet.

Then he'd gone to the kitchen to start dinner, but the sight of his mother's kitchen, so meticulously kept, so ruthlessly white, left him feeling immobile and hollowed out all over again.

She wasn't here to soothe away the problems. To make dinner, to keep the house freakishly clean. She was gone, but he couldn't even grieve right. All those things she was supposed to do were now his responsibility. He didn't have time to miss her.

When the doorbell rang, Trevor moved into the living room feeling like some outward force was moving his body. It wasn't until he saw Callie on his doorstep that he remembered she was coming.

"Not one crack about the..." She trailed off, her brows furrowing into concern. "Whoa. What happened to you?"

"Callie, hey. Um, I'm sorry. I think we're going to have to take a rain check on dinner."

"What happened?"

Trevor let out a long breath. He didn't know how to explain it. More, he didn't want to explain it, because it meant admitting some crappy stuff about himself. "Shelby's pretty pissed at me right now. I don't think your presence at dinner would help the situation any."

Callie leaned against the doorframe giving no indication she was going to go and let things be. "Why is she pissed at you?"

Trevor swallowed, but there was a discomfort in his throat that made it hard to complete the action. "She found out I'm on a leave of absence, not home for good."

"Ouch."

Trevor shook his head. "I guess it's best it came out now." Why was his voice so uneven, his hands not quite steady? He cleared his throat and tried to get a handle on what was working through him.

Callie rested her hands on his shoulders, but he still couldn't pull together enough control to make out any more words. When she pulled him into a hug, he simply rested his chin on her shoulder and closed his eyes.

Real men didn't cry. How many times had his parents stressed that Steeles didn't cry? It was a horrifying thought that the lump in his throat was some kind of precursor to that. He'd just hold on to Callie until the feeling passed.

"Um, it's going to be okay, you know?"

Leave it to Callie's attempt at comfort to help him regain a little control. Trevor pulled back and managed a smile. "Sure."

"I'll go talk to her."

He wanted to hug her again, because he knew that was the last thing she wanted to do. "No, not now." He wanted to leave it at that, but as he turned into the house, the memory of Shelby's words sharpened in his gut again. "She said I was a crappy brother."

"That's not tr—"

"No, it is true." Trevor didn't turn around to face Callie,

instead he looked at the picture of his parents on the mantel of the fireplace. They smiled at him, and he felt those opposing forces that had driven him away. "Mom and Dad always put so much pressure on me. I got out whenever I could. I pushed them and Shelby away. I shut them all out. I hung out with you or got a job halfway across the country. I got tired of always having to be better. Sometimes I just wanted to be what I was."

She rested her hand on his shoulder. "Let's order a pizza, watch the game. Then one of us will go talk to Shelby."

A diversion. It was definitely what he needed. "No, I said I was going to cook. I'll cook." Hopefully it would take his mind off of everything to do something. "You can help."

When he turned to face her, the skeptical smirk was almost enough to make him chuckle. "Okay, you can watch."

Shelby sat at her desk, staring blindly at the homework in front of her. Tears blurred her vision. Hearing the sounds of dinner being made and two voices—one male and one female—reminded her of a time when both her parents had been alive. It made her so sad she didn't know what to do except cry.

Mom always yelled at her when she cried, saying it was a sign of weakness, but Shelby was giving herself some reprieve. Mom had cried after Dad died, even if she'd tried to hide it.

Shelby immediately recognized the female voice as Callie's. At the moment, she hated Callie and Trevor with a painful rage, hate and desperation twisting inside her.

For as long as Shelby could remember, Callie had been a sore point in the Steele household. The only real arguments she could remember her parents having had been over Callie's influence on Trevor. In fact, it was the last thing they'd fought about before Dad died.

Shelby had always hated Callie's ability to cause argument in her family. It had been a childish hate at first, but it had grown with her. She didn't care if Callie had turned over a new leaf, and neither had Mom. They'd both been convinced Callie was rotten at the core. On those rare occasions Shelby had been foolish enough to think Callie was actually changing, Mom would remind her that no matter what happened, Calloway Baker was simply no good.

Why Trevor or Dad had never seen that was anyone's guess. Maybe men just being stupid.

Laughter floated up through the vent and Shelby scowled down at it. Maybe Callie didn't have anything to do with Trevor going back to Seattle, but she did have something to do with stealing him away while he was home.

The fallen tears had blurred away the work of at least two of her physics problems. In a fit of anger, Shelby ripped the paper out of her notebook and crumpled it into a little ball.

It wasn't fair. She'd had such a great day at school. It had started off awkward and weird, but then Dan kind of swooped in and saved her, acting like nothing happened in the two weeks she'd been gone. He'd been like a knight in shining armor or whatever, and stuck by her side the entire day trying to make everything as normal as possible.

He'd walked her to her car after school and asked if she wanted to go to prom with him. Though tears still dampened her cheeks, Shelby smiled at the memory of him telling her if she didn't want to go to prom, he'd still want to hang out with her on prom night. Best of all, he'd told her to take her time deciding.

Like he really liked her. Shelby had been so excited all the way up to the moment she pulled into the driveway at home and realized Mom wouldn't be at the house to share her excitement. So she'd cried and cried and cried.

Then she'd gone inside, ready to cry on Trevor's shoulder and tell him all about her day and feel some of the comfort that came from an adult presence. But he hadn't been home. He'd been off at AIF. With Callie.

She'd listened to the messages and Trevor had walked in looking happy. Everything had crumbled into a haze of fury at that point.

Anger and sadness melded together to make her feel sick and upset all over again. Was this how life would be from now on? Even the happy stuff would be ruined by all this loss?

Trevor was all she had left and he didn't want her. He wanted Seattle. He wanted to help Callie. He wanted everything but what his little sister needed. Anger began to overtake the sadness, and Shelby liked that better. She liked anything better than feeling sad all the damn time.

Shelby used her palms to wipe the tears off her cheeks. She was going to be valedictorian, go off to UNI, then write Trevor off for good. There were plenty of people in the world who had no one in their lives and they survived just fine. Let him go back to Seattle. She'd survive.

Besides, Dan was going to UNI in the fall too. Maybe going to prom would turn into, like, a real relationship so she could at least have someone.

"Hey."

Shelby's head snapped up to see Callie standing in her bedroom doorway. "What the hell are you doing here?"

"Here in your house or here in your room?" Callie asked casually, unaffected by Shelby's angry demand.

"Both. Neither." Shelby focused on the anger, mustered her best withering look. "I know why you're here." She stopped abruptly when Callie crossed her room and shoved a plate of food at her. Shelby stared at it, but Callie shoved again.

"Take it."

Not sure what else to do, Shelby followed directions.

"So, why am I here?"

Shelby looked down at the plate, then set it on her desk. She tried to remember the speech she'd practiced giving Callie the night of the funeral, but came up empty. She focused on finding the best way to get Callie gone. Mix the truth with total disdain. "Trevor thinks you have some sort of insight into how I'm feeling. I knew you weren't the brightest, Callie, but I gave you more credit than this."

Callie didn't say anything, just arched an eyebrow.

Shelby pretended she was trying to teach something to a dimwitted five-year-old. "Do you really think *you* of all people can help me through this?"

"No, I don't." Callie shrugged like it didn't matter. None of Shelby's meanest insults seemed to be penetrating Callie's unusually affable demeanor.

"Then why are you in my room?" Shelby didn't like the way Callie studied her schoolbooks or the pictures on the wall. She didn't like Callie's tall body taking up space in the small, feminine room Mom had helped decorate after Dad died. It was one of Shelby's favorite memories, painting and picking out bedding with Mom.

"I do know what you're going through. Regardless of my social or intellectual status."

Shelby turned to her homework. "You don't know anything about me."

"Maybe, but you probably went back to school today because you hoped it'd be a distraction. It probably wasn't as easy as you thought. Because after something like this happens, people treat you differently. It's worse in high school." Callie paused, and when Shelby snuck a sideways glance at her, she noticed Callie was frowning and looking at the ground.

It was weird seeing Callie act unsure, almost vulnerable, but Shelby refused to soften, even as Callie continued.

"I had friends who were so uncomfortable they would ignore me altogether. I was younger, but when my grandma died your brother was the only one who treated me the same. Not like I was a leper or a charity case. He was probably one of the few things that got me through."

Shelby didn't want Callie of all people to understand, but it seemed she did. Still, Shelby held on to the resentment that Trevor had given Callie comfort, but he'd failed her. Except failed wasn't the right word. He'd been letting her cry all over him since the funeral. But he'd lied to her. He obviously didn't want to be around her.

Forgetting her previous mission to write off Trevor, Shelby focused on the fact Callie always managed to get her hooks into Trevor and steal him away. Like Mom always said. Callie had some kind of unhealthy hold on Trevor, and it was their job to break it.

Realizing Callie was studying her in the silence, Shelby shot her a nasty look. "Maybe I have better taste in friends than you did." Nope, but Callie didn't need to know that.

"Maybe." Callie shrugged again, didn't seem hurt by the statement. "Look, I know you have it in your head that I'm not good enough to take out your trash. Your family is into the college thing and the law-abiding do-gooder thing and I never fit that mold, so I get it. I'm not good enough for Trevor so you hate the fact we're friends. I'm willing to put that aside and help you if you need it. Maybe you don't."

Maybe some of that were true, but not all of it. Maybe Shelby did need help, but not from Callie. Not from some community college dropout loser. "Why would you want to help me?"

"Because I figure after everything your brother has done for me, I owe him."

"Good to know this isn't actually about *me* then." Shelby poked at the food on her plate with a fork.

"You've been nothing but a bitch to me your whole life. Why would it be about you?"

Shelby had no earthly clue why that made her want to smile. She refused to indulge. "Whatever. I'm fine. I don't need your pity or help."

"Fair enough, but if you change your mind you know where to find me." Slowly, Callie made her way out of the room. Shelby did her best to bite her tongue, but half the question tumbled out like it had a will of its own. "Do you think...?"

Callie stood in her doorway, knob still in hand. She didn't prompt or leave, just stood there.

Two choices: tell Callie to leave and ignore the burning curiosity to get someone's opinion who knew what it was like or to take a chance that Callie might be honest and give her some perspective.

She was too emotionally wrung out to suppress anymore, so, keeping her eyes glued to the plate of food, Shelby went ahead and asked. "Do you think if I go to prom it'll be weird and awkward?"

Callie was quiet for a moment as if she was giving it some serious thought. Shelby wished she'd kept her stupid mouth shut. She wished Callie would answer the question already.

"It's your senior prom. If you want to go, it shouldn't matter if other people are weird or awkward about it. I regret not going to mine." Callie smiled, but it was a nasty kind of smile. "But you're so much smarter and better than I am, maybe you wouldn't regret it."

"Maybe I'm a bitch to you because you're such a bitch to me."

"Maybe, but I don't think that's it."

No, it wasn't. She'd been nasty because Mom hadn't liked Callie. Mom had always been nice to Callie's face though, and Shelby thought someone should act how they felt.

"Well, see you around, Shelby. If you have any other questions, you can ask, even if you're bitchy about it. Your brother is desperate to know what to do with you, so I'll answer."

The sentiment was nice in a veiled way, but it filled Shelby with guilt over what she'd said to Trevor earlier. Maybe he really was trying, maybe he did actually care, and maybe she should cut him some slack. He was, after all, giving up a big portion of his life to be there for her, even if it was only for a short period of time.

Shelby scowled down at the plate of food. She really hated Callie Baker. That woman always ruined everything.

Chapter Four

Callie headed to the main office to find Em for lunch. The freakishly hot late April day had sweat trickling down her back and she was in serious need of some air conditioning.

Mary was on the phone when Callie stepped into the office, so she skirted the glass display cases and took the stairs to Gramps's upstairs office.

The steps were narrow and walking up them had memories crowding Callie's mind. When she'd been young, she'd raced up the stairs after a long day at school to see what Gramps had for her to do.

He'd been gone two years now and the large upstairs office still smelled like his cigars and old magazines. Callie usually avoided it if she could because the memories were too painful in this particular place, but Em had been working up here all morning looking for some book.

Callie crested the stairs and looked around. It was the same. Piles of mail, magazines, newspapers everywhere. Airplane knick-knacks scattered throughout. They hadn't gone through his things. It had been a silent agreement to let everything stay where it was unless they needed something. Should Lawson ever come back and take his rightful spot that might change, but for now there was something sadly comforting about coming upstairs and knowing it would be like Gramps was still around.

Across from the stairway a window took up almost the whole wall. Beneath the window was a long bench Gramps used to take naps on. When a person sat on that bench, they could look out and see the majority of AIF. It was one of Callie's favorite spots. Or had been.

And that's where Em was—sitting on the bench with her nose pressed against the glass. She looked back at Callie and grinned, her gaze quickly returning to the window. "Come look."

Callie crossed the cluttered office to the big window. Em pointed to the grass runway below. The riding lawn mower was parked and next to it stood Trevor.

Shirtless.

"Um." Like Em, Callie's eyes were immediately transfixed. He was using his T-shirt to wipe the sweat off his forehead, and the motion caused muscles to move and bunch under sweat-slicked skin. He could use some sun, but other than that Trevor was pretty much flawless.

"So far this is the *best* part of Trevor being a volunteer." Em practically giggled.

"How long have you been watching him?" Though the question held some accusation, Callie wasn't walking away from the window either. In fact, she was pressed against the glass almost as close as Em was.

"Just a few minutes." Em waved a hand briefly in Callie's line of sight, but Callie's gaze didn't falter.

"Not creepy at all, Emerson." Sarcasm dripped from the words, yet she was doing the same thing. She should look away now. Step back from the window. And she would.

In a few minutes.

"Callie. Seriously." Em pointed toward the window, her gaze never leaving Trevor. "Look. At. That."

Couldn't stop if she wanted to. It wasn't that Trevor was super hot or something. Okay, maybe he was, but she was a woman and any woman with a beating heart would want to watch *that*. Any woman would feel a certain amount of lust over flat, hard abs and strong, powerful shoulders. Didn't mean a woman had to act on it. She was just having a normal reaction.

Except that reaction was being caused by her best friend. A guy she was determined not to think about naked. Anymore. Mustering all her strength, Callie pushed away from the window and headed for the door.

"Where are you going?"

When Callie looked over her shoulder, Em's nose was still pressed to the glass. Callie grunted in disgust. "To tell Fabio down there to put a Goddamn shirt on."

"But—"

Callie tramped down the stairs, unable to hear Em's argument. Without a glance at Mary, she cut through the back of the office and the Canteen to make it to the runway, focused on the task at hand. Callie tried to reach the itch between her shoulder blades. A weird, uncomfortable feeling was lodged there.

Trevor was still standing next to the silenced mower, shirtless, except he was now gulping down water from a big thermos. His neck moved with each gulp and the close up view of a shirtless Trevor?

Hot damn.

Old Callie fought to break free and do something really stupid, like—good God—get within touching distance, but new Callie wouldn't acknowledge one dirty thought. Not one.

"This isn't a soap opera," she shouted. If she was keeping a distance between them it was just because old Callie seemed to be getting stronger. And old Callie's fantasies made every inch of her as hot as Trevor looked.

"Come again?"

She planted her feet, mustered her best intimidating look.

"Put a shirt on, Steele."

"Why?" He set the thermos down on the seat of the mower and began crossing over toward her. "It's hot."

Oh, yeah, it definitely was. "I'm your boss. Just follow orders."

Trevor leaned against the fence a few feet away from her. "Why? You enjoying the view?" He waggled his eyebrows.

Callie rolled her eyes, hoping she could rationalize the pink on her cheeks being from the heat of the day. "Please. You'd need a few more muscles and some tattoos to affect me." He really didn't, but she would never admit that to him. Let him think she had a thing for muscle-bound bad boys instead of lean, rangy good guys.

"Who says I don't have any tattoos?"

Callie narrowed her eyes, studied him. Her pulse jumped. "You don't have any tattoos."

"Just because I don't have any above the waist doesn't mean I don't have one." He cocked his head, grinned.

Something strange and unnerving clutched in Callie's gut, but she ignored it and matched his grin with a skeptical smile. "All right. Prove it."

Trevor began to unbuckle his belt and Callie thought her heart was going to jump right out of her chest, but then he stopped. "Okay, you got me. No tattoo."

Callie realized her mouth was hanging open. She quickly snapped it shut.

"What about you?"

"What about me?" she asked, really wishing she had a drink of water at this point. Her throat was so dry she couldn't swallow and she was having trouble settling on a coherent thought. Damn heat.

"Any tattoos?"

"You'll never know." She got a weird and uncomfortable feeling Trevor was flirting with her. Which was crazy. The heat was messing with her brain. Obviously. She hadn't been acting like herself since Em had told her to come look. The thought of Em watching from above reminded her of her purpose, which was definitely not looking at how low Trevor's jeans hung at his hips.

"Em's up there drooling all over you, and I'd prefer it if we could get some actual work done today."

Trevor looked up at the window and Callie watched as Em ducked out of view. Served her right.

"Em's drooling all over me?" His grin grew wider.

The new feeling that worked through her was not lust, interest or fighting old Callie, but it was an emotion she wanted to ignore just as much as those.

"You would get a perverted thrill from Em drooling all over you," Callie muttered with a disgusted wave of the hand. "She's blonde and pretty and perfect, just your type."

Trevor now stood only a few inches away from her, and Callie used every ounce of willpower to keep her eyes on the trees in the distance. Okay, maybe she peeked at his bare chest, but only for a second. Just long enough to note the smattering of dark chest hair.

Jesus. Maybe she was having a stroke.

"If I didn't know you as well as I do, I'd say that sounded almost like jealousy."

Callie snorted. "In your dreams." She turned on a heel and began to stomp back into the office. If her heart beat a little harder at the accusation it was only because...

Damn it, she was running out of rationalizations. She picked up the pace, hoped Trevor didn't notice.

"I'm not a teenager anymore, Callie," he called after her. "I prefer a woman with a bit of an edge these days."

She kept walking. He was going to have to stop this pseudo flirting or old Callie might get her way after all.

When she walked into the Canteen, Em was moving toward her with an uncharacteristic frown on her face. "I am so mad at you right now."

"What?"

"You told him I was looking at him!"

"So? You *were* looking at him." Callie brushed past Em, an uncomfortable weight squeezing her lungs so she couldn't get a full breath.

"So were you."

"Well, he was quite thrilled with the idea of *you* looking at him, so why don't you go bat your eyelashes at him and I'm sure he'll ask you out." Callie had no idea why she felt so angry, so out of control. Had no idea why these stupid, jealous-sounding words were coming out of her mouth. She was *not* jealous. She was *not* crazy. And she was *not* going to let the sight of one man shirtless get her worked up like this. Pathetic.

"Oh, get a grip, Callie."

Callie stopped in the doorway between the Canteen and the office and took a deep breath in then out. "On what exactly?" she asked, managing to make her voice sound syrupy sweet.

Em stepped into view, her uncharacteristic frown now matching the uncharacteristic irritation reflected in her bright blue eyes. "Even if Trevor had eyes for anyone but you, I wouldn't go out with the guy you're practically in love with."

"In love with?" Callie sputtered. What a ridiculous accusation. She was not the fall-in-love-with-your-best-friend type. Especially when he was a goody-goody. A freaking FBI agent. The former mayor's son. It was crazy to think someone like her would be in love with someone like him.

No matter how good he looked without a shirt.

Jesus.

"Yeah. In love with." Em planted her feet as if to block the doorway, slender hands resting on her hips.

"You're so far out of your mind, Emerson."

"Am I?"

"Yes, and you'd think after everything Luke did to you, you'd be over all these stupid romantic fantasies. It was one thing when you were a teenager, but grow up."

Em's face paled, but the battle light didn't go out of her eyes. "Luke has nothing to do with this or with me. But if you want to be a bitch and bring it up to change the subject, fine. It only proves my point." Em turned and walked out of the room, her long, pink skirt swishing behind her.

Callie sank into one of the chairs. She wasn't quite sure what Em's point was, but she was positive the sinking feeling in her stomach had everything to do with hurting Em's feelings and nothing to do with what Em had said.

Nothing at all.

For three days Shelby hadn't said one word to Trevor, and he'd have been lying if he said it wasn't kind of nice. When they weren't talking, he didn't have to worry about mopping up tears or hearing nasty accusations.

As much as it was less pressure to live in the silence, each day without true interaction, the guilt twisted deeper. His only respite was AIF. He didn't know what he'd do without it. Even on days where he spent the majority of his time on a mower, he felt useful. Shelby made him feel ineffective, useless no matter what he tried to do.

Still, he made sure he got home before Shelby every day. Of

course, today he'd miscalculated how long grabbing a six pack and some cookies from the grocery store would take since about five people stopped him and asked how he was doing, how Shelby was doing, and what they could do to help.

Trevor knew it was kindness, but he'd never understood the small town penchant for sticking your nose in other people's business. No matter how many times Dad had tried to explain how that was the great thing about small communities.

He wanted his privacy, and if he needed help he'd ask for it. He didn't need DeeDee Hawbeker clucking her tongue over him buying beer and cookies and nothing else.

So not only was he late, he was also irritated by well-meaning people and his dead father's words. If Shelby was still freezing him out when he went inside, so the hell be it.

Trevor stepped into the house already feeling deflated. Damn, he wanted to get back to Seattle.

"You *are* a crappy brother," he muttered aloud, tossing his keys onto the little end table near the door. He should be thinking about Shelby, not himself, but he couldn't manage the selfless guardian role.

Trevor moved into the living room and it took him a minute to realize sounds and smells were coming from the kitchen.

He stepped into the room to find Shelby baking cookies. And some *guy* sitting at the kitchen table.

"You're home," Shelby practically sang, her smile bright and kind of creepy. The boy looked up at Shelby nervously. Though Trevor knew he shouldn't be okay with his kid sister having some guy in the house without any kind of supervision, the skinny kid with scruffy hair and black-framed glasses didn't pose much of a threat.

"Yeah, I'm home."

"This is Dan." Her voice was still oddly chipper as she bent over to shove a pan of cookie dough into the oven.

Dan stood, wiped palms on his pants that were too tight in Trevor's estimation and held one out. "Hi, Mr. Steele. It's nice to meet you."

Trevor shook the boy's hand, but before he could verbally respond, Shelby jumped in.

"Call him Trevor." For the first time, there was no pleasantness in her voice, just edge.

Trevor was about to tell this Dan kid that he could and should call him Mr. Steele, before it dawned on Trevor why Shelby didn't want Dan calling him Mr. Steele.

To Shelby, Mr. Steele was their dad, most definitely not her brother. Trevor forced a smile. "Nice to meet you too, Dan. What are you two up to?"

"Physics homework." Dan's voice squeaked slightly as he sat back down, staring intently at the open book in front of him.

"I'm baking us some cookies for a snack," Shelby said, her voice and demeanor back to sing-songy.

Trevor wasn't sure if he was forgiven or if Shelby was putting on an act for the sake of *Dan*, but it was kind of nice having her talk to him again. He went over to the counter and leaned against it. "Do I get any cookies or are you going to tell me to get out of the way and go watch some cartoons?"

She smiled a little since it had been exactly what he'd always told her when he'd be doing *his* homework and she'd been underfoot. "You can have two cookies. Actually, I have something to run by you while Dan is *still* working on the *first* problem."

Poor Dan scrunched down in his chair. "It's hard," he muttered.

Shelby's smile broadened and Trevor got the feeling he should start worrying about Dan even if the teen wasn't threatening looking. Shelby was eighteen, after all. Now he was responsible for... Trevor grimaced. All that teenage hormonal... He couldn't think the words when associated with his sister.

"What do you want to run by me?"

Shelby turned her attention to wiping off the counter. "Well, Dan is taking me to prom."

Trevor looked over his shoulder at the young man's back. "Oh, he is?" Trevor was glad to see Dan shift in his chair.

"I need to get a prom dress. Mom already gave me the money before, but I need someone to take me dress shopping."

"Uh."

She rolled her eyes. "Not you. I was thinking maybe I could ask Em and Callie to go with me."

"Em and Callie?" Surely he'd heard wrong. Really, really wrong. Or maybe he'd suddenly fallen asleep and this was some sort of crazy dream. Maybe she'd poisoned him and this was a hallucination.

But she just stood there, wiping the counter, waiting for an answer.

"You want... I'm sorry, I don't understand. You want someone you don't like and someone you barely know to take you prom dress shopping?"

Shelby scrubbed the immaculate white countertop harder. "I think I've been wrong about Callie."

Trevor was rendered speechless, but he wasn't fooled. Shelby was up to something. He didn't have a clue as to what, but all his best undercover training told him to go along with it for the time being and investigate later.

"Okay. I'm glad to hear that." *I don't believe you for a second, but good try lying.* "I'm sure Callie and Em would be glad to help you, but isn't dress shopping something you'd want to do with your friends?"

Shelby stopped her work on the counter and turned her back to him under the guise of checking on her cookies. "They already have their dresses."

Out of the corner of Trevor's eye, he noticed Dan looking over his shoulder at Shelby and frowning almost worriedly at her.

Hmm. "You're sure you want to ask Em and Callie?"

"Actually, I was hoping maybe you'd ask them for me." She looked up, smiled hopefully, but she twisted her fingers together, a sure sign there was more to this innocent act.

"I see."

"I'm free all weekend," Shelby added.

"Uh huh."

"And it doesn't have to take a long time."

"Right."

"Trevor." She worked on her best pathetic pleading look. "Please."

"Why can't you ask them?"

"Because, like you said, I barely know Em, and Callie and I aren't exactly friends."

"Which is why this makes no sense to me. It's not that I think it's a bad idea. I just don't get it."

Some irritation crept onto her face and her pleading look turned harder, more frustrated. She definitely had a plan. One she didn't want him to know about, and she didn't like him not giving in and playing along without a few questions.

"It's weird, but I need an opinion besides my own, and my friends are busy." Trevor could tell she wanted to say something other than busy and began to wonder for the first time if she was having problems at school. She hadn't talked about her friends much since he'd been back. Maybe there was something to that.

He grimaced at the thought of trying to navigate the twists and turns of the teenage girl psyche. Maybe it'd be best to leave that alone and let Callie and Em deal with it.

"They're older and have done the prom thing. Em's always nice, and Callie..." Shelby frowned a little. "Like I said, I want to start over there. Maybe she's not as bad as I thought."

Trevor watched as Shelby struggled to spit out the words. Shelby was a halfway decent liar, but not good enough to hide the fact she still didn't like Callie and struggled to lie about it.

"I'll ask them." He didn't think denying her request would help him figure out what she was up to. Better for Shelby to think he was fooled into complacency.

"Maybe you could go call them. Like, right now?"

Trevor frowned, but quickly smoothed it out into a casual smile. "Sure. Just make sure to save me some cookies." He pushed off the counter and gave Dan the once over while the teen pretended to focus on the physics book in front of him.

Trevor left the kitchen. On the one hand, maybe Shelby was being genuine. Maybe she was that desperate for a female role model or whatever, and if she was having problems with her friends, maybe it was prompting her to look at the way she treated people. It was a plausible enough explanation for a turnaround when it came to Callie.

Trevor didn't buy it. Shelby had something up her sleeve, something he wouldn't like. Trevor sank onto his bed. He had some investigating to do, but where to start?

A few minutes later, his thoughts were interrupted by hesitant footsteps and then the squeaky voice of a teenage boy. "Mr.... Tr... Mr. Steele?"

Trevor looked over at the poor kid hovering in the hallway, vibrating with nerves. "Yeah?"

"Um, I told Shelby I had to go to the bathroom so I'm just

going to come out and say this. Kiley and Sarah had this big mother-daughter prom extravaganza thing last weekend so, I think Shelby's feeling a little weird about things, you know? That's really why she doesn't want to ask them."

Trevor looked at his tapping fingers for a moment, that old familiar guilt cropping up. "That explains a lot." But not everything. Certainly not the one-eighty with Callie.

"And, um, I figure Shelby said I don't have to, but I wanted to make sure it was okay I take her to prom. I mean, okay with you. I mean, I'm a good kid," Dan finally managed to squeak out. "And I have to be home by one prom night, so I'll have her home by twelve thirty, unless you want her home earlier. I mean, you're her brother, but you're also her guardian so even though she doesn't think... I think... "

"Relax, kid," Trevor muttered. He felt for Dan, but he also didn't like the idea of being anyone's guardian. Especially when it came to prom night stuff. Too weird. Too uncomfortable. "Twelve thirty is fine."

Dan smiled and Trevor thought about his own prom night. He'd finally gotten into Tina Lavina's pants after the dance, and then they'd gotten really drunk in her parent's basement. One of his few forays into breaking the rules.

"Thanks, Mr. Steele," Dan was gushing. "I'll make sure to show Shelby a good time."

The thought of good time had Trevor changing his tune a little. Maybe he couldn't do the emotional, feminine guardian crap, but he could certainly play the role of protective guardian.

Trevor stood from his bed, leisurely made his way over to Dan, but kept his stare fixed on the kid until Dan's smile began to wilt. "No drinking, no drugs, you lay a hand on my sister and I'll break it." Trevor offered a sunny, pleasant smile. "Also, please remember, I own many, many guns." Trevor patted Dan on the shoulder. "See ya 'round, Dan."

The role of guardian was enjoyable for the first time. Now, he had to figure out what Shelby was up to, and maybe he'd start feeling like he was doing the right things.

Chapter Five

Callie tapped her foot on the tile floor. A buzz of activity swirled around her. Women wrangling children, teenagers in giggling packs, old couples walking slowly just to walk.

She hated the mall. Hated the continuous hum of noise and the different places and all the bright lights and colors. It was too stimulating, too overwhelming.

Adding Em's enthusiastic prom dress talk, Shelby's creepy alter ego trying her damnedest to be nice, and a trip to the mall was worse than normal. Callie's foot tapped harder. She wanted to go home, wanted to go to her shop, where she could lose herself in some rock music and the relaxing comfort of banging on metal for a while.

"Which one do you think she'll pick?" It had been Em's suggestion to give Shelby some alone time in the store after their hour of shopping with her. All so Shelby could make her own decision without "feeling any pressure" and then meet them in the food court for lunch.

"I could give two shits."

Em frowned. "Oh, you have to admit it was kind of fun." Her smile was immediately back in place. "Besides, she was actually considering that bright blue one you picked out. It looked great on her. Who knew you had a knack for this?"

"I don't."

"Don't you think she had fun?"

"I think that kid is up to something." Callie drummed her fingers on the sticky table in the same cadence of her foot tapping. This whole trip idea had been weird enough, Shelby spending an entire hour and a half being nice to her? That was downright alien invasion material.

"You're being paranoid."

"She hates me. She has always hated me, and there is absolutely no reason for her to have stopped hating me unless she is up to something."

"Maybe she realized—"

"Nope." Callie refused to believe Shelby had changed overnight, refused to believe there wasn't still some of that age-old hostility in Shelby's responses before she ironed them out with niceties. "She didn't realize jack. She's up to something, and I'm going to figure out what it is before I end up shackled in a basement somewhere."

Em shook her head, hair bouncing in time. "You're being ridiculous."

Callie didn't respond, instead watched as Shelby made her way over to them, hanging bag in hand.

"Which one did you pick?" Em wiggled in excitement.

Shelby slid into a seat and didn't make eye contact with either of them. "The blue one."

Those were exactly the kinds of reasons Callie couldn't get over the feeling an ambush was coming. Shelby didn't actually want their help, and almost seemed regretful and irritated she'd ultimately picked a dress Callie had suggested. Each time Callie tried to bait Shelby into a nasty response, Shelby would almost take it, but then the angry flash would disappear and be replaced by a creepy politeness.

"Wonderful. Let's buy you some lunch."

Callie studied Shelby's face, but Shelby worked up a smile. "Sounds good."

They went up to the sandwich place and ordered, retreating

to the sticky table, food in hand. Though Em managed to keep the conversation flowing all through shopping, as they sat down to eat their food it seemed as if all topics had been exhausted.

"So." Shelby offered into the awkward lack of conversation. "Sounds like Trevor is really helping you guys out at AIF." Shelby bit into her sandwich, looked at Em and then Callie, and then quickly back down at her food when she saw Callie staring at her.

"He's been a lifesaver," Em agreed. "AIF is a lot of work for three people, especially in the spring and summer. Adding one person, especially a volunteer, has helped us immeasurably."

Shelby nodded as she chewed and swallowed, but Callie didn't miss Shelby's covert attempt to check the time on her cell phone. "I bet you guys wish he could stay and help past September."

The picture began to come together in Callie's head. The purpose for this sudden forced niceness. This odd girls' afternoon.

"We can get by after the fly-in. Besides, we're hoping Lawson will be home soon. You probably don't remember Lawson. He's our cousin. He moved to California, oh gosh, fifteen years ago."

"But, what if he doesn't come home?" Shelby asked, effectively cutting Em off from a long, rambling story about Lawson.

"Oh, well."

"I mean, if he doesn't come back, or even if he does, wouldn't you wish Trevor had stayed?"

Callie shook her head. Up until that moment Shelby had done a good job of keeping her cards hidden, but now they were all out on the table. For a moment, Callie almost felt sympathy. When you lost your parents so young, it was hard to lose anyone else. Callie could understand the desperation in Shelby's question. She could even empathize with it, but that didn't make what Shelby was attempting to do right.

"This is why you're being nice."

Shelby's eyes shot to Callie, a flash of guilt in her frown before she smoothed it out. "What do you mean?"

Callie waved an impatient arm. "Drop the act. You're trying to butter us up so we'll help you convince Trevor to stay."

The innocent look immediately left and was replaced by a scowl. "So?"

"So?" Callie shook her head. She'd been this self-absorbed once, and she wished it could make her more sympathetic, but what Shelby needed was a cold dose of reality. "That's a shitty thing to do. Even for you."

"Don't you want him to stay?" Shelby demanded, slumping in her chair and crossing her arms across her chest, the perfect picture of teenage sullenness.

"I want him to be happy." Callie hoped her voice sounded calm rather than snippy. "If you cared about him like you should, you'd want that too."

"Why can't he be happy here?" It was nearly a whine.

"Because he can't. He won't be."

"Who cares?" Shelby spat. "I deserve to have someone at home. I deserve to have him stay. Haven't I been through enough already? Why does my life have to change? Why does his life get to come before mine? I don't want to go to Seattle on breaks from school. I want to come home."

Sympathy petered out, because while Callie could sympathize with Shelby's loss, Callie had gone through worse. "You don't own the market on loss," Callie said through gritted teeth. "Or on getting the short end of the stick."

"Oh, and you do?" Shelby countered. She leaned toward

Callie. "Your mom died when you were a baby. You never had one to miss. You probably don't remember your dad either. You have no idea what it's like to lose your parents when you know exactly what it means and exactly what little is left."

There were tears in Shelby's eyes now, and Callie had to fight the sting of her own. "You're a selfish brat if you think making Trevor miserable will weaken the pain of losing your parents."

"Guys, maybe we should—" But Em's quiet protests were lost as Callie stared long and hard at Shelby until the sullen teen looked up.

"I lost a lot of people at a very young age, so don't kid yourself into thinking you know better than me just because you think you're smarter or superior. Losing means learning, and you need to learn that making other people unhappy won't make you feel any better." God, it had taken Callie a long time to learn that lesson. Even now, there were some days it was hard to remember.

Maybe she was taking the harsh road, but if she could impart any of what she'd learned on Shelby it would be well worth it. "I won't let you sabotage Trevor's life because you can't see past your own hurt."

Shelby sank deeper into her chair and sneered through the tears in her eyes. "You think you know him so well because you love him or something?"

Irritation and anger clawed through. What the hell was with everyone accusing her of being in love with Trevor? "I'm a little tired of getting that particular accusation. I can care about your brother without being in love with him. It's called friendship."

"It sounds pathetic," Shelby shot back.

"You know what? I'm done. I'll wait in the car." Ignoring her half-eaten sandwich, Callie pushed out of the chair. Em didn't try to stop her. She was still too busy gaping at the exchange she'd just witnessed.

The anger increased with each step away. Callie couldn't place the source of it, but it bubbled hot and heavy in her chest.

She could blame it on being used, but she'd known all along Shelby was using her. She could blame it on everyone thinking she was in love with Trevor. Couldn't two members of the opposite sex just be friends? Couldn't two members of the opposite sex who had a kind of weird attraction to each other still be friends without everyone accusing the woman in the duo of being some kind of lovesick, pathetic moron?

Callie wrenched the car door open and slid inside. It was such a double standard. She bet no one ever accused Trevor of being in love with her. Not that he would have any reason to be. What exactly did she have to offer? A bad attitude, a snarky mouth, and a crappy way with people.

Callie groaned and rapped her head against the steering wheel. She was losing her mind, and she wanted to blame it on everyone else. On Em for being perfect, on Shelby for being such a bitch, on Trevor for being Trevor, but the bottom line was all of her weird feelings and conflicting emotions were her own damn fault.

Because no matter how disgusted she was with herself over it, there was a part of her, a very large part, that liked the idea of convincing Trevor to stay. A part of her that might have gone along with the plan if Shelby hadn't been so sneaky about it.

Which made Callie a total moron. About as much as sitting here sulking in her car did.

She wasn't in love with Trevor, no matter what Em or Shelby or anyone might think, but if she was being honest she knew there was a danger with him. If things had been a little different, if she were a little different, or if he were, there was potential for *something*.

She didn't want to think about that potential, that something. Since she'd been a baby, all of the people she'd loved and counted on deserted her. Like some sort of curse, death swept them away. Truly letting herself feel what she could potentially feel with Trevor would leave her open to all that hurt again.

She could count on one hand the people she cared for unconditionally, the people who returned that feeling, and of that small handful, Trevor was the only one who wasn't blood. The only one who could walk away and break all ties to her without the word family bringing him back.

Callie was desperate to keep that handful intact.

The passenger car door opened and Em slid in. Callie swallowed down the lump in her throat as Shelby moved into the backseat with her dress. No one said a word, and Callie was more than happy to drive in complete silence.

When Callie pulled the car into the Steele driveway twenty-five long, silent minutes later, Trevor was using a weed eater along the edges of the front yard, biceps flexing under the weight of the long machine.

Callie put the car into park, but didn't make a move to get out. She was glad when Em didn't either and Shelby climbed out of the backseat.

Trevor leaned into the open window, an easygoing smile on his face. "Everything went okay?" She could smell grass and sweat on him, and when he leaned into the car, he was closer than she felt particularly comfortable with.

Callie looked at Shelby skirting the front of the car. Shelby's expression was a mixture of anger and pleading.

Something about it had Callie censoring her words.

"Yeah. Great." What would be the point in telling him about Shelby's little plan or their painful argument? It'd make him feel guilty about letting Shelby down. She didn't look at Trevor, even though she could practically feel his breath on her face.

"Thanks," Shelby said. "For taking me."

Callie shrugged.

"Let us know if you need any help getting ready on prom night," Em offered.

"You guys want to stay for dinner?" Trevor jabbed a thumb toward the house. "We could order a pizza."

"Nah, we gotta get back. Work to catch up on." Still, Callie didn't dare look at Trevor, afraid he would see the lie in her eyes, afraid he would see other things in them as well.

Trevor tapped the sunglasses down on her nose so she was forced to look at him. "You okay?"

"Fine." Callie pushed them back up. "See you Monday." Without giving anyone another chance to talk, Callie shoved the car into reverse and began to back out the drive.

Once on the highway, Em finally interrupted the silence. "Why didn't you tell him?"

Callie shrugged, kept her eyes glued to the road. "It'd make him feel bad." Though her eyes weren't on Em, she could feel Em's studying gaze and it had Callie hunching her shoulders.

"You're not going to try and convince him to stay?"

"Hell no," Callie spat. She would be a good friend when it came to this. Selfish wants wouldn't change her mind. "He doesn't want to be here."

"Maybe."

"I know Trevor well enough to know that staying in Pilot's Point is his own personal nightmare."

"Or maybe you're scared."

"Scared?" Callie might be hard on herself about a lot of things, but she'd never considered herself a coward.

"Yes, scared. Of what you'd have to deal with if he did stay."

Callie ground her teeth together. What was it with people? They always had to stick their noses where they didn't belong. Airplanes never poked into her personal life, never asked her how she was feeling. Much better companionship. "Could we please get off this idiotic merry-go-round? I'm tired of it."

"I'm saying this because I care about you." Em touched Callie's arm briefly, and the quick glance showed that Em's eyes were wide and concerned. Callie hated that look. It always made her feel guilty when she had no reason to be.

"You keep walls up, Cal. With all of us."

"I don't know what you're—"

"We'll start with me. You pretend you're fine with the relationship I have with Tom and my mom. I know it hurts you, and it makes you feel like you missed out on something. By never expressing those emotions, by ignoring them, you're putting up a wall between us that keeps us from being as close as we could be. It's a gulf that divides us, and it makes me sad that it does. But it's your wall to keep me blocked enough that you feel safe."

Callie swallowed against the emotions that flooded her throat. Maybe part of that was true, but she didn't consider it a wall. By not expressing some of those stupid feelings, she was keeping her and Em as close as they could be. Expressing them would only make that gulf wider. It would be doing what she'd just warned Shelby against doing, hurting Em so Callie could feel better. It wasn't right.

"Then with Law. Whenever he calls you never express how

angry you are with him. Not once in the past year have you asked him to come home or told him how much it would mean to you—to us. You pretend you totally understand why he's still in California and you pretend it's okay. Another wall."

"I am fine with your family situation, and I do understand why Lawson is still in California. He's got kids, Em. I'm not a total selfish bitch."

"Maybe intellectually you understand, but it's obvious that emotionally it hurts. You're not a selfish bitch, but you try to be because it hurts less than all the caring you'd do otherwise." Em's voice was soft, almost pleading. Callie knew it was meant to be comforting, to be helpful, but it only served to have her pushing her foot harder onto the accelerator. If they got home, she could make her escape from Em's psychoanalysis.

"Then you add the fact you're not being honest with yourself or Trevor about how you feel about him. How many more walls will you build?"

"I know exactly how I feel about him," Callie muttered. Okay, maybe not exactly. Sometimes she got a little fuzzy on what she was feeling, but she did know what she wanted to feel for Trevor and that was platonic friendship. Neither of them would benefit from anything more.

Em sighed. This time when Em's hand reached out to touch her, it rested on Callie's elbow and remained there. "I've let you deal with everything that's happened in your own way, probably for too long. Now, it's time you faced some of the issues all this death has caused. I'm worried about you. I want you to be happy. Life keeps going. We should be happy."

"Em, cut the hippie bullshit, please. You're not a shrink, and I'm fine."

"Deflecting. Another wall. Do these walls make your life what you want it to be?"

Callie's throat constricted, and she squeezed the steering wheel hard. Maybe Em wasn't totally off base because all the normal tactics weren't getting her sister to back off. She'd try a little honesty. "Maybe they're what I need to make it through the day."

On a sigh Callie recognized as defeat, Em's hand slipped off Callie's elbow. "Maybe. Or maybe you're keeping yourself from truly being happy because you're too afraid of feeling good. I don't totally disagree with what you said to Shelby, but I wonder if it's another lie. Maybe it's not the people you love you're trying to protect. Maybe it's yourself."

Callie didn't like either answer. She swallowed. "Is there something so wrong with protecting myself?"

"If it leaves you alone and unhappy, I'd say yes."

"And your suggestion is?" Her tone was snippy, but there was a part of her buried deep under all the sarcasm and fear that really wanted to know.

"Let some of the walls down. Maybe you'll find out you can be happy after all."

Callie pulled the car into AIF, looked at the home her grandfather had built, the place that meant the world to her. If she let some of those walls down, what more would she lose?

Maybe it was time to find out.

Chapter Six

Women made absolutely no sense to Trevor. At one point in his life, Callie had made sense, but the more he spent time with her, the more he realized she was just as confusing as every other woman on the planet.

It had been over a week since the weird little shopping trip, and ever since things between everyone had been a little off. Trevor had never gotten to the bottom of the whole thing, but something had happened, something had altered.

Shelby was now quiet and accommodating at home, there was some kind of awkward distance between Em and Callie, and when he was in a room with any three of them, they seemed to be studying him, trying to figure out some problem.

But he didn't have a damn clue what problem he represented. He felt about as edgy as they all were acting.

The sky was darkening as Trevor pulled into AIF. Shelby was out with Dan and he'd been too bored to sit around the house all evening. He was feeling restless, missing Seattle, missing having a life that didn't revolve around his teenage sister.

If he sat around the house much longer he would be tempted to read through his email reports, which a downward spiral into wondering if he could get out of Pilot's Point earlier than his original six-month plan.

So, he'd decided to head out to AIF. The only place he didn't actively wish for his old life.

Lights shone from the small window of Callie's shop, and

the quiet tinkling of music melded with the cacophony of spring peepers from the ponds.

A cool breeze rustled the leaves of the trees, and the sky to the west glowed as the last sliver of sun disappeared. Some of the dissatisfaction lifted, filtered away as if it was sinking with the sun.

He didn't know what it was about this place, but he was beginning to think it was magic, and he was beginning to understand what made the Bakers so fiercely loyal to a bunch of metal buildings and antique planes.

Trevor stepped onto the concrete step of the shop and looked in the open door only to find the cluttered room empty, despite the faint strains of a rock song from the ancient radio in the corner. Frowning, he stepped inside and noticed the door attaching the shop to one of the hangars was also open.

When he stepped into that doorway, the image that met him stopped him in his tracks. Callie wasn't working on the plane, she was sitting in the cockpit. The main hangar doors were closed but she looked out at them as though they were open sky.

She looked unbearably sad, miserably lonely, and it made his heart ache.

When he stepped into the hangar, the sudden movement had Callie's head jerking to face him. "Hey," she greeted, quickly climbing out of the cockpit and jumping down to the ground below. "Thought you were gone."

She skirted the plane's tail to cross to him, but her eyes didn't meet his.

"Yeah. Shelby's out on a date. I got bored."

"Oh. I'm just..." She looked up at where she'd been and trailed off.

"Can't think of a plausible lie?"

She shrugged, still not making eye contact. "Guess I was daydreaming."

"As hard as you work, I'd say you could use a little daydreaming time." But it hadn't looked like the happy daydreaming she should have been doing, and he desperately wanted to see her happy. "What kind of plane is this?"

Her eyes took in the length of the plane as she ran her fingers across the bottom of the tail almost reverently. "Stearman."

He studied the glossy blue and yellow machine. He didn't know shit about planes, but it looked nice and well loved, even if it was a glorified deathtrap in his estimation. "Isn't this the one you've been working on?"

"Yeah. Gramps lent it to a guy, and, to make a long story short, this guy busted it all to hell before we got it back. Then, I kind of put it away." She looked at the plane the way a woman would look at her child. A kind of pride, an undeniable love and adoration.

To Callie, it was more than metal and screws; it was a memory. Which was why he couldn't figure out why she seemed so sad. Planes and flying was something that always made her happy.

"You okay?"

"Yeah." She shoved her hands into her pockets. "Why?"

He knew if he told her she looked sad, she'd get pissed. He went about it a different way instead. "You haven't been yourself the past few days. Kinda quiet. Haven't picked one fight."

Instead of laughing like he'd hoped, she frowned. "Maybe you don't know me anymore."

He frowned in return, didn't like the idea. Of all the people in his life, he knew Callie the best. Or thought he did. "I know that plane means something to you."

She moved up to the front of the plane, trailing her fingers along the length of it as she did. "I learned to fly in this plane. Actually, more than that, my dad took me for my first ride in this plane."

She smiled, and some of the sadness lifted into the pleasantness of memory. "This was the first plane Gramps bought when they started AIF because it was the same kind he soloed in. Then when Dad learned to fly he soloed in this one, and when it was time for my first solo, I did too." She held her arms out, almost as if she could give the plane a hug, she would. "I love this thing. Like part of the damn family."

She turned to face him, the smile still on her lips. "Let me guess," she said with a little laugh. "You think I'm nuts."

"Actually I was thinking you're beautiful when you're happy." The words slipped out before he could change them to friendly rather than eerily close to romantic.

Her mouth gaped open for a second before she turned away from him. "Ha. You're funny." But she didn't sound amused.

"Callie, I'm—"

He moved toward her, but she expertly cut him off. "I'm going to sell it. Hopefully." She rested her hand lovingly on the glossy yellow of the lower wing.

That stopped him in his tracks, made him forget the beautiful comment. "Why would you sell it?"

"AIF needs the money."

He moved so he could see her face. His heart tripped to see tears in her eyes, even as she tried to blink them away they spilled onto her cheeks.

He'd seen Callie cry before. Remembered with perfect clarity the way she'd sobbed into her grandpa's side at her grandma's funeral. He'd been fifteen, standing between his parents, having no idea what her pain must have felt like. He could still remember the hard, cold wind whipping its way through the funeral, could remember the preacher's droning words, could remember how his heart had twisted at the sight of Callie crying when he thought she'd been the strongest girl in the world.

This kind of crying was different, though equally wrenching. She didn't sob or make a noise. The tears kept spilling over, dousing her cheeks, her hand clutching the plane as if she could keep a hold of it.

"I'm such an idiot. It's just a fucking plane." Her voice squeaked and choked.

"It's more than that." He moved over to her, tentatively reached out to wipe her wet cheek with his thumb. "You said so yourself."

She shook her head, sniffled. Maybe he was wrong. She didn't just look beautiful when she was happy. There was something achingly beautiful on her face now as well. He so rarely saw that kind of naked emotion there. It drew him in, had rational thought dimming in the face of her proximity, her tears, her emotion.

He didn't know what he was doing and for this brief, blinding moment he didn't care. Meeting Callie's brown eyes, their lips hovering centimeters away, he couldn't think about consequences. All he could think about was kissing her.

It was possibly the longest minute of his life. Both seemed unable to end it, yet neither moved forward. They stood, frozen in time, eyes locked in a confusing battle of *what are we doing*?

Trevor's heart thumped hard against his chest, almost painfully, and yet, there was something warm and sweet working through his limbs. A kind of longing he wasn't sure he'd experienced before. Not just blood-pumping lust.

Something deeper, more complex.

When he finally worked up the guts to close that last centimeter of distance between them, just as their lips met for the briefest, faintest second, Em's voice rang out in the still air around them.

"Callie!"

They stepped away from each other, and though they'd broken the physical connection, their eyes were still locked. When Em came into view, she didn't pause before her words tumbled into the moment and crushed it completely. "I just got off the phone with Lawson. He got custody. He's moving home." Em's grin looked like it might split her face in two. "Lawson's coming home!"

Callie wrenched her gaze from Trevor, her breath coming out in an audible whoosh. Trevor wished he could manage it, but his breath was caught in his lungs, unable to escape.

"Home? For good?" Her voice was raspy, uneven, and that loosened some of the tightness in his chest. At least they were both feeling unsteady.

"For good," Em squealed. "Stop working and come home. I've got a million things to tell you."

"Yeah, I'll be there in a minute."

"You can come too, Trevor. Callie has some beers hidden away in the cabin somewhere. Twinkies and Cokes too, which she thinks I don't know about."

It was an attempt to lighten the weight of the room, but neither Trevor nor Callie could work up the appropriate smile of response.

"No, thanks, I should be heading home. Gotta sit on the porch with a shotgun for when Dan drops Shelby off."

Em smiled at the joke, but Callie didn't. Even Trevor was having a hard time coaxing his mouth to curve upward.

"Well, I'm heading back to the cabin. Don't be too long, Callie."

Callie nodded and the minute Em was out of sight she sagged against the plane, looking like she'd been punched in the gut. It was a strange reaction to news she'd been hoping for.

"Aren't you happy?"

"I don't know what I am."

He hoped she wasn't just talking about Lawson, because he was feeling a little confused himself.

"I'm relieved," she managed. "It won't magically solve everything, but before Gramps died we were all doing about five people's worth of work, then me and Em had to try and take all that on. Your help has been great, but Law being back—it's balance. We each get to focus on what we're good at. My family will finally all be here. All be home."

Then she looked at him, studied him again in the way she'd been studying him all week. He wanted to ask what that look was all about, but when he opened his mouth, a good-bye tumbled out instead.

"I'll get out of your hair. See you tomorrow."

He backed out of the hangar and turned around once in the shop. He reached his car and promised himself that if he ever got bored again, he'd take his chances with work email.

Callie trudged to the cabin feeling like she'd been through the gauntlet. First, Trevor had called her beautiful and all but kissed her, then the thing she'd been waiting on. Lawson was actually coming home.

Things never could happen one at a time. They always had to happen in a blast, so she couldn't adequately respond to any one event at the appropriate moment.

After all, what should she have done when Trevor walked in on her feeling sorry for herself, missing her dad, and feeling sick over the thought of selling the Stearman? She thought she'd done the right thing. She'd been honest. Maybe she'd tried to deflect him a little bit, but she'd explained the significance of the plane. Hadn't backed away from the memory or emotion.

She hadn't put up a wall or brushed him off. It was supposed to be progress. Was it her damn fault she hadn't been able to hold it together? She hated to cry, but sometimes she couldn't keep it all under control. For a moment, it had felt good to let loose, to let emotion pour out. Then Trevor had touched her cheek, and it hadn't felt friendly. It had felt as good as that emotional release.

But the moment that followed and the way his eyes held hers. The way his mouth had been so close and had so briefly brushed hers. Callie didn't know what to think of it. She hadn't initiated anything. Nope. That had been all Trevor.

What the hell did *that* mean?

Now, Lawson and the boys were coming home. Everyone would be in their rightful place. Until September, when Trevor would leave again. Of course, Seattle was his rightful place, but she was getting used to having him around.

Callie climbed the stairs of the cabin's porch, each limb on her body a heavy, immovable weight. The last thing she needed was another piece of her life to be conflicted about.

Callie took a deep breath of the spring evening, tried to gain some strength from it. She still felt heavy and uneven.

One thing at a time. First, she'd deal with the news of Lawson coming home. Then she'd figure out what to do about Trevor.

When Callie opened the door and stepped into the small living room of the cabin, Em was curled up on the old, floral print couch with a notebook and pen in her hands.

It made Callie smile. There was some comfort in coming home to Em, exactly as Callie had known she'd be, already planning and organizing. No matter how many things happened at once, no matter how much Callie struggled to deal with every blow, she could always trust Em to be that steady, predictable rock.

"You don't waste any time making to-do lists." Callie tried to hold on to that warm feeling of love. Lawson was coming home. She had to work on thinking positively, and having their little family together was positive.

"Never too early." Em's grin stretched so wide Callie thought it must hurt her face. "A million things to do the next few weeks."

"When's the move home date?"

"The boys' last day of school is May twenty-third, so he's hoping to be home by the thirtieth."

Callie nodded. It gave Lawson, and Sue for that matter, a lot of time to change their minds. Callie didn't say that, instead she took a seat in the rickety rocking chair in the corner and pulled her knees up to her chin, letting the chair sway back and forth. "What's first on the list?"

"We've got to get the main house clean and ready."

The weights in her arms felt heavier and Callie rested her chin on her pulled up knees. More work, as if they didn't have enough. She meant to keep that sentiment to herself, but she muttered it before she had a chance to censor herself. "Great. Another thing to do."

"How can you say that? Lawson's coming home."

Callie wished she could muster half of Em's enthusiasm, but all she could think about was the time and energy it would take to get the big house ready for three inhabitants.

Just like Gramps's office, the house down the gravel road stood exactly as it had two years ago. The emotional toll of going through everything that had been Grandma and Gramps's would be huge.

"Everything will be like it was supposed to be." Em's voice was dreamy and almost childlike. "The Baker grandkids running AIF. Like we always planned."

Yes, like they'd always planned. Callie could still remember huddling together on the porch of her grandparents' house with Em and Law, talking about how cool things would be when they were old enough to run AIF. They hadn't thought about Grandma and Gramps being gone, hadn't thought about how hard it would be to make ends meet, and had instead dreamed of all the good the way kids do.

Callie felt tears sting her eyes again, but she wasn't about to cry twice in one day. Instead, she offered some practicality in a quiet voice. "It doesn't magically solve all our problems. AIF could still fail."

Em's smile didn't falter, not for a second. "This isn't just about AIF. It's about family. We'll finally all be in one place."

Callie closed her eyes. "I know. I'm sorry." It was hard to be honest about this one thing. She'd kept her concerns about Lawson's return mainly to herself. And it was hard to be honest, period. She'd spent most of her adult life ignoring feelings, shutting them out. Breaking the instinct to keep it that way would take time and effort.

Em wanted to close that gulf between them, so Callie was determined to keep trying. For Em. Maybe for herself too.

"I guess there's a part of me afraid it won't happen. I don't want to get my hopes up. We have to remember to be practical if we want to save AIF."

"You worry too much." Em's smile was reassuring. "Have

some faith."

"I'll work on it." She would really try to work on faith.

Em scrawled another thing on her to-do list so casually Callie figured the conversation was over, but instead of silence, Em kept talking. "Do you want to talk about what was going on between you and Trevor?"

Callie opened her eyes and looked up. "Huh?"

Em rolled her eyes, tapping her pen against her paper. "I may be naïve, but I know a moment when I see one. That was a definite moment. What was going on?"

"Nothing." Callie replayed the moment in her head. "He said I was beautiful." She frowned at Em's goofy grin.

"That's sweet," Em said in that dreamy, romantic voice that always made Callie cringe.

"No, it's stupid. Weird. He didn't mean it. Couldn't have."

"Well, how did he say it?"

Again, the moment replayed in her mind. The way Trevor's eyes had held hers, the way his voice had been low and serious. Honest. Trevor never lied to her. Callie took an unsteady breath. "He said I was beautiful when I was happy."

Em issued one of those little *aw* noises, and Callie scowled.

"Then what?" Em demanded, leaning forward in her seat. Her to-do list balanced precariously on her knees, but she didn't notice. "Tell me."

"Then..." Callie's eyebrows knit together, the memory of being so close to Trevor clogging her lungs all over again. She looked down at her knees, tried to focus on the here and now, but the memory took over, causing her hands to tremble just a little.

It had felt like an eternity standing there, eyes locked to Trevor's. His breath had been warm on her skin, her heart had sped up at the proximity of their bodies, but she hadn't been able to break the moment until he had. "He almost basically kissed me." Exasperated, Callie looked up at Em. "Why would he do that?"

Em's smile was sympathetic. "You don't want me to answer that."

Callie looked down at her knees. Come to think of it, she probably wouldn't like any answer to that question. "No, I don't."

"What's next?"

"Nothing. Nothing happened and nothing is going to."

"Why not?"

Because I'm scared. Because I'm unsure. Because I'm not what he needs/deserves/wants. But none of those reasons spilled out. Callie's throat closed so she couldn't squeak a word.

"You need to figure it out. September will be here soon enough."

Trevor's impending departure was as much a reason as all the others. Trevor was the only man she'd ever wanted a future with and the only way to ensure that future was to remain friends. If they made it into something more and then he left, it would all be over.

Keeping him at arm's length wasn't a wall. It was what had to be done. Callie was positive Trevor would be feeling the exact same way.

Chapter Seven

"Are you sure I need this much hairspray?"

Trevor stifled a yawn as Em put the finishing touches on Shelby's prom ensemble. The whole thing was taking forever, and he didn't know why he was being forced into the role of audience. A teenager getting all dressed up for some dance wasn't his idea of Saturday night entertainment.

Then again, the options in Pilot's Point weren't any more fascinating than this.

Still, he really *really* hated when they asked for his opinion. What did he know about dresses or makeup or up-dos? Zilch. When he was eighteen he certainly hadn't noticed his date's hair or makeup. He'd had other things on his mind, and the thought of those things made Trevor sink farther into the couch and scowl.

"If you want to make it through the dance without a hair out of place we'll need one more spray." Em's tongue pressed to the corner of her mouth as she worked to secure Shelby's hair.

"If you used the earth killing kind of hairspray, it'd probably only need one coat." Callie earned a warning look from Em.

Trevor snuck a glance at Callie, who sat on the same couch as him but as far away as she could get. Two weeks since their weird, pseudo-kiss moment and they hadn't found even footing.

Somewhere in the rational side of his mind he knew he should broach the subject with her. It was the not talking about it that was making things so weird. Unfortunately, his rational side hadn't been able to coordinate with his mouth yet.

"There." Em looked expectantly at the two-person audience on the couch.

Trevor straightened, searched for the right words. A compliment, he assumed, was expected. "Uh, you look nice."

Em rolled her eyes. "Nice?" Em turned to face Shelby and took her by the shoulders. "Shelby, you look gorgeous." Em's reassuring smile had Trevor relaxing a little bit. Maybe he sucked at the whole prom thing, but at least he had someone in tow that could give Shelby what she needed.

"Blue was a much better choice than yellow." Shelby turned to smirk at Callie, but it lacked the kind of fierce heat their interactions used to have. Something had cooled off between the two. Trevor didn't know what it stemmed from, but it was nice not to have to referee.

"Dan will *love* it," Em added, stepping back to admire her work.

"Dan better *love it* with his hands to himself." Trevor earned a disapproving look from Em and an additional one from Shelby.

The doorbell rang and some of Trevor's tension eased again. Shelby looked excited. She looked happy. Though she was obviously trying to play it cool, she couldn't dim the smile on her face or stop checking herself out in the mirror.

It didn't have anything to do with him, but he was glad she could have those feelings in this moment. He didn't want her to be sad, and with the help of the Baker women, she wasn't.

How weird was that?

It took him a few moments to realize that three pairs of eyes stared at him expectantly. "What?"

"Open the door, moron. Girl's gotta make an entrance."

Trevor frowned. Of all people, he didn't expect Callie to get the girly parts of prom, but he pushed off the couch and went to the door as Em scooted Shelby out of the room.

When he got married and had kids, he hoped to God they weren't girls. Living through one prom night as a kind of guardian was enough for his life experiences.

On the other side of the door, Dan stood in his tux, looking a little pale. The teen clutched a plastic container that housed a little pink corsage.

"Hi, Mr. Steele."

Trevor tried not to laugh when Dan's voice cracked in the middle of the greeting.

"Hey, Dan. Now, before I let you in, I'm going to have to frisk you."

Dan didn't look worried, but he did look confused. "Um, okay."

"It's a joke." Trevor moved out of the door and gestured Dan inside. Okay, maybe it would be a *little* fun to have girls. "Lighten up, kid."

"O-okay," Dan agreed.

"Hey." Shelby stepped out from where Em had hidden her away. "Please ignore my brother. No one gets his jokes."

Trevor watched Dan smile and fidget a little with the plastic container in his hands. "Oh, it's okay. Um, here." He shoved the corsage toward Shelby, hands shaking.

Either this whole dance thing was a first for poor old Dan, or he was acting the nerdy role to keep Trevor from being suspicious about his nefarious teenage motives.

Trevor was pretty sure it was the former.

"Why don't you put it on her?" Em handed the plastic container back to Dan.

With shaky hands, Dan helped secure the corsage around Shelby's wrist. It went a long way to soothe Trevor's nerves at anything crazy happening.

"Well, we better get going so we can meet Haley and Jacob."

"Home by twelve thirty. Not one drop of alcohol, and Dan, watch those hands." Again Trevor had to try hard not to laugh when Dan immediately dropped his hands from Shelby's arm. "You go anywhere besides prom, you text me."

"You don't get to tell us what to do."

Trevor only had to raise an eyebrow to have Shelby backing down.

Her shoulders slumped and she sighed. "Text any change of location. Home by twelve thirty. Got it."

"Don't forget to have fun." Trevor grinned at Shelby's scowl, but she couldn't hold it and smiled in return.

"Thanks." She turned around to face Em and Callie. "Thank you both for everything tonight."

Callie only shrugged, but Em offered a beaming smile and said, "Our pleasure. Enjoy yourselves."

Dan and Shelby eventually made it out the door, and Trevor felt weird. He'd done his best, enlisted people to help out with the whole prom situation, and he hoped Shelby hadn't felt like it was less.

But Trevor was reminded that his mother should have been there, and it hurt even him that she wasn't. As Em and Callie began to gather their belongings, Trevor felt a sudden odd panic. He didn't want to be alone tonight.

"You girls want to stay for dinner?"

"Sure," Em piped up, but Trevor's eyes were on Callie. She didn't meet his gaze.

"Yeah, sure," she echoed, sounding anything but.

"I'll walk up to Bennie's and grab us a pizza." Em picked up her purse and slid it onto her shoulder.

"You don't have to do that. We can call some place that will deliver."

Em was already halfway to the door. "Don't worry about it. Short walk. Besides it'll give me a chance to see if Pete's working. Work up a little discount." She winked over her shoulder before she disappeared out the door.

Trevor got the distinct impression he and Callie were being left alone on purpose. Unfortunately, he didn't know what to do about it.

"Em and Pete got a thing going?"

Callie looked at her feet. "I don't know if I'd classify it as a thing. She goes in and flirts. He gives her a discount on pizza. Since it's about the only way I get a meal that isn't veggie frou-frou gunk, I hope they get married and have lots of little baby pizza makers."

Trevor forced a chuckle out, but quickly, uncomfortable silence settled over the living room. He really hated that he'd somehow managed to make things awkward between them, and he had no idea how to fix it.

"Want a beer?"

"God, yes." She pushed off the couch and followed him into the kitchen. Awkward silence followed them as Trevor pulled two bottles from the fridge. He held one out for Callie, opened his mouth to say something and nothing came out.

Callie took the outstretched bottle from his hands. Their fingers brushed, but she showed no outward sign of reaction.

"Wanna go drink it out on the porch? I'm going to pass out from all these hairspray fumes."

Callie nodded and silently followed him to the front door.

The warm day was slowly cooling into the perfect spring evening. The sun had begun its slow descent. Around them, bugs created a low hum of noise, only punctuated by the distant shrieks of children playing or the rumble of a car pulling into its garage.

The two big trees in the front yard gave an illusion of separateness from the rest of the neighborhood so as he and Callie sat on the small concrete stoop, almost close enough to touch, it wasn't hard to pretend they were all alone.

Maybe he couldn't talk to Callie about what was happening between them, but it didn't mean he couldn't talk period. "Should I be worried about this whole prom thing?"

Callie smiled, took a slow sip of her beer. "Nah. Shelby's a good kid, and Dan looked like he might spontaneously combust if they even held hands. He's afraid of you, which was adorably naïve. I think you're safe."

"I don't want her to be messed up because I couldn't do the right thing here. I can't be her dad, but at the same time it doesn't seem right to just be her brother either."

Callie patted his shoulder, and it was the first initiated physical contact since that stupid moment. Maybe they were on their way back to normal.

"Don't be too hard on yourself. You do your best, Shelby will do her best, and everything will work out."

Trevor shook his head and looked down at the cement below him. A small trail of ants made their way across the cracked surface. "I guess you're right. With all her faults, she's got a good head on those shoulders. I mean, she's not like..." He censored the thought, but a few words too late.

"She's not like me."

"That's not what I was going to say." At Callie's raised eyebrow he set the empty bottle down. "Okay, that *is* what I was going to say, but I knew before I said it that it wouldn't come out right, so I didn't say it."

Callie shrugged, picked at the label of the bottle. "You're

right, though. Shelby's got that kind of maturity I didn't manage to scrounge up until, oh, a year ago. She won't make the mistakes I did. She'll be the one who makes all the right choices."

Trevor looked at Callie, hated that he'd put sadness back in her eyes. That he'd inadvertently pushed her guard back up. The only way he knew how to break it down again was to go back, go back to where things weren't so murky. "You know, I almost asked you to prom senior year." He chuckled, but when her laugh didn't meld with his, warning bells sounded in his head.

Her mouth gaped open as she stared at him, like he'd just admitted to cross-dressing or something.

"What? It's not that shocking, is it?"

"No. Yes. I mean." She furrowed her brow and looked down at the ground. "Matt Barns told me you were going to ask me, but then you didn't."

"Matt told you?"

She nodded, and suddenly he realized he hadn't traveled into mood-lightening territory at all. Now they were stuck in some kind of time warp. Eighteen and hideously awkward.

"What changed your mind?" Her voice was so quiet, so meek he wasn't sure it came out of Callie's mouth.

"I don't know." He struggled to recall the events of an April so many years ago. "Mom didn't like the idea for starters."

"Why not? I thought she liked me."

"Seriously? My mom couldn't stand you." It surprised him to see the look of horror on her face. "I thought you knew that."

"She was always so nice to me." Suddenly Callie was that insecure girl she'd been, but the bravado had been stripped off. It nearly stopped his heart.

"I thought..."

He squirmed. "It's not that big of a deal. Mom was so rule oriented. You never were very good at following rules. She didn't approve. It's nothing to be upset about." But he could tell she was, and he couldn't figure that out.

"You didn't ask me to prom because your mom didn't want you to?"

"Well, that wasn't the whole reason." She was angry. He didn't understand it, but Callie was sitting there angry at him for some dumb thing he'd done in high school. They were talking about a dance ten years ago. Callie could hold a grudge, but it was a *dance*. So not Callie.

"What was the whole reason?"

Trevor had to think about that. Why had he chickened out from his first instinct all those years ago? The fear of Callie laughing at him and saying no? That had played into it. She'd dated older guys, dangerous guys. He'd never been her type. Not romantically anyway, and he hadn't really been sure enough of himself to suck it up. But the main reason...

"You scared the shit out of me."

"What?"

He took a deep breath, tried to put words to what he'd felt back then. "Unpredictable doesn't begin to describe it. You were always moving, always reacting. There was so much hurt under it all. Even when we were laughing or having fun, you were so riddled with grief. I didn't know what to do with it, and I guess I was selfish enough not to want that to be a part of prom."

She was quiet for a long moment, and some neighbor's screen door slammed closed. "That's not selfish," Callie finally said, but her voice was less than convincing, and Trevor didn't know how he'd ventured into such weird territory.

Apparently he was making all the wrong moves when it came to Callie.

"Pretty sure it's the definition of selfish." He studied her and had no idea what he saw. Whatever it was, whatever emotions played there were new to Trevor. He didn't know where to go from here, didn't know how to pull them back into the present. Which was also weird territory, but not nearly as confusing as this.

Callie shook her head, her tense shoulders sagging. She stared hard at the bottle she held in her hands. "No. Prom is a one-time deal. It should have been fun. If I remember correctly you got into Tina's pants that night, so you had your fun."

"Callie." He didn't know what to say. Somehow, ten years later, she was making him feel like a total asshole. Then it dawned on him. "You didn't go."

"Not my scene." She shrugged, but the movement was jerky. "I probably would have said no even if you'd asked me. Could you imagine me in one of those prom get-ups? Please."

But he could tell by the way she stared intently at the bottle, tracing the circle of the opening with her thumb, she was lying. She hadn't gone because he hadn't asked her.

Maybe she had been right a few nights ago. Maybe he really didn't know her at all.

Em appeared at the walkway with two pizzas in hand and Trevor was thrust into the present. Here he thought he'd left teenage angst behind when he'd gone off to college.

Apparently, it was still alive and well.

Callie slammed her alarm again and again until the offending buzz stopped. She'd been up until three the night before working on the Stearman, so six had come way too early.

Trevor's words from the night before had haunted her, kept her working long past bedtime, long past the time when her muscles screamed at her to stop. At this rate, she'd have the Stearman done way before the fly-in.

You scared the shit out of me.

There were a lot of things she wasn't proud of when it came to that time between her grandparent's deaths, but she couldn't get a handle on the fact she'd been scary. At the time, she'd felt strong and in control. Yeah, it had been hiding a manic sense of grief, but who knew Trevor had seen beyond that into the scared, hurt little girl she'd been?

She would have gone to prom with Trevor if he had asked. She would have done the dress thing and the hair and makeup crap and probably felt like an idiot most of the time, but she would have gone because it was *Trevor*.

But she'd been too scary. His mom hadn't liked her.

Callie didn't understand why finally understanding this mattered. She was a different person now. She wasn't going to magically win Mrs. Steele's approval from the great beyond, and she wasn't the same raucous, hurting hellraiser. What did it matter?

She was a businesswoman. She was an adult who was trying very hard to cope with all that life had thrown at her, and doing an okay job.

Why should something that happened ten years ago, something so completely unimportant, rattle her? It was a high-school dance, not significant in any damned way.

Callie sat up in bed and scrubbed her hands over her face. "Get it together," she muttered into the darkness of her bedroom. She could go back to sleep for another hour, but that would be an hour lost at AIF. Still, she didn't get up.

Instead, she reached over and pulled a box out from under her bed. Callie had never been one for snapshots, mementos or anything that might remind her too much of what she'd lost, but Grandma always had been. Albums, collages, scrapbooks. Grandma never had enough in the world of memories.

There were no family portraits in Callie's room. Callie didn't like to fall asleep or wake up to the ghosts of her past staring at her blankly from pictures on the walls. A few airplane prints hung, breaking up the otherwise misty gray around her. For a long time, that misty gray had suited her, no matter how many times Em complained about how depressing it was.

Callie took her eyes off the walls and pried the lid off the box now in her lap. She pulled out the scrapbook Grandma had made and given to her on her fifteenth birthday, a few short months before her death.

Callie couldn't remember the last time she had thumbed through the heavy pages of pictures decorated with stickers and frames, butterflies and rainbows and flowers. All things Callie was not.

She only looked at one page though. The first one. At the top of the page in big pink sticker letters read *The Baker Family*. Beneath was one of the few pictures that existed of her mother, father and her. Callie was an indecipherable bundle of pink blankets, but her parents' beaming faces were what Callie had always cared about.

She was now six years older than her mother was in the picture, two years older than her father. The older she got, the more she could see each of them every time she looked in the mirror.

Her mother's straight black hair and dark brown eyes, the pouty lips Callie rarely used to her advantage. Her father's sharp nose and chin.

When a tear dropped onto the picture, Callie slammed the book shut and shoved it into the box, but before she could toss it under the bed, she stopped herself.

If she really believed she had changed, that she was not the girl who scared people off, it was time to start embracing that. Swallowing, Callie reopened the scrapbook. Using her fingernails, she carefully pried the family picture off the heavy paper.

She pushed off the bed and walked over to the hand-me-down set of drawers. She stared at herself in the mirror for a moment, and then tucked the picture into the corner where she would now look at it every day.

They were her family. Gone? Yes. But still hers.

Though her muscles ached and her eyes were gritty from lack of sleep, the newfound strength worked its way through her.

Callie gathered her clothes for the day, looked at the picture in the mirror, the gray misty walls, and smiled. She had been a mess, but she didn't need to be anymore.

Full of this newfound confidence, Callie marched into the cabin's kitchen where she knew she would find Em concocting something healthy and granola-y for breakfast.

"I think we should paint my room."

Em blinked up at Callie. "Okay. Did you have a particular color in mind?"

"Not gray. Something less depressing."

A smile spread across Em's face. "Pink?"

"Don't push it."

Chapter Eight

"I think it's stupid. They're adults."

Shelby frowned at the road in front of her, even though she really wanted to gear that scowl at Dan.

She liked Dan. A lot. He was funny, smart, and he never tried to be someone he wasn't to fit in. She liked that best. He was shy and nervous sometimes, but Shelby was beginning to realize that was with the boyfriend/girlfriend stuff. The more she got to know him and the more time they spent together, the less he fumbled or flustered.

Though the fumbling was kinda cute.

On the flip side, the closer they got the more Dan voiced his own opinion—even if it differed from hers. Shelby wasn't a big fan of that.

"Adults sometimes need a push in the right direction too," Shelby replied, maneuvering the car around a curve.

"Except you're doing it for you, Shel. Not because it's right for them."

This time, Shelby did scowl over at him. "Can't it be both?"

"Could be." His eyes were watching the farmland pass by. Then he looked over at her and smiled that really cute smile that crinkled up his eyes and made her heart do weird things in her chest. "But I don't think it is."

Shelby let out a humph of breath and focused on the road. What did it matter who it was right for? Trevor and Callie had a thing for each other, obviously. She was going to try and push them together a bit. It didn't matter why.

"This was your idea."

"No, my idea was having a joint graduation party. Your idea was to have it at AIF in some complicated plot to get your brother and Callie together."

"Dan, do me a favor," Shelby growled. "Shut up."

"Yes, ma'am."

It was hard to keep the scowl on her face, because she liked that about Dan too. He didn't get moody when she snapped at him. He agreed to let the subject drop.

Sometimes, when Shelby was feeling a little sad or missing Mom, she liked to imagine what her life would be like in ten years. A lot of the time, even if it was silly or lame, she liked to imagine that Dan would still be in her life. That this, right here, would be it. And she'd daydream about that until it made her smile enough that she was ready to feel happy again.

Mission accomplished. Shelby pulled her Civic into the parking lot of AIF with a smile on her face and determination in her heart. She was a firm believer in making your own happiness. If life was supposed to make her happy, it was doing a crap ass job. She would have to make things happen rather than wait for them to happen.

Shelby stepped out of her car and shaded her eyes against the sun. AIF was a weird place. A cluster of gray and white buildings surrounded by green grass and, farther in the distance, leafing trees. All in the middle of nowhere farmland.

Shelby didn't really get it, but driving up on a bright sunny May day, even she had to admit it was kind of pretty.

"We can go up to the office and see where they are." The grass around the buildings was freshly cut, which Shelby knew to be Trevor's doing. Around the fences, bushes and wildflowers grew in what Mom would have been sure to call wild and unkempt. Shelby thought it was kind of beautiful.

Focusing on the task at hand, she squared her shoulders and began marching toward the office. AIF's secretary would hopefully be able to tell them where Callie was and then Shelby could put the whole plan into action.

If this one failed, as the prom dress friendship mission had, so be it. She'd keep coming up with new plans until she got what she wanted.

"Good morning," Mary greeted them. Shelby didn't know the older lady very well, but Mom had always said she was odd. Only behind her back of course. Now that Mom was gone, Shelby felt uncomfortable around the people Mom had always complained about. "You looking for your brother?"

"Oh, no, ma'am. Actually, I wanted to talk to Callie."

"She and Em are with your brother. Just missed 'em, actually. They're heading down to the big house. You're welcome to follow. Take your car around the fence where you came in and take the gravel road away from the highway. Can't miss it."

"Thank you."

Shelby ignored Dan's disapproving expression. She needed Trevor, and if she got him to stay, he'd always be there. If she needed to come home for the weekend to escape a roommate, or if she needed to borrow money, or get her car fixed, Trevor would be right there. She might not have her parents, but she'd have him.

It wasn't wrong of her to want that, to try and make sure that happened, no matter what anyone said or thought.

They climbed back into her car and Shelby gingerly drove down the curving gravel toward the "big house", cringing at each dinging sound on her precious car. She had never been past the main buildings of AIF, so she had no idea what was hidden beyond the random clutches of trees. Finally, at the last turn around a pond lined with big cottonwood trees, the big house came into view.

Shelby leaned forward to get a better look, intrigued by the unique building before her. It was big. Not huge or anything, but bigger than her home. It had a weird, slanted, A-frame structure, and the wood of the outside looked at home with the trees that surrounded it on three sides.

The house was seemingly held up at the sides by two sloping wooden porches. The expansive lawn around the house was cut, but everything looked a little dilapidated, a little sad. Even the blooming fruit trees couldn't cheer up the lonely, bleak exterior.

Trevor, Callie and Em stood outside the house talking about something, that is until they heard her car on the gravel and all turned with mixed looks of confusion on their faces.

Again, Shelby squared her shoulders. The plan had been to get Callie alone, avoid Trevor. Maybe it was better that they were together. Em was kind of an outlier, but it wasn't anything Shelby couldn't handle.

"You sure about this?"

Shelby flashed a bright smile at Dan. "What's not to be sure about?"

He shrugged and then stepped out of the car with her. Before Shelby could open her mouth in greeting, Trevor was crossing to them with that *oh I'm so smart and intuitive* FBI agent look, but Shelby was determined not to crack.

"What are you doing here?" His tone was casual, but he studied them each carefully even if his smile remained one of concern.

From her peripheral vision Shelby could tell Dan was squirming and she had to fight the urge to roll her eyes. When it came to Trevor, Dan was such a wimp.

"We wanted to talk to Callie and Em. Just for a sec."

Em and Callie crossed over, Em looking all bright and cheerful and Callie looking a little different. She was dressed in black and jeans and everything, but she was smiling. It wasn't that nasty smile before she said something rude either.

It was like a real, happy smile. That put Shelby off her stride for a minute.

"What's up?"

Shelby surveyed the group in front of her, determined Em would be the least likely to see right through her, so she focused in on Em's blue eyes. "Dan and I had a little idea we were hoping we could run by you."

Shelby concentrated, blocking Callie and Trevor's skeptical looks completely out of her line of vision. "Dan and I have been talking about having a joint graduation party. His mom can't really help out and I, well..." She slid a look at Trevor and saw exactly what she wanted to see. Guilt.

Maybe that was wrong of her. So be it.

"We thought maybe we could have our party out at the airport. You've got the Canteen and big open space. It'd be great for a big barbecue. We'd do all the work. We'd want to kind of rent the space."

"You want to rent out AIF for a party?" Em cocked her head, mulling over the surprising suggestion.

Shelby nodded.

"We can pay you," Dan offered into the silence. "I mean, not a lot. There aren't a lot of places to have parties around here and I've got kind of a big family coming into town. Plus, if it's okay, there might be a couple other kids who would want to have their parties with us."

Shelby couldn't read any of their faces, but eventually Callie stepped forward.

"You don't have to pay us."

Shelby watched as Em's mouth dropped open a little. "They don't?"

"We'll do set-up and clean-up too," Callie added.

"We will?" was Em's shocked response.

"In return," Callie continued, ignoring her sister's incredulous looks, "you and Dan volunteer at AIF all summer. Say, ten hours a week."

Shelby didn't have time for it to sink in before she was already trying to argue. "But—"

"You'll have to be in charge of your own food stuff, but I bet Trevor being the great brother he is would help you out with that."

"You... We..." Shelby was too blown away to formulate a response. She looked helplessly at Dan.

"That sounds really cool, Ms. Baker," Dan said eagerly. "You sure?"

Shelby gaped at him. Was he high? This was *not* the plan.

"We need you guys' help more than we need your money. One night for a couple slaves all summer is more than worth it."

Shelby looked at Callie, who was grinning. Somehow Callie had thwarted her plan without knowing it.

"Well, I'll take you guys up to Mary and we'll figure out the best day for all of us," Em said, still looking a little shell-shocked.

Shelby finally found her voice. "Okay."

"I think I would have rather had their money," Em muttered to Callie, but Shelby caught it and watched Callie double over with laughter.

"Cracks me up when she gets all penny pinching," Callie said to Trevor, and Shelby watched a moment pass between them. Shelby couldn't pinpoint what the moment or look was about, but Shelby liked to think it might be a precursor to what she was trying to accomplish.

With the right kind of push, she'd make sure those two fell head over heels and Trevor wouldn't think about leaving Pilot's Point ever again. Maybe Callie's plan actually helped her do that better. If she spent ten hours at AIF a week, there'd be all kinds of opportunities to push Callie and Trevor together.

Shelby scurried after Em, smiling from ear to ear.

"That was weird."

Callie looked to where Shelby's car had disappeared in a cloud of dust. "She's got another scheme up her sleeve."

"Yeah, but I never figured out the first one. Which is pathetic. I must be losing my touch."

"Time to get you back to Seattle and hot shot FBI agenthood." She hoped it sounded more joking than it felt. And really hoped it took his mind off that first scheme, so she didn't feel compelled to explain it.

Trevor turned to take in the house. "You want to wait for Em?"

Callie didn't turn. Needed to get her bearings first. "No, let's go ahead and start. Putting it off won't help anything."

They were down to two-and-a-half weeks before Lawson and the boys would be showing up ready to make the Baker house home. It was time to suck it up and get to work. Callie and Em would work on sorting things after hours, but first they needed to look and see if any repairs would need to be made, and if Trevor could do any of them.

Today was inspection. Tonight and the coming evenings would be the emotional task of going through everything.

Callie took a deep breath and turned to face her second childhood home. She'd spent the first eight years of her life in the cabin she and Em now shared, but after Dad had died, she'd lived at the big house with Grandma and Gramps.

If she let them, the memories would crowd around until she couldn't breathe. Instead, she focused on the job at hand. Tonight would be about memories. Chances were she'd end up crying then with Em, so there was no way in hell she was going to cry now. Especially in front of Trevor. Again.

"We'll start in the basement. Work our way up."

Maybe her hand shook a little as she pushed the key into the hole and opened the door, but the musty air that greeted her took away any of the remaining trepidation.

This wasn't right. The building was a house meant to be lived in—not locked up. Lawson and his boys would live in it and love it the way it was meant to be. Grandma would like that. Gramps would too.

With the harsh sun-blocking curtains on every window, the house was dark and eerily quiet. It almost felt haunted, and that had Callie going around to every window and moving the curtains out of the way so that sunlight filtered in.

All the furniture was covered with thick drop cloths, and though Callie itched to throw them off, it would be best if things remained covered until closer to Lawson's arrival.

"It's so weird," Trevor said in a low, reverential tone. "Seeing it like this. I haven't been here in so long."

Callie shrugged, hoping to alleviate the heavy feeling on her shoulders. "It'll be up and running again in no time."

She moved across faded orange carpet to the big, wooden stairs that led to the basement. They needed to check the heater, make sure there weren't any leaks or cracks, menial things that would need to be taken care of before people could move in.

That would hopefully keep her mind off the heavy musk of dust and the choking feeling of ghosts.

At the bottom of the stairs, Callie reached up and pulled the string. It had been years since she'd lived here, but she still remembered its exact location. When the single bulb popped on, it revealed more musty, dirty air and a whole hell of a lot of work.

Gramps had been a packrat, and like his office at the airport, the basement was full of stacks of magazines and other airplane paraphernalia. They didn't have to organize all of it, but if three people's belongings were going to fit some of it had to be sorted.

The faintest hint of cigar smoke leaked its way through the overwhelming stench of grime and almost had her smiling.

"This is a lot of work, Cal."

"Yeah." But it would be healing work. It would hurt like hell, but going through everything, really putting it away instead of ignoring it, that would be a really positive step toward what she was trying to find.

Balance. Hope. A future.

"We won't get to everything before they get home, but I want them to have at least something of a fresh start. They've had a rough few years, too."

She surveyed the mess and tried to determine a good starting point, what needed to be done and what could be left for Law. She moved into the room that had once been Gramps's home office, flipped on the light and felt all the strength leak out of her.

Gramps's leather chair was covered in an inch of dust. On the table next to it were his glasses and a book marked with a bookmark. A bookmark she had made him at school in the fifth grade, with poorly drawn airplanes, laminated by her teacher.

Callie swallowed, tried to refocus. Tried not to think he was gone for the day and would be back.

The familiar feeling of being beat down returned. She'd made it a few days feeling decent about herself, so it made sense this would knock her back some. Healing? Was it even possible?

"What do you think?"

She looked at Trevor, really looked at him. The way his black hair was starting to grow out, enough that if she ran her fingers through it, it wouldn't feel scratchy. His eyes were focused on the mess of the basement, and they were so blue it didn't seem natural.

Broad shoulders tapered down, and his white T-shirt clung to his flat stomach, hard muscle under smooth skin. From all the work outside at AIF, his previously fair skin was now tanned.

What was so wrong with wanting him? With, for once, taking what she wanted? New leaf? Fuck it. She wanted something more than this new leaf of feeling sad and doing the right damn thing, she wanted to *feel* something besides all the bad.

Changing? Yes, she was changing. Healing from years of loss and pain and not knowing what to do with it all. Why not do something good, experience something amazing in the midst of all this new, hard stuff?

"I think you should kiss me."

He opened his mouth to speak, but no sound came out other than something akin to a squeak. It made her smile because it made her feel powerful. And it made her feel *good*.

She didn't give him a chance to act or not act beyond that little squeak. She fisted her hands in his shirt and pulled his mouth to hers.

There was nothing tentative in her movement, much like her grief-fueled kiss years ago. But, it was different. She felt different. There was no alcohol prompting her decision, no debilitating sadness weighing down her limbs. This wasn't desperation. No, this was freedom, and as Trevor's lips began to move against hers, as his arm banded around her waist, she felt only one thing.

Good.

Callie gripped Trevor's arms, enjoyed the hard muscle there as his teeth scraped against her bottom lip. Some sound came out of her she wasn't familiar with, almost akin to a whimper as Trevor pushed her against the cement wall.

His hands roamed down and cupped her ass so that they were pressed hard together, center to center. She could feel his erection, and the thought of having him inside her had that strange noise escaping her throat again.

His tongue tangled with hers and his hands slid back up, over her sides and across her ribcage. She arched toward him, desperate for something, anything more. One hand cupped her breast and explored it until he found the sensitive nipple, while his other hand cupped her neck and pulled her mouth harder to his.

"Callie." Her name from his lips, said so rough, so desperate, had the heat in her core exploding to something almost unbearable. Then he let his teeth scrape down the side of her neck and she was sure she was going to explode right there.

"Put your legs around me," he instructed in a voice she had never heard. It was dark and authoritative and pretty much the sexiest thing ever.

She wasn't used to following orders, but she was pretty

sure she'd do just about anything for that voice.

When she hooked her legs around him and he lifted her off the ground, it was kind of hard to catch her breath. Until they crashed into the long table full of random rusty airplane parts.

Parts rattled onto the ground, Trevor all but dropped her, and she awkwardly found her footing before falling on her ass.

A laugh bubbled up through arousal as she found her balance by gripping the table. "Well, shit." But his hands were on her again, on her waist, pulling her back into him and any laughter was forgotten. "Hold on a sec," she muttered, narrowly missing stepping on a few pointy screws.

"I know, I know." His hands dropped from her waist and he stepped away, strangely agitated. "You're going to say we shouldn't do this because it'll wreck our friendship and I'm leaving in a few months and—"

Shocked at the sudden change in everything, and that he was putting words in her mouth, Callie stood where she was and put her hands on her hips. "Actually, I was going to say we need to be careful or one of us will need a tetanus shot." She gestured at the mess around them and watched as he looked at it, his eyes refocusing on something other than her.

When he looked up at her, eyes dark and intense and so incredibly blue, she let out a long, steadying breath. She could practically read his mind. And his mind was shouting *abort*.

Without a shadow of a doubt she knew Trevor was about to pull the rug out from her. Again.

"Callie." Trevor looked at her, really looked. Her eyes were so dark they almost weren't brown anymore, her chest heaved, and she looked as though she was trying to rebuild that wall between them. Her cheeks were flushed and her hands gripped the table behind her.

Such a fucking mistake. He couldn't get that message across to the rest of his body, but his mind knew this had been a mistake.

"I know. What you said. It's true."

But her voice wasn't steady and her eyes searched his for some kind of answer. Some kind of rebuttal.

He didn't have one, but he did have the truth. If they didn't get it out now, then this type of thing would keep happening until they ended up in bed together or never speaking to each other again. The former was extraordinarily enticing, but what he really wanted, needed was Callie in his life. Not Callie as some kind of fling.

Trevor took a deep breath and framed Callie's face with his hands. "I don't want to hurt you."

She was confused for a moment and then she tried to look down, but he couldn't let it be that easy. She deserved more, and she had to see it not just hear it. "Believe me when I say there is a part of me that would like nothing better than to finish what we started."

"Yeah, that part is called your dick." When he didn't even crack a smile, she shrugged a little, tried to wriggle away. "Jeez. It was a joke."

"I don't want to joke. I want to be honest. I want to..." God, he *wanted* to kiss her again. To feel the soft expanse of her skin. He *wanted* to take her clothes off slowly and...

Trevor closed his eyes, tried to erase the images careening through his mind. "I want to explain because I don't want things to be weird between us again." He reopened his eyes. "You mean too much to me for us to go down this road. Because, bottom line, I'm leaving."

She wiggled again, but he held firm and she stilled. "I get it, Trevor. Really." Her eyes refused to meet his.

"That doesn't mean I shouldn't say this." He waited and waited until she finally met his gaze again. "I don't want to be the one that hurts you. Maybe that's egotistical of me to think I could, but I don't want to be the one who walks away and leaves you hurting. I'll have to walk away, Callie. You know that."

"Yes, I know." Her voice was soft and it caused him to gentle his hold, to brush the pads of his thumbs across her jaw.

"Don't," she said, a slight crack to her voice, and that hint of vulnerability was the only thing that had him dropping his hands.

She took a step away from him and wrapped her arms around herself. Like magic, she pulled herself together, hiding all the little chinks in her armor, all those pockets of vulnerability, and suddenly she was Callie standing in front of him. Strong, invincible, in charge, and he wobbled in her shadow.

"Now, brace yourself, Trevor, because I'm going to be really honest here." She tried to smile to lighten the mood, but it didn't reach her eyes. It didn't reach anything. "You could hurt me."

She let that hang in the air for a minute, her eyes holding his, her hands clutching her arms as if that was her grip on strength.

"Callie."

"So, you're right. We can't do this because I'm starting to think I'm finally getting to a point where I can heal. Finally getting to a point where I *want* to. I think that means letting myself have a real relationship if the right guy comes along."

Something clutched in his heart, but was immediately gutted by her next words.

"You're not the right guy, Trevor."

He should nod and accept that, but he couldn't. He had to know it wasn't that simple. "Because I'm leaving."

She stepped toward him and traced his hairline with her finger before she met his eyes again. "Because I'm Pilot's Point." She dropped her hand. "And you're not." Flat. Final. Sure. He wished he could feel any of those things, mostly sure.

He took her hand in his, squeezed. "Is it pathetic we're letting addresses keep us from doing this?"

She shook her head almost vehemently. "No. They aren't just addresses. You're FBI through and through, and without AIF, I'm nothing. It's more to us than *just*. It's who we are."

He swallowed and when she pulled her hand away, he let it fall, let the connection end. For the first time in his whole life, he wished he could be Pilot's Point. He wished he could stay.

Chapter Nine

Trevor jammed his thumb against the remote. Some crappy teenage girly music blasted from upstairs. Outside, the weather reflected his mood. Dark, windy, the threat of rain and thunder in the distance.

The windows were open and he knew he should shut them, but the smell of an impending spring storm kept him from completing the action.

He'd lived in Seattle for four years, but it had never become home. That was okay; he hadn't been looking for a home. Staying in Pilot's Point held no appeal, but there were things he'd missed about it, things that felt comforting now.

Spring thunderstorms. Fresh Iowa corn on the cob. Callie.

The crux of his shitty mood. He couldn't get the taste of Callie out of his mouth, the memory of her long, lean body pressed against his, or the fact he'd been the one to back away. Again.

Everything he'd said to her had been the God's honest truth. Just the thought of hurting Callie had his stomach cramping painfully. He didn't want to be the one who walked away from her willingly after all she'd lost so unwillingly.

So he'd backed away, when it had been the last thing he'd wanted to do. Things remained fine between them. Normal. Except for the fact every time he saw her, heard her voice, or thought about her, images and sensations of that basement moment flooded his mind.

Then his thoughts would run toward the dangerous.

Because there was a problem he hadn't figured out. He was leaving whether or not they were sleeping together. Whether or not there was more beyond friendship. He was leaving. What was the point of staying apart?

Not hurting Callie, and maybe not hurting himself. Hell, if he could always remember those two very important pieces of information.

Thunder boomed and he raised his beer in a silent cheers to it. He wanted a storm that would shake the windows, that would pelt rain down on the earth and slash the sky with lightning. He wanted something to feel more out of control than himself.

Shelby's horrific music finally shut off, followed by the sound of her footsteps on the stairs. He watched her come down and couldn't quite understand how his baby sister had turned into a woman.

A woman who was as mysterious to him as the woman who'd been his best friend for as long as he could remember.

"Hey," she offered, walking in front of the TV screen.

He didn't return a greeting. Instead, his bad mood leaked out. "Do me a favor when you go back upstairs? Put your headphones on so I don't have to listen to that shit."

Shelby rolled her eyes before disappearing into the kitchen. She returned with a bag of chips and plopped next to him on the couch. "We need to talk about graduation."

"What about it?" He had no desire to talk or think about graduation, about that big event everyone should have their parents for. It made him think about the future. Weddings, babies and all the things and ways he'd have to play parent to his little sister. The pressure built in his chest, and he tried to chase it away with another swig of beer.

He was leaving her too. Taking away something from

Shelby by not staying in Pilot's Point, especially when it was so obvious she wanted him to. But, he couldn't live with all those demands choking him. No amount of thunderstorms would take away that heavy weight in his chest every time he thought about all he was now responsible for.

A scarier thought snuck its way into his mind. What would change if he went back to Seattle? Would that weight disappear? Or would it still be there? Every time she came to visit during break, every summer she would hate being away from her friends, stuck with him.

"I have two tickets. I gave my other two to Dan, but I thought maybe you'd want to bring someone."

Trevor tried to focus on her words, tried to push the other thoughts out of his mind. "Bring someone?"

"Yeah, to keep you company." She crunched into a chip, didn't look at him. "Graduation is so long and boring. Maybe if you brought Callie you'd have someone to talk to."

Trevor leaned forward and tried to get a better look at her face. "You're suggesting I bring Callie to your graduation?"

"Sure. It's not like I'll have to hang out with her."

Who was this woman? Why couldn't he read his own sister? Frustration melded with guilt to produce an even heavier weight. "What's with you?"

"Nothing is with me." She looked over at him defiantly. "What's with you?"

Because he didn't want to answer the question, he polished off the bottle of beer. "Will it bother you if I sit here and get shitfaced?"

"Does it matter if it bothers me or not?"

It surprised him she thought her feelings had no meaning to him. It squeezed his heart to see her terrible effort at apathy. "Yeah, it matters."

She straightened a little, looked at him considering. "Then, yeah, it would. If you expect me to handle my problems without alcohol, you should set the example."

Guilt made the self-pity bubble up and over. "I never had to set an example for you, Shelby. You came out perfect."

"You're wrong," she said quietly. "Mom always told me I had to be like you."

"Mom always told everyone to be like something or someone else. Never could satisfy that woman." It was the first time he'd ever vocalized anything remotely negative about his mother since she'd died. He felt like shit for it, but it was true.

"Don't talk about her like that."

He jerked his shoulder, his hands itching for another beer or ten. "Whatever."

"She was trying to make us better people," Shelby continued, her voice earnest as if she was trying to convince herself as much as him.

"It worked, didn't it? We're decent people. Smart, talented and successful. But it kept me way the hell away. So far away I couldn't even be here when she—"

"You didn't know."

"Does it matter?" Nothing seemed to matter. Hurt was blooming in his chest and he wanted it gone. He wanted to *be* gone.

"You came. You're here." After a long pause, she rested her hand on his arm. "It matters."

Trevor sat there for a long moment, looking at his sister's hand on his arm. She was trying to comfort him. Maybe it did a little to wash away some of that guilt.

"Dan really likes baseball." Shelby gestured at the TV screen. "You should talk to him about it sometime."

Trevor sighed. Time to lighten the mood. Let go of all the

angst eating away at him. He'd focus on Shelby. On her life. "You really like the kid, don't you?"

"I guess." She tried her hand at apathy again and failed miserably as her mouth curved into a smile. It did more to ease the pressure, the ache. She was happy. He wasn't ruining everything. At least not yet anyway.

Trevor stared at the TV, then the empty bottle in his hands. "I like him too. He's a good kid."

"Does that mean you'll stop trying to scare the crap out of him?"

"Nah, best laughs I've had in a long time." Trevor was surprised to find he could smile, he could tap into that sense of enjoyment he got from messing with Dan's head.

"Jackass."

He wanted to hug her for figuring out how to pull him out of his dark mood. Instead, he rested his arm behind her shoulders. "I love you, Shelby. I know I don't say it enough, but I do."

"I love you too. You don't have to say it. You're here. That's enough."

Here. Where he didn't want to be. Four more months of this. Of dealing with his feelings for Callie, of dealing with all the myriad of things with his teenage sister. It was overwhelming, and yet, sitting on the couch with Shelby, watching baseball, he didn't feel so lost and helpless. He kind of felt right.

Callie stepped into the library then mentally cursed herself for not checking to see if Em was actually there. Em was nowhere to be seen, but Trevor was standing on a ladder replacing light bulbs in the ceiling fan. His T-shirt rose up, exposing a strip of abs Callie could remember running her hands over. His cargo shorts hung low enough she could see the black waistband of his boxers and *shit* she did not want to be alone with him.

"Found another one." Mary walked in holding a box of light bulbs. Callie had never been so happy to see Mary in her entire life. "Oh, hey, Cal."

Callie didn't know whether to laugh or bang her head against a wall when Trevor bobbled on the ladder. They might be acting like things were normal between them, but things definitely were not.

"I was looking for Em."

"She had to run to the bank. Whatcha need?"

A less active imagination. A crappier memory. Instead, Callie smiled at Mary. "Nothing. Gotta get back." Yeah, because the planes might run away if she wasn't there. With her back to Mary and Trevor, Callie rolled her eyes.

"Hey, uh, wait a sec." Trevor climbed down the ladder as she reluctantly turned around. "You busy Wednesday night?"

"Uh." He was acting shifty, nervous, and it made her wary of agreeing to anything. Especially with Mary standing right there, grinning like a crazy person.

"Course she's not busy. Girl never does anything but work now that she's turned over this new leaf. Take her out, Trev. Nice as the new leaf is, girl needs to get away from these planes once in a while."

Mortified, Callie could only stare at Mary. Mary snickered, and Callie was no longer even remotely grateful for her presence.

Trevor's face remained blank. Some trick. Callie wished she knew how to keep her face from blushing like a shy teenager.

"I thought you could go with me to Shelby's graduation.

She gave me an extra ticket and it'd be nice to have someone to talk to." He attempted a smile. It sucked. At least there was some indication he was as embarrassed as she was.

"That's not much of a date."

Callie glared at Mary, and in unison with Trevor retorted, "It's not a date."

Mary held her arms up in mock surrender. "Of course not." Sarcasm dripped from each word. "I'll just get out of your way so you can discuss..." She made air quotes with her fingers. "Graduation."

Callie fought the urge to scream. They had enough to deal with without other people starting to call them on their newly weirdly blurred friendship. One little mistake and now she had to walk on eggshells around her best friend. Not fair.

That was what she got for letting herself have something good. And, damn, it had been *good*.

"Look, you don't have to go. Really. I can handle it myself."

"No." Callie gave a firm nod. Mary's teasing would not screw her out of being a good friend. Her mistake of kissing him and, well, a lot more than kissing would not screw her out of friendship with Trevor. She was determined to keep that, even with the weirdness between them. Weirdness would fade. Eventually. "I'll go."

Somehow his expression was both relieved and disappointed. She knew the feeling.

"Great. Well, I should get back." He gestured at the ceiling fan with the light bulbs.

"Right. Me too." But they both stood for a minute, not moving, just looking at each other. Nervous, unsure Trevor wasn't as lethally sexy as bossy, very sure Trevor, but he was damned cute.

Which meant Callie was well and truly screwed. With that thought, she got the hell out of the library as quickly as her feet would carry her.

Chapter Ten

Callie pulled on the hem of her skirt as she stepped out of her car at the Steele house. The only thing she'd had suitable to wear to a graduation had been the black dress she'd worn to Mrs. Steele's funeral, and it didn't seem right to wear that again.

She would have gone shopping, but there hadn't been time. Lawson and the boys would be home in less than a week and she and Em spent every AIF-free moment going through the belongings of their grandparents.

Callie tried not to think about it. Part of it had been amazing, like having them back for a few fleeting moments, but then she had to remember they were gone, and the amazing turned into something painful. In the past, she would have given up that amazing to avoid the pain, but now it seemed worth it.

Callie took a deep breath in and let it out. Now was not the time to think about it.

Self-conscious, Callie pulled the skirt down again. It was borrowed from Em, so about an inch too short. She looked mildly ridiculous in the flowery print, but she'd managed to find a shirt of her own to go with it—a short-sleeved button-up shirt in white she was pretty sure she'd never worn.

She walked up to the Steele house and knocked on the door. Trevor answered almost immediately and it had Callie stepping back in surprise. She was kind of counting on those last seconds to compose herself.

"Hey. You're late."

"Sorry," Callie muttered, trying not to pay attention to how good Trevor looked in a suit. She'd never thought she'd be the kind of woman attracted to a guy all dressed up, but he made it look so damn appealing.

When she thought about him looking appealing, she thought of all the other *appealing* things he could do with his hands, his mouth, and... She really had to stop this.

"Is it hot out?" he asked, frowning out at the sun.

"Not particularly. Why?"

"Your cheeks are all pink."

"Oh." She didn't know what else to say and fidgeted as he took in the rest of her appearance.

"You look different."

Callie's mouth twisted and her nose wrinkled. Well, at least there was no danger of compliments sweeping her off her feet. "Okay."

He shook his head. "That didn't come out right."

"Don't worry about it. I'm no supermodel."

"It's not that. You're not wearing black and you've got lipstick on."

"Miracles happen every now and again. Are we ready?"

"Yup." He stepped out onto the porch, so close the pine smell of his soap drifted toward her. Damn. Why did he seem so unaffected? Like nothing had ever happened in that stupid basement. Apparently he was doing a lot better at blocking it all out than she was.

Callie stepped away, started walking toward the garage. When she looked back, Trevor hadn't followed her.

He was staring at her legs and possibly her ass, and as he realized he'd been caught, he started to walk and tried to pretend he'd just been checking his pockets to make sure he had everything.

But Callie had seen that same flash of something she'd seen in the basement, and it made her smile. Momentarily.

All of Trevor's words the other day in the basement had been true. She'd meant every word she'd said in return, but Callie couldn't shake the feeling that before September came around they were going to end up giving in. And it was going to be a disaster.

Callie waited impatiently as Trevor opened the garage door and unlocked his car. The quicker they got to graduation, the quicker they were surrounded by a bunch of people, the better.

Wordlessly, she slipped into the passenger seat, desperately trying to keep the stupid skirt at a respectable level.

"Thanks for agreeing to come. It'll probably bore you to tears. Hell, it's going to bore me to tears, but it'll be nice to have someone to talk to."

Callie kept her hands on her skirt and her eyes on the windshield. "No problem."

"Liar. You're swamped and this is the last thing you want to do."

Callie had to laugh, couldn't resist the urge to look over at him. His profile looked so strong, so untouchable, but she knew he was feeling a little off, a little sad Shelby was graduating and his parents weren't there.

The urge to reach out and touch his face, just a simple sympathetic gesture, had her clasping her hands on the hem of the skirt and facing forward again. "No, it's nice to have a break. Besides, Em and I are almost done with what needs to be done at the big house. Lawson will be here before we know it, and Dan and Shelby will be helping. We'll have plenty of hands to get us ready for September. They can do without me for one night."

"Thanks. Let me guess, that's Em's skirt?"

Callie shifted uncomfortably. "Yeah. Didn't have time to go shopping. Sorry."

"It looks nice. You look nice."

This time when she looked over at him, he was frowning, and his knuckles were white on the steering wheel.

The laugh bubbled up, quick and uncontrollable. As it broke out, it kept building until she was laughing almost uncontrollably.

"What's so funny?" Trevor asked, but his lips were curved upward.

"I don't know," Callie said between breaths. "We're such a mess. Such a ridiculous mess." She tried to get a breath but ended up laughing some more. "Why am I here, Trev?"

"We might be a mess, but I still need you."

That had her sobering some, had something warm and scary melting her defenses. "Then stop looking at my legs."

He grinned, that handsome, cocky grin exactly the same as when they'd been in high school. "I'll do my best, but you should probably know they're really nice legs."

All laughter was now efficiently dead, and they were back to where they started. Awkward silence and both pairs of eyes staring hard at the road.

When Trevor pulled his car into the busy lot of the community college's auditorium, Callie felt unwanted memories press against her mind. Maybe it was silly, but the community college still reminded her of the unmitigated failure she'd experienced there, and it left her feeling out of place.

She didn't know if Trevor sensed that, or if he simply needed some reassurances of his own, but he took her hand in his and smiled. "Just until we get inside."

Callie nodded and swallowed and tried to ignore the surroundings and the warm feel of her hand in his. She knew his calluses were new from working at AIF, just like hers were old from always working with her hands.

Nowhere more than here did she feel their differences. Trevor was educated and polished. Callie was lacking in both. Still, she let her hand rest in his as he pulled her through the groups of people, waving absently at those who called his name, or hers, until they spotted two empty seats. Once they sat down she could pretend half the town wasn't staring at them wondering what the hell was going on *there*.

Before they could reach and claim the seats and blissful denial, Dana stepped in their path.

"Well, well, well, what do we have here? I certainly didn't expect to see you tonight, Callie."

Callie forced her lips into a smile, even if her jaw was clenched together. "Dana."

"And, Trevor, it's been so long. Sorry to hear about your mom."

Trevor shrugged, tried to move past Dana, but the large woman effectively blocked any way out.

"Don't you two look cozy." She smiled, looking down at their joined hands with the predatory gleam of a true gossip.

Callie dropped her hand from Trevor's immediately. "Just offering some moral support to an old friend."

Trevor didn't take the hint and he slipped his arm around her shoulders. "I don't know what I'd do without Callie's moral support."

Dana practically drooled, and Callie could tell she was already searching the auditorium for people to tell. "Well, I'll let you two find a seat."

When she was out of earshot, Trevor's arm went back to his

side and Callie marched toward the empty chairs, determined to keep her mouth shut. She lasted a minute before whirling around.

"Why'd you do that? By the time graduation starts half this auditorium will think we're a couple. And by the time it's over, all of Pilot's Point will be yapping about it."

His look darkened, hardened. "None of their business."

"No, but that sure as hell isn't going to stop them." She plopped into the empty seat and sighed. It wasn't bad enough she was trying to convince herself she wasn't having a thing with Trevor, now she'd have to convince the whole town?

"I thought it might help."

"Help?"

He slid into the seat next to her, watching the stage where people were setting up. "You still haven't gotten that permit from Dana, have you?"

"No."

"Dana and my mom were friends. I thought throwing myself into the ring might help."

"You've been away a long time, Trevor. I don't think you hold as much weight as you think you do."

He scowled and didn't respond. Which was good. She was just going to sit here and be silent and hope like hell the next two hours flew by.

It was much different than her high school graduation. She and Trevor's ceremony had been at the high school, crammed into the small gym with no air conditioning. She could remember sweating and being miserable.

This building was bright and airy, comfortable and modern looking. As the procession started and the graduates marched in with their familiar red and white robes, Callie had to swallow hard against the memories. She'd been a mess at her graduation, missing everyone, feeling useless and directionless.

She was eleven years removed from high school graduation. Nothing about that night really mattered now, but she felt like that girl all over again. She should have known better than to agree to this. Why had she?

Because of Trevor. Didn't it always come back to him? How pathetic.

The graduates processed, sat, were greeted by speakers. The student council president gave his speech and then it was Shelby's turn to be announced as valedictorian and give her speech.

Callie sat, trying not to fidget, trying to fight the urge to bolt and run for the doors. An administrator Callie didn't recognize stepped up to the podium and began to introduce Shelby's accomplishments.

Callie looked at the poised eighteen-year-old who smiled at the audience as the principal read off her amazing feats. *Congratulations, Shelby, you're making me feel like an idiot and you're not even trying.*

Shelby took the podium looking very grown-up and self-possessed. Looking so much like Mrs. Steele Callie had to take a breath. When she snuck a look at Trevor, she knew he saw it too. His jaw clenched, his fingers tensed on his legs.

Then Shelby began to speak, and even Callie was pulled into the girl's words.

"Parents, teachers, administrators, family members and friends. Today is the day that most of us sitting in caps and gowns have been dreaming about for a very long time. It's our ticket to adulthood, to doing what we want. We have a long way to go, but this is our starting point.

"For the past four years, I have worked hard—so hard—to achieve this honor. I was taught and believed wholeheartedly that hard work will get you whatever you want, and I have always been determined to get exactly what I want."

Shelby took a deep breath and Callie watched as Trevor took it with her. He was so vested in this. Callie wondered if he noticed anyone besides himself and Shelby in the large auditorium.

"But, this year, I've realized something. Hard work can't give you everything. There are too many things outside our ability to control." Shelby's gaze landed on Callie, then Trevor. "No matter how hard I worked, I couldn't stop my mother from passing away. I could not stop my world from changing drastically. And that was a hard thing to learn, to accept."

Shelby swallowed and looked down at the cards in front of her, the only sign she was remotely affected by talking about her mother. Then she looked up, eyes clear, voice strong, and continued.

"But it wasn't an excuse to give up or not work. It was a rug pulled out from under me. In our future, we will all have that metaphorical rug pulled out from under us, probably more than once. What matters, what will always matter, is what we do in the face of it."

Well, that hit home too much for Callie's comfort. She didn't like getting perspective from a teenager.

"Will you dust yourself off and keep working? Will you stay on the ground and give up? Only you can choose. We stand here on the edge of our adult lives, and only we can choose what paths we take. Not our teachers, not our parents, not our friends. They can guide us, shape us, influence us, but they cannot make our choices for us.

"I promise myself, standing on this stage, that I will always get back up. I will always work hard no matter what curveball life throws. Because it's worth it. I hope you'll do the same.

Congratulation, graduates. Thank you."

Shelby stepped down and Callie looked over at Trevor. His jaw was clenched tight and there was something so sweet and completely different about the emotion on his face.

"You're so proud," she whispered into his ear, feeling oddly proud herself.

His smile was sheepish. "Yeah."

"It's sweet." She squeezed his hand, and when he held on, she didn't try to take it away. As Shelby's class crossed the stage, one by one, Trevor and Callie watched, hand in hand.

Shelby fought her way through the crowd of classmates and their families trying to get to the seats Trevor and Callie had been sitting in. She tried to focus on that image. Trevor and Callie sitting next to each other, watching her speak the words she'd slaved over. If she didn't focus on that image, she'd have to see all the families around her. All the parents with tears in their eyes as they held on to their freshly graduated daughters and sons.

Shelby's throat constricted, but she refused to cry. *Steeles don't cry.* Her parents weren't here, but she couldn't change it. Crying wouldn't change that horrible sense of loss. Crying wouldn't ease the fear she was going to be completely alone. So she wouldn't cry. She wouldn't. *Steeles don't cry,* Mom's voice repeated.

Finally, she spotted Trevor's head above the rest of the crowd, and her heart constricted along with her throat. If she didn't look at his eyes, he looked so much like a younger version of Dad. If he were Dad, she wouldn't have to worry about the panic clogging her throat. She wouldn't have the words *please don't go* pounding in her head every time she was near him.

Her vision blurred momentarily, but it was clear by the time she reached Trevor.

Trevor smiled, and she focused on his eyes because they didn't make her think about Dad.

"You did good, kid," he said, and his voice wasn't quite steady, which made Shelby's heart wobble uncertainly in her chest.

Don't cry. Steeles don't cry. Don't cry. "Thanks," she managed, sliding a glance toward Callie.

"Your speech was great, and you know I wouldn't say it if it weren't true. You're..." Callie's mouth twisted into a frown. "Pretty smart, I guess."

Shelby smiled, and tried her best to be genuine, without thinking about what Mom would have said or felt about Callie being here. "Thanks. I-I'm glad you came."

A couple people walked by and patted her on the shoulder, congratulating her on her speech. Some friends stopped with hugs or smiles or promises to meet up later at Project Graduation, and Shelby began to feel as if she was above it all, watching from somewhere outside her body.

Dan appeared, helped bring her back to earth. "We should go turn in our cap and gown, Shel. They won't let you into Project Graduation if you forget."

Shelby nodded, looked at Trevor. Graduation was over. He'd promised to stay until September, but his real responsibilities were pretty much done. She was eighteen, a high school graduate. She could take care of herself.

She didn't want to take care of herself. Her vision was blurry again and she felt rooted to her spot.

"Go ahead. I'll see you tomorrow." Trevor offered a smile.

Tomorrow. He'd be there tomorrow. But in September he'd

go back to Seattle. Forever away. Just visiting him would require a plane ticket. What if she needed him? What if she needed help? Again Shelby looked at Callie and all she could do was hope, hope with everything she had, something was going to keep him here. She needed him. She couldn't say it to his face, but deep down she needed him.

"Yeah, I'll be home bright and early."

Before she could turn with Dan to leave, Trevor pulled her into a hard hug. "I'm so proud of you," he whispered into her ear.

In that moment, the tears won. She forgot about everything else around her and sobbed into Trevor's chest. All the walls she'd built to keep the pathetic part of her from escaping crumbled in the moment.

"Please don't leave me," she said, knowing her voice was weak and pathetic. She didn't care, not right now.

He didn't say anything, but he held on until she was ready to let go.

Chapter Eleven

Gutted didn't begin to describe the clawing, empty feeling in his chest. Trevor pulled his car into the driveway and sat, foot on the brake, staring at the house in front of him.

Callie watched him in that quiet way she had acquired since the last time he'd been home. Two years ago she would have ignored what had happened, which he would prefer at the moment, or she would have told him to get over it.

He could still feel Shelby clutching him, could still feel her body shake as she'd said those words. *Please don't leave me.*

That lump was in his throat again, and he couldn't swallow it away. The weird burning sensation behind his eyes. All of those same things he'd dealt with when Shelby had accused him of being a terrible brother, of caring more about everyone else.

True, hurtful words, but they were no match to Shelby's desperate plea. Trevor shoved the car into Park, not bothering to pull into the garage. He was being suffocated, pressed under a huge rock. He couldn't breathe.

Without saying a word to Callie or sparing her a glance, he pushed out of the car, tearing at his tie. He couldn't take a full breath and his heart began to hammer in his ears.

Jesus, what was happening?

"Trev?"

He stopped halfway to the house, bent over and rested his hands on his knees, desperate to catch a full breath.

"Trevor." Callie's voice was calm and her hand was strong

and reassuring as it rested on his back. "Calm down. Just relax. Everything will be all right."

He squeezed his eyes shut, horrified when something liquid and warm leaked out. He was not crying. No way. Not a chance. *Steeles don't cry. Not ever.*

Callie's hand rubbed right under his shoulder blade, and slowly her soothing words helped ease the rapid beating of his heart. "It's all right. Everything will be fine. Slow down. Try to take a breath now."

Trevor swallowed, managed one breath in and one breath out. He brushed at his cheeks with the back of his hand, hoping the darkness around them hid the action. He jerked his body upright. "I'm okay." His throat felt raw and achy.

Callie's hand remained on his back, rubbing a calming circle. "Was that a panic attack or something?"

"Hell if I know."

"What did Shelby say to you?"

Trevor looked up. Callie's expression was something between fear and anger, her question somewhere between concern and accusation.

"She said..." Trevor cleared his throat, opened his mouth to say the words, but they wouldn't come out. Not without the lump, the weird heat behind his eyes. "Doesn't matter."

Callie stepped in front of him now and placed a hand on his chest, just above his heart. "Tell me what she said."

He put his hand over hers. There was something in the moment he wanted to keep. This strange sensation wrapping around all the pain and fear and misery. Callie's hand on his heart, he wanted that.

He cleared his throat again. "She said she didn't want me to leave." *Please don't leave me.* Those words would haunt him no matter what he did.

"I know that hurts. I can't imagine how hard that is for you." Callie's hand moved to touch his face, but then she changed course and wrapped her hand around his wrist, freeing the hand trapped against his heart.

"Maybe I should stay."

"She's laying the guilt on, and some of it's on purpose." Callie's voice was strong and forceful where he felt anything but. "You have to stay strong. You have to do what's right for you. It might take her a while to get it, to appreciate it, but neither of you gets anything out of you staying. She isn't losing you if you leave. You can't let her make you think she is."

Trevor agreed, but he couldn't figure out why Callie was so adamant about it. "Don't you want me to stay?"

She froze at the question, and the anguish on her face had his heart shuddering to a slow, painful stop, but she quickly closed it off, built back the wall. "I want you to be happy."

He nodded, but part of him wondered if she was telling the truth.

"I should get home. Are you going to be okay?"

Trevor stood there for a long time, not sure how to answer. He wasn't okay, but Callie couldn't help him. No one and nothing could. He was stuck in an impossible situation. No matter what happened in September, he'd be hurting someone.

"I'm fine," Trevor lied, passing her on his way to the house. "See you tomorrow." He didn't look back, afraid if he did he'd fall apart again. He pushed into the house, Shelby's words echoing in his head.

Chapter Twelve

"Aw, he's grumpy."

Em poking Trevor in the ribs didn't help the situation. He wasn't in the mood for teasing any more than he was in the mood to get up at the ass crack of dawn on a Saturday to prepare for Shelby's graduation party.

That wasn't the source of his bad mood, though. He wanted it to be, but the real reason was he'd been sleeping like shit for three days. Ever since Shelby had begged him not to leave her.

If he'd felt guilty before, this was a whole new level of heart-rending guilt. Escape wasn't even a fantasy anymore, because it made him feel as disgustingly guilty as everything else.

Trevor lifted another twenty-four pack of water out of his trunk and hefted it into the kitchen of the Canteen. His limbs were heavy with fatigue, but he ignored it. Em and Callie had been exchanging worried glances over him all week, but he pretended he didn't see. It was the only way he knew how to get through one day and then the next. Ignore everything but what had to be done, and hope the answer to all of his problems would fall into his lap at some point.

When he returned from the Canteen, Callie and Em had their heads together but stopped talking when he got within earshot. He didn't react and picked up the boxes of soda from his trunk, repeating the process of dropping them off in the Canteen.

When he came for the last load, Em was gone and Callie was sitting on his trunk.

"You're going to have to move."

She shook her head. "Nope."

"I've got one load left. Then I have to go to town and get all the barbecue stuff and then I've got to pick up the cake." *And then I've got to fling myself off the nearest tall building or mountain. Except, oh hey, there aren't any of those around Pilot's Point.*

Callie hopped off the trunk but didn't get out of his way. Instead, she stood defiantly in it. "You look like hell."

"Thanks." She looked pretty and fresh as she hadn't had a chance to get all mucked up with engine grease yet. Both the jeans and the T-shirt she wore were tight enough to show off every slight curve. "You look hot."

She frowned a little. "It's not hot out here."

"That's not what I meant." He took a step closer, feeling like he was standing on some kind of ledge. A breeze ruffled through the air and he could smell what he assumed was her shampoo, a hint of coconut.

She tried to create a disapproving look, but it came out half-assed when she didn't fight off a smile.

It eased some of the edges, but left a strange feeling in its wake. A recklessness he didn't know what to do with. He reached out and touched her ponytail, rubbing the ends between his fingers.

"Back off, Steele." She gave him a light push so his hand dropped. "You've got too much on your mind right now and it's making you crazy. You need some sleep."

"You're damn right I've got too much on my mind," he muttered. He could feel the snaps on his control unlocking one by one. It was rare, and it felt freeing. Control and doing the right thing was apparently overrated.

"I know you're hurting. You're letting all this guilt eat you alive. Shelby's pushing your buttons on purpose. Don't let her."

He grabbed Callie's wrist and backed her against the car. "It's not just about Shelby." The guilt was, but the edginess wasn't. Being around Callie every day added another layer to all the twisting emotions inside of him.

"Come on. This is about graduation and Shelby and her wanting you to stay, and you not belonging here." She wrestled her hand free, though he kept her caged against the car. "Instead of letting her get to you, you need to be clear. You need to make her understand Pilot's Point can't be your home, and she can't be selfish enough to demand it. You have to—"

"You know what, Callie, this new leaf is wonderful. But back the fuck off, okay?"

Her face immediately changed from friendly and earnest to something he recognized. A flash of hurt quickly covered by a slash of anger. "So, you're allowed to give advice, but you won't take it?"

"You think that because you're finally getting your life together ten years too late you have any kind of insight into what I've got to deal with?"

He should have backed off. He should have kept his mouth shut, but there was an anger inside of him that had to be unleashed or he was going to explode. Losing control might have felt freeing, but danger lurked in all that freedom.

"Taking a shot at me make you feel better?"

"You would know."

"Fine. You want to take your anger and frustration at the situation out on me. Do it." She angled her chin like she was expecting some kind of blow. "You want to take all that guilt Shelby is laying on you and throw it in my face. Have at it. If it'll make you feel better, go ahead. Unlike your sister, I—"

Trevor's hands curled into fists and he took that last step

toward her so their bodies were pressed together. When he spoke, his voice was little more than a growl. "Stop pretending like half of what I'm dealing with isn't wanting to get you naked right this very second."

That knocked some of the fight out of her, but her fists didn't loosen any more than his did. "You're being a jackass on purpose."

His eyes took a slow tour of her body, tormenting himself with what he knew he shouldn't have. "Are you so sure about that?"

"Yes." Her voice was strong, but the breath she exhaled afterward wasn't steady. Still, she met his gaze and let him crowd her. "Taking it out on me doesn't change your reality. And I'm not sleeping with you so you can blow off a little steam."

The words deflated him because that's what it had sounded like, and maybe that's even what he'd meant. Hell, he didn't know anymore, but with the power of his anger gone he felt defeated and lousy and like one sorry son of a bitch.

As if she could read all of those feelings in his face, she reached out for his hand and uncurled his fingers with hers. "You need some sleep." Her voice was soft and comforting. Either new Callie was really good about not holding a grudge, or he was such a pathetic mess Callie felt sorry enough for him to let go of anger. "Come on." She took his hand and she pulled him through the Canteen and then the main office.

"There's a lot of work to do."

"Em and I are used to a lot of work. If you're going to be any use to us tonight, you need some sleep."

"I will. Tonight. Today there's too much to—" She stopped in front of the stairs that led up to Fred's old office.

"Up," she instructed, pointing.

"Callie."

"You be a good boy and maybe you'll get a reward." She smiled and batted her lashes at him, and if it hadn't caused such a disturbing electrical current he might have asked her what kind of reward. Instead, he turned and took the stairs.

"Now, go lie down. We've got a pillow and blanket all set up. Take a bit of a nap. Em and I will take care of some things, and then we'll wake you up in time to go get the cake. Deal?"

He didn't want to lie down, didn't want to face all his swirling problems. If he was running around getting crap together for the party, he could at least partially pretend he wasn't a man torn into a million different pieces. "And what do I get if I follow orders, ma'am?"

"What do you want?"

She stood with her hands on her hips, chin angled up like she was daring him to answer honestly. He stood next to the makeshift bed and managed his best reckless smile. "I can't have what I want."

She pushed him down onto the window seat and then leaned over him to pull the curtains closed. It made the room murky, though not quite dark.

"Then I guess your reward is a few hours of rest." She pulled a blanket on top of him though it wasn't cold enough to warrant it. "This is a magic sleeping place. All your problems disappear for a few hours. And when you wake up, you'll know exactly what to do." Her voice was soft and dreamy, like a mother telling a fairytale to her child.

"Really?"

"No." She smiled down at him, and if he weren't so tired, if he hadn't been such an ass to her this morning, he would have pulled her down on top of him. "But a few hours' sleep might bring back the Trevor I know, not the bastard currently invading his body. That *would* be magic."

"I'm sorry for what I said." He wanted to reach out and tuck the stray strand of hair behind her ear, but he knew she'd move away from him if he did. "Not the getting naked part, the ten years too late part."

She shrugged, plumped up the pillow under his head. "It was true."

"No, it wasn't. And it wasn't fair to judge you when I'm such a fucking nightmare right now."

She studied his face with a look he couldn't read. "I figure I've lashed at you plenty. You owe me. We'll call it even. I bet when you wake up, you'll feel a million times better."

He wanted to believe a little sleep would cure it all, wanted it to be possible. "Are you taking care of me?"

She looked at the hem of the blanket rather than his face. "Maybe." Then she brushed her lips across his forehead. "Get some sleep, Trev."

Before she'd even gotten down the stairs, he was asleep like the dead.

Callie hopped out of the Stearman. For looks purposes, it still needed a few tweaks, but she'd gotten the plane itself up and running in time for Shelby's graduation party and, to soothe Em's frugal soul, she'd been offering rides to the party-goers for five bucks a pop. She'd made a small fortune off of Dan and his brother and cousins and couldn't keep the smile off her face.

It had been too long since she'd flown. Wrapped up in the day-to-day of AIF, working on the Stearman, prepping the big house for Lawson's impending arrival. It had been months since she'd taken to the sky. Part of her had forgotten the simple joy in maneuvering a small plane over the world below. She was above it all, in control. Nothing gave her quite the same rush as flying.

Well, almost nothing. Trevor was making his way through the crowds of people, toward her. Ever since he'd gotten some sleep, he'd returned to the normal Trevor, not the broody, miserably guilt-ridden, depressed Trevor who had been going through the motions ever since Shelby's graduation.

Hell, he was smiling now as he crossed toward her, and that was some kind of miracle.

It didn't seem fair he looked so good in baggy khaki shorts and a blue polo shirt that brought out his eyes. She was sure she looked the same as she always did, dressed in jeans and a black shirt, probably dirt on her face and her hair a mess from flying around most of the evening. What could he possibly find alluring about that?

There were half a dozen women drooling over Trevor as she watched him continue to cross to her. They all looked put together, clean, charming.

But he was walking to her, his eyes focused on her, and she knew that he wanted *her*.

Dangerous ground. Her mind always seemed to be traveling there. Somehow she'd turned over the new leaf and completely lost the ability to block out any attraction to Trevor.

"Hey." They were far enough away so the crowd was a low buzz, so they could be hidden by the plane or the darkening sky.

"Hi. Want a sunset ride? It'll cost you double."

He looked at the plane suspiciously. "Nah, I'm good."

Callie shook her head. "You face down criminals with guns and you're afraid of a little flying?"

"I'm not afraid of flying. I'm afraid of hurtling to my death in a tiny piece of scrap metal."

"Wuss."

"Besides, you'll cut the engine halfway through, pretend we're crashing until I'm about to puke, and then laugh the rest of the damn flight."

"Dan and his cousins loved it."

"Better men than me, I guess." He grinned and leaned against the airplane, facing west and the setting sun. They couldn't have had better weather for Shelby's party, and now the sunset was the perfect capper—a riot of purples and blues and oranges and pinks, the kind of sunset that made the biggest cynics sigh.

"I haven't had a chance to thank you for this morning. I don't know what was wrong with me, but I needed that sleep. Or I'd probably be around here snarling at everyone." He reached out and took her hand in his, squeezed. "You're a life saver."

Callie shrugged, squinted at the disappearing sun. "I guess it was my turn. You're usually the one saving my ass."

His fingers linked with hers and she had to fight the urge to curl them around, to hold him there in this perfect moment.

"You know, right now, watching this sunset with you, this is the first time in two months I've wondered what it might be like to stay and the answer is, it wouldn't be the end of the world."

Her hand dropped from his. Hearing him say it, watching his profile glow in the orange swath of fading light, had her heart doing an uncomfortable dive in her chest.

Not with hope. No, she refused to call it hope, but it was something akin to hope and it was tempered with a very large dose of fear.

What if he did stay? Didn't that put the events in her

grandparents' basement into a new and very possible light?

Fear multiplied. Her fingers curled into her palms, as if she could fight her way out of this blinding new fear.

No. He was just talk. A trick of some sleep, a great party and a beautiful sunset. She'd lose him in the predictable way— on a flight out of Pilot's Point with everything as it should be. She wouldn't have to be crowded with worry. She'd lose him to Seattle, the way she was supposed to.

He turned to face her then and everything shifted inside of her; the fear gave way to unknown warmth. He cupped her face with his hand and she tried to step away, but his other arm rested on her hip and pulled her toward him.

"Let me kiss you, Callie. Just for a minute. Or two."

His lips skimmed hers, a feather-light touch. There was such a big part of her desperate to give in to it. Give in to him. She was so certain it was going to happen sooner or later. Why not let it be sooner?

When his tongue skimmed her bottom lip, she gave in, let herself be pulled into the perfect moment.

It was unlike any kiss they'd ever shared. It was soft and sweet, nothing demanding or impulsive. A completely new experience. A low, humming buzz along her skin, a slight shiver in her heart, and the slowest warming in her core.

His thumb whispered along her jaw, his other hand grazing up and down her side, but it never became anything more than druggingly sweet, achingly innocent.

Then he pulled away. He was always able to, and she always took it. Every good moment, every bad moment, he brought them all crashing to a halt. "We can't keep coming back to this place." She hated that her voice was breathless, that she couldn't pull away from the warmth of his body.

"I know." He didn't sound as convincing as she wanted him

to. His fingers traced her jaw, her neck, and she tried very hard to fight off the shiver.

"I don't want to ignore this anymore." His lips touched hers again, a brief, light touch, then her cheek, then her other cheek.

She had to hold on to his arms to steady herself against the shuddering feeling inside of her. "But—"

"I'm thinking about staying."

It was like a bucket of ice water being dumped over her head. Him actually uttering the words, and not in some kind of guilt-induced heat of the moment. He was really thinking about it, really considering staying. "You can't." She clutched his arm, desperate to convince him this wasn't the answer. Only she didn't know where the desperation came from.

"Yes, I can. I could probably get my old job at county. The bottom line is Shelby. She's made it impossible for me to be happy in Seattle. It isn't her fault, but if I go back there the guilt is going to eat me alive. I'll be just as miserable as if I stayed here, but if I stayed at least there'd be you."

Her heart flipped even as panic leaped into her throat. *As miserable.* Maybe if he thought there'd be a chance to be happy she could accept it. Maybe if she knew without a shadow of a doubt these feelings wouldn't fade if he stayed. Maybe if he could somehow promise forever.

But he couldn't. If he stayed, if they pursued this, she could lose him in a million different ways. Ways she couldn't predict. Not just to Seattle, or boredom, or life. To the realization they were too different, that she wasn't good enough for him, that someone else who came along would be better. It would drive her crazy until she drove him crazy too. She had to know how he would leave her, because some way, somehow he would.

Love always left her.

He was watching her and she knew she had to say something, but it was hard to do anything in the grip of all this panic.

"Trevor, you can't stay." She sounded as scared as she felt.

"I just told you why I can."

"But, it's a mistake. It would be a mistake. You're not thinking clearly. You're letting guilt influence your choices." She tried to take a calming breath, but it was shallow and ineffective.

"The guilt is there, Callie. I can't ignore it. It's there and it's killing me. Jesus, I don't get you." He pulled away completely, shoved a hand through his hair. "You keep saying you want me to be happy and I'm telling you maybe, somehow, I could be if I stayed here and you're still desperate for me to leave. I don't get it."

"This isn't about me."

"But it is. It is about you. You don't want me to stay. Why not?"

"I—" She couldn't find an answer, nothing, not lie or truth or something halfway in between could work its way out of her lips. "I don't know."

"Figure it out." He looked out at the sun, his face hard and his hands tucked into fists. She wished she knew what to say, wished she knew what to do. All she could feel was a drumming panic pumping through her veins and a tightness in her chest that kept any words stuck somewhere between mind and mouth.

Callie closed her eyes, Em's words pounding into her brain. *You keep up walls with us, Callie. Maybe it's not the people you love you're trying to protect. Maybe it's yourself.*

"I don't want to be the only thing that would make you happy. Even if I thought I could be, I don't want that kind of pressure."

Callie opened her eyes, surprised the words had come out of her mouth. Now that they had, it was a light bulb moment. The ding, ding, ding of a right answer. Beyond not wanting to ruin their friendship, beyond not being sure she could do the serious relationship thing, was the very real fact she couldn't take on the responsibility of his happiness. It was hard enough taking responsibility of her own. She'd never be able to live up to it.

"You're right." He sounded tired again, exhausted beyond measure as if this conversation was taking away all the energy he'd gotten from the nap. "That isn't fair. I don't want to put that kind of pressure on you." He shoved his fingers through his hair. "God, this is such a mess. How did I get here? I had a plan. It was a good plan."

"Plans rarely work out when it comes to stuff like this," Callie murmured. "You've got a lot on your plate." Hesitantly, fearfully she reached out to touch his arm. A friendly gesture. She hoped. "It takes a while to sort things out. You've got time. You don't have to decide to stay or not today. You've got months. Think about what you really want."

He nodded and visibly swallowed. "I want you, Callie."

The words wreaked havoc on her system, and she was about five seconds away from giving in, from ignoring everything she'd just said. The whispers of fear coated her brain just in time to pull herself together.

"I don't think that's a very good idea, under the circumstances. Attraction isn't everything and if we give in, it has the potential to ruin a lot." She tried to believe the truth in her words, tried not to let her mind rehash that kiss. "It's not a good idea."

"No, it isn't." He grabbed her chin, gave her a hard,

frustrated kiss. "But that's not going to stop me from thinking about it. You're a part of this. If I decide to stay, I'm not going to give a shit about potentially ruining anything."

When he walked off, Callie felt no closer to a resolution than she had when she'd been honest about some of her feelings with him.

So much for breaking down walls. It hadn't helped a damn bit.

Chapter Thirteen

"This is our last chance to get the permit in time since it takes ninety days to jump through all the hoops once Dana signs off on it."

Shelby looked at the binder Em had been putting together, then at the bathroom door where Callie had disappeared almost half an hour ago.

"Maybe I could go with Callie. Dana and my mom were pretty tight. I could help."

Em smiled so wide it made Shelby want to squirm, especially when Em slung an affectionate arm over Shelby's shoulders.

"Aw, you've fallen under the spell."

"Huh?"

"The AIF spell. You love it. You want to help. Just like your brother."

Shelby squirmed away from Em, who was right even if Shelby didn't want to admit it. In the week Shelby had been volunteering for AIF she'd given way more than the ten hours she'd promised. There was something comforting about being there. Being a part of something. A weird something. Almost like a family.

Not that she would *ever* admit it to anyone. But she got it, why Trevor was always eager to leave in the morning. AIF was so different than the Steele house with its interminable silences and ghosts around every corner. AIF was a breath of fresh air, a place to feel relaxed.

"Of course, I think your brother might have some ulterior motives to being around here so much." Em wiggled her eyebrows, and Shelby's stomach jumped with hope.

"What ulterior motives?"

Em closed the binder and nodded her head toward the bathroom door. "My sister, I'd guess. Don't you think?"

"I heard a rumor in town that they're together," Shelby whispered conspiratorially, hoping to get some kind of confirmation besides whispers and gossip.

Em leaned her head closer, keeping her gaze glued to the bathroom door. "I heard that too, but I haven't seen any solid proof. They've been acting the same as they always do around here. Have you seen anything?"

"No." Shelby frowned. "Dan said his cousin said he heard from somebody they were making out at my graduation party."

Em chewed her bottom lip. "I don't know. You know how rumors are, and I think Callie would have mentioned it."

The bathroom door opened and even if Em and Shelby hadn't been discussing Callie, they both would have stopped talking. Callie stepped out looking like an entirely different person.

Her straight black hair was pulled into a French braid and she was wearing a business suit. It was black, but the dark purple shirt underneath was a really good color for her.

She wore makeup. It was subtle and businesslike, and if Shelby didn't know better, she would have thought Callie a high-powered professional. Even her black heels were fashionable, though Mom would have said they were a little too flashy for business.

"All right, Shelby. How do I look?"

Surprised, Shelby frowned at Em then back at Callie. "Why are you asking me?"

Callie straightened her jacket, stood with shoulders back as if she was bracing herself. "Because I know you'll be honest."

Shelby fidgeted in her seat, torn between integrity and habit. Integrity would mean telling the truth, habit would be a nasty comment wrapped around the truth. "You look sophisticated." *For trash*, Mom's voice added in Shelby's head. Shelby frowned at the voice; there were times when it really got on her nerves.

"I'll be damned," Callie muttered.

"It's true." Em looked pleased and hopeful. "Dana won't be able to look at you and see Bad Girl Baker at all."

From Callie's grimace, Shelby knew Callie didn't share Em's confidence.

"Let's cross our fingers, toes, everything." Again Callie straightened her jacket and for the first time Shelby noticed the nerves. Callie's hands weren't steady and she kept moving around the room as if she couldn't sit still.

"I want to go with you," Shelby blurted, pushing away from the table before she realized what she was doing.

Callie's brows knit together. "What for?"

Shelby thought of Em's story of the numerous refusals and Dana's stupid reasons for not giving AIF the parking permit. Shelby knew how easy it was to dislike Callie, but it wasn't fair Dana was hurting AIF to hurt Callie. "I want to help."

"You Steeles certainly think a lot of yourselves." Callie crossed her arms over her chest. "I don't need help."

"Dana and my mom were friends. I know what they think of you." Shelby was determined now. She wasn't backing down. "I can help you change Dana's mind."

Callie and Em exchanged indecipherable looks.

"What's in it for you?"

The accusation hurt, especially since for once Shelby was

trying to be nice. "I want to help."

"Want to help or want something to lord over me so I'll help you get Trevor to stay?"

Even though Shelby knew she deserved the slight, the rational part of her mind was no match for the irrational part that bristled at Callie's accusation. The part that felt unjustly vilified. Except when Shelby really thought about that feeling, those words, they were all her mother's.

Shelby squeezed her eyes shut, hoping to shut Mom out too. She loved her mother, missed her more than anything, but she was eighteen and she wanted her own voice in her head— no one else's.

Her own voice wanted to help, even if Mom wouldn't have approved. Of course, if Callie felt so inclined to help talk Trevor into staying, Shelby couldn't see that as being a bad thing.

Shelby took a deep breath and met Callie's squinted gaze. "Does it matter why? Shouldn't you take whatever help is offered? Em said this is your last chance, and if I can help, and I'm offering to help, just accept it. Everything else be damned."

At Callie's sharp intake of breath Shelby knew the words hit home.

"Fine, but you screw this up for us, you better disappear. Even your brother won't be able to save you from my revenge."

Shelby scrambled after Callie's hasty exit, grabbing Em's binder on her way out. Once they were in the car, driving away from AIF and toward downtown Pilot's Point, Callie broke the silence first.

"Dana and your mom were friends, huh? Did they have an 'I hate Callie Baker' club or something?"

The words were surprisingly bitter. Shelby didn't think Callie cared what other people thought, but the idea of an "I hate Callie" club wasn't too far from the truth, so Shelby kept her mouth shut.

"Jesus," Callie hissed. "Didn't they have anything better to do than hate me?"

Shelby didn't have a response for that either, because if she were being honest with herself, she kind of agreed with Callie, which was a sad state of affairs.

"I give you credit. You've always been honest about how you feel about me. Never pretended or faked being polite. I appreciate that."

Shelby fidgeted in the seat, her hands sweating from clutching the binder so hard. "I never did understand why Mom was so nice to people's faces but so mean behind their backs. It seemed dishonest to me."

As soon as Shelby said it, she regretted it. Saying those things, to Callie of all people, felt like the worst kind of betrayal.

"Well, hell, how am I supposed to keep being a bitch to you when you say that?"

Shelby smiled, couldn't help herself. No matter how many times Mom's words pounded into her brain about Callie being bad, about Callie being incapable of change, Shelby couldn't see it. Callie was different, and the thought of her with Trevor wasn't totally self-serving anymore. Trevor and Callie kind of complemented each other, and it was obvious to anyone with half a brain they had the hots for each other.

"As long as we're being friendly, I want to talk to you about something."

Shelby's smile immediately died. She did not like the sound of this.

"I know you want Trevor to stay in Pilot's Point, and I get it. He's your brother and you want something and someone to call home. It makes sense."

"I'm guessing there's a but here." Shelby slumped in her

seat, kept her eyes focused on the window, prepared to ignore whatever lecture was coming.

"Whatever happened at graduation really hit him hard. Hard enough that he's feeling so guilty he's talking about staying."

Shelby straightened in the seat so fast the binder clattered onto the floor below. "He is?"

Callie frowned at the reaction, clutched the steering wheel tighter. "Yes, but don't start celebrating just yet. If he decides to stay, it's only out of guilt. He was a wreck after graduation. I've never seen him so lost. But in a couple years, that guilt will wear off and he's going to be stuck here, somewhere he never wanted to be while you graduate college and start your life somewhere else."

Shelby's heart twisted. She'd never meant to make Trevor feel bad with what she'd said at graduation. No one was more embarrassed by that moment than her. Being so pathetic and needy with him was not part of her plan, and she'd been so mortified by it she'd pretended it never happened.

It never occurred to her that honesty and emotion would have affected Trevor enough to get him seriously thinking about staying. She'd gone the manipulation route because she'd been so sure that would be most effective.

Her stomach churned into queasy waves as she realized why she'd thought that. It had been Mom's method of choice when getting what she wanted. Shelby leaned her head against the cool window and closed her eyes.

"You okay?"

Shelby swallowed. No, she wasn't okay. Ever since Mom had died, ever since her strong influence had left the house, Shelby had been realizing more and more all the ways she didn't want to be like her mother, and all the ways she was. It made her feel disloyal and weak all at once. If she loved her mom, shouldn't she want to be like her?

"Shelby?"

"I'm okay," Shelby rasped.

"I thought you'd be ecstatic."

Shelby opened her eyes, stared at the buildings of Pilot's Point in the distance. "I want Trevor to stay, I do. I just..." She shook her head. She *should* be ecstatic, but she couldn't fight the feeling she'd somehow done something wrong.

Callie reached over, tentatively patted her shoulder. "He should stay because he wants to, and he doesn't want to."

"I don't want him so far away. I don't want to be..."

"Alone?"

Shelby swallowed, nodded.

"It probably doesn't mean shit to you, but you're part of the AIF family now. You're always welcome."

Some warmth worked its way through the conflicting feelings in her head and stomach. "It means something."

Callie smiled. "Good."

"I still want him to stay." More than anything. "But I guess you might be almost kind of right about... Well, it shouldn't be out of guilt."

Callie's smile widened. "Be careful, you might give me a heart attack here."

The past two months came into sharp focus. She'd been a selfish child, and maybe that was okay with everything she'd had to deal with, but it was time to start making some adult decisions. Some adult decisions that weren't based on her mother. "I guess I kind of almost owe you an apology."

"For what?"

"I guess most of my life I treated you a certain way because my mom didn't like you."

Callie shrugged and seemed uncomfortable. "Well, for most of your life I deserved it."

"Yeah, you did." Callie snorted, but Shelby couldn't be amused by her own words. Too many emotions fought for prominence. Betrayal was winning pretty steadily. Her mother would never approve of this discussion, of Shelby's new almost-respect for Callie. But Shelby had to do what she felt was right, even if that made her feel guilty. "I love my mom." Her voice cracked a little, but she wasn't going to cry.

"Of course you do. I liked your mom too, until I found out she hated my guts."

"I don't want to hate you or manipulate Trevor, but, Mom's voice is in my head." That sounded crazy, and stupid. She should have kept her mouth shut. Why was she telling this to Callie anyway?

"You can love your mom and not listen to that voice, you know? I mean, look at your brother. He took all the good things from your parents, but got rid of most of the rest. He did what they wanted, but he did it his own way." Callie's lips curved into a small, faraway smile, and, for Callie, Shelby figured that was as close to gushing as she got.

"You are *so* in love with him."

Callie snorted. "I am not. We're *friends.*"

"Yeah, friends who want to have sex."

Callie gaped at her and Shelby shrugged.

"What? I have half a brain and eyes, don't I? It's pretty obvious. And very disturbing."

"Jesus Christ," Callie muttered, shaking her head.

"Well, whatever. You care about Trevor, right?"

Callie's jaw tightened in tune with her hands on the steering wheel. "Right."

"Why don't you want him to stay then?"

She frowned at that, squeezed the steering wheel again and stared hard at the stoplight above her. "Because I want him to be happy."

Shelby leaned forward to pick the forgotten binder off the ground. "That doesn't seem like a whole answer to me."

"It's the only answer I've got."

Shelby smiled, hugging the binder to her chest. Suddenly she felt a lot better. Callie and Trevor were getting closer and closer, and there were two and half months until September. Plenty of time for them to finally admit their feelings for one another.

Shelby just had to decide if it was still manipulation to give them a little push in the right direction.

Trevor stared at the list in front of him. He'd labeled it the Happiness List, and so far there wasn't a whole lot to be happy about.

Seattle was killing Pilot's Point. It had his job, freedom, his own place that didn't remind him of his parents, a decent gym, Puget Sound, stuff to do at night. All he had for Pilot's Point was less guilt and Callie, and she'd been right to tell him that wasn't fair.

So, he had made a deal with himself. As long as Seattle outranked Pilot's Point on the happy list, he'd plan on going back. If Pilot's Point ever made some kind of miraculous comeback, he'd stay.

He couldn't understand why part of him hoped for the miraculous comeback.

The low murmur of voices outside the door was a welcome distraction. Dan was likely dropping Shelby off from their date.

Trevor didn't eavesdrop, but if the voices went silent for too long, he usually pretended he had to take out the garbage or get the mail.

Shelby knew what he was doing, but it wasn't going to stop him from doing it. In fact, he had a really great idea for the next time. He'd go dig out one of his old gun holsters and put his gun in it as he walked out with the trash. Unloaded of course, but Dan didn't need to know that.

Trevor added "scaring Dan" to his happy list, though he wasn't quite sure it counted. After all, Shelby and Dan wouldn't be a part of Pilot's Point come August. He scratched an asterisk next to it.

The voices quieted, but only for a moment before Shelby pushed the front door open. Casually, Trevor folded the list and shoved it into his back pocket.

"Hey."

"Hey." Instead of disappearing to her room like she usually did after a date with Dan, she sat down next to him on the couch.

"Who's winning?" she asked, staring at the TV screen.

He hadn't been paying attention, so he had no clue. "Lost track. I heard something interesting today."

Shelby fidgeted, kept her eyes on the screen. "What's that?"

"You went with Callie to meet with Dana."

Shelby shrugged defensively. "Yeah, so?"

"Let me repeat that. *You* went with *Callie* to *help*. You see how this is a hard thing for me to understand."

Shelby rolled her eyes. "Maybe Callie's not the worst person in the world."

Trevor clutched his chest, gasped. "Oh my God, the world must be ending."

"You're such an idiot," she muttered, but even Shelby

couldn't keep from smiling.

Miracles must exist because he was beginning to think Callie and Shelby were actually on the path to friendship.

"I've been thinking," Shelby said. She shifted and pulled out a folded piece of paper from her own pocket. "About graduation."

Trevor sat up a little straighter, swallowed. They were finally going to talk about it? Shit. He'd really prefer to leave it alone.

"I shouldn't have said... I was sad and missing Mom and Dad and I didn't mean it." She stared intently at the paper in her hands and Trevor was glad he didn't have to meet her eyes.

Trevor opened his mouth to say something to diffuse the moment, to shrug it all off, but no words came out.

"All of a sudden I kind of panicked. All those other people had these big families and I thought if you left, I'd be alone."

"Even if I'm not here, you're not alone. You can always call, visit. I'm not leaving *you*."

"I know." She began unfolding her piece of paper. "You'd do almost anything for me."

It was the almost that had guilt stabbing at him.

"I do want you to stay in Pilot's Point, but I think there's a compromise somewhere."

"A compromise?"

She shoved the wrinkled piece of paper at him. "Here."

It was a printed out sheet of paper with a list of FBI Agencies in the Midwest. Next to each city's listing were handwritten notes of how far away each one was from Pilot's Point and UNI.

"I don't want you to be miserable," Shelby said, her eyes meeting his for the first time. "But Seattle is so far away. I don't know how everything works, but I thought maybe you could

163

transfer closer. Somewhere I wouldn't have to hop on a plane if I needed you."

Trevor's mouth gaped and he looked down at the list. *Kansas City, 220 miles from Pilot's Point, 330 Miles from UNI. Springfield, IL, 169 miles from Pilot's Point, 330 miles from UNI.*

It went on and on, going through the majority of the field offices in the Midwest. A lot of work had been put into this list, and, well, it made sense. It was another option.

Like he needed another fucking option.

The realization dawned on him quick and clear, and when he looked up at Shelby, his jaw clenched hard. "What did Callie say to you?"

Shelby's brows knit together. "Nothing."

"Then where'd all this compromise bullshit come from?" He pushed off the couch, letting the piece of paper fall to the ground. Now it wasn't just stay or go, it was stay or go or, hey, move to any handful of FBI offices.

Trevor had no doubt Callie had gotten to Shelby somehow. Shelby wanted him to stay. Compromise was not in a Steele's vocabulary.

Shelby stood too, clenching her fists together. "It's not bullshit. It's better than you going back to Seattle. I want you to be happy."

"Now I know Callie said something to you because a day ago you could give a shit about my happiness."

She snapped her head back like it'd been a blow. Almost immediately tears filled her eyes.

Great. Congratulations, Trev. You're the biggest tool in the world. Why don't you go slap her in the face while you're at it?

"Just like you didn't give a shit about mine before Mom died?" She didn't cry, she held on to those tears, but that didn't help Trevor feel any less like an ass.

"Shelby—"

"Screw you, Trevor," she all but spat. "I was trying to be nice, to find a solution that would make us both happy."

"You're right." Trevor held up his hands in surrender. "You're right. I'm sorry."

She seemed skeptical of his sudden turnaround, but he didn't have the energy to fight her anymore. What was the point? They never seemed able to find the same wavelength. The idea they never would made him immeasurably sad.

"I'll go throw this away." She picked up the discarded piece of paper.

"No, I want to keep it," Trevor replied, holding out his hand.

On a sigh, she handed it to him. "Do whatever you want. I'm done caring." With that she trudged up the stairs like the weight of the world was on her shoulders.

Trevor sank into the couch, stared at the paper.

Fuck.

Chapter Fourteen

Callie kicked at the ground while Em sat placidly on the porch swing. Callie couldn't sit still—placidly or otherwise. Nerves dictated she move.

Lawson and the boys would be arriving any minute.

It hadn't been that long since she'd seen them. Without fail, Lawson always brought the boys home for Christmas, even if Sue didn't make the trip with them. But those visits were brief—a flurry of activity, food and wrapping paper, and then they'd be off again.

This was different.

After running AIF jointly with Em for two years, they were about to add a new voice to the mix. The extra hands would be welcome, but Callie had a few reservations about Lawson taking over Gramps's role after so long.

The role of president wasn't one Callie wanted. Callie wanted to focus on planes, just like Em wanted to focus on her library and museum. It made sense, but Callie couldn't help but wonder if they were handing over a big piece of power to someone who had no idea what he was getting himself into.

It was Lawson's rightful place, and yet he'd left AIF at eighteen when Sue demanded they move to California so she could pursue her acting career. Twelve years he'd been gone. What did he know about Antiques in Flight now?

Wrong thinking. AIF was in the blood. They couldn't punish Law for caving to his wife's demands. Of course, if he hadn't knocked up the biggest bitch in Pilot's Point when he'd been sixteen, he never would have left with her.

Callie sighed, squinting down the gravel road. Didn't matter. Law had made his choices and they were what they were. Now he was choosing to come home and AIF would have to support three more Bakers.

Failure became more of a burden. As if on cue, that burden arrived.

The sound of gravel popping under tires had Em standing. Callie could make out a small SUV flitting behind the trees. For reasons Callie couldn't understand, tears sprung to her eyes.

Lawson was home. Her family was in one place. When Lawson stopped the car and stepped out, Callie had to actively blink back those tears.

Em rushed into Lawson's arms, tears already on her face, as always leading with her heart. Callie hung back, feeling caught.

It seemed forever ago Em had accused her of having walls built up, of never expressing to Lawson all the frustration she felt, all the reasons she wanted him to come home. Because she'd held that in, she'd mainly held herself apart. So much so it was hard to move now.

When Em finally relinquished Lawson, it only took his hazel eyes landing on her with trepidation to have her crossing the short distance between them.

She paused for a moment before powering through the uncertainty and letting her heart do the leading too. She hugged Lawson, hard, and said the words she felt. "I'm so glad you're home."

"Me too, Cal," he replied, returning her hard squeeze.

Brandon and Evan stepped out of the car, gingerly stretching their cramped limbs. They were two younger versions of Lawson, the Lawson Callie remembered as a boy. Gangly with shocks of dark brown hair and skin tanned by the sun.

Brandon, the oldest at fourteen, didn't look too enthused to be here. He had Sue's eyes, a vibrant, cat-like green. His scowl looked permanent, like it had become his relaxed expression. Callie recognized something in it. The hurt of abandonment and the desperate attempt at toughness behind it.

Sue had always been a shitty mother, but Callie doubted Brandon or Evan felt they'd be better off with her half a country away.

"We're glad you're here." Callie pulled Brandon into a hug. He stiffened, but after a moment hugged her back.

"Thanks, Aunt Callie."

Callie smiled, she liked the familial endearment even if it wasn't technically, biologically accurate.

Evan bounded around to where Callie stood, bouncing up and down with a sunny, ten-year-old enthusiasm, a direct contrast to his brother even if they looked so much alike. Callie bent down to bring him into a hug too.

Lawson went to the trunk of the car and popped the lid. Inside were the haphazard belongings of three very disorganized men. Evan looked around as if he'd landed on an alien planet. Brandon kept the scowl on his face and hefted a big backpack onto his shoulder. The three Baker men paused for a second, looking at the house before them.

"You're home," Em said, completely unfazed to be shedding a few more tears.

Callie and Em helped to unload the car, slowly picking away at the squished boxes, bags and random items until the car was empty and the contents had been put inside.

Lawson brought the last load in, set the box down in the kitchen, and looked around.

"Wow, this is weird." He let out a breath. "It's exactly the same."

"Yeah, and it's yours." Callie patted his shoulder.

The grin made the skin around his eyes fold into wrinkles. "You have no idea how happy that makes me."

Callie couldn't fight it any longer, and a few happy tears spilled over onto her own cheeks as well.

They did their best to get everything settled, the necessities unpacked. Well, mainly Em, Lawson and Brandon did all that while Callie kept Evan busy and out of the way. They ate dinner together, like a family, and something about the whole evening had Callie feeling whole.

She wasn't sure she'd ever felt that in her adult life.

After Lawson put Evan to bed and Brandon went to his room to try and get his computer connected to the Internet, the adults retired to the porch. The same porch they'd spent summer nights on as kids, catching lightning bugs or dreaming about the future.

Lawson sat on the swinging loveseat, his ankles crossed on the bench in front of him. Em sat next to him, curled into the corner. Callie took her usual spot on the railing. The night above was clear and perfect and for the first time in a long time, optimism won out.

Her family was in one place and AIF would be okay.

"Am I really here?"

"Home sweet home," Em replied, moonlight illuminating her wide grin. "Just wait until we go up to AIF tomorrow."

Lawson shook his head. "I can't believe it's real. I've been dreaming about this for years."

"Then what took you so long?"

Lawson and Em's heads both snapped toward her and Callie winced at her own words. She hadn't meant them to come out sounding so harsh. Especially with how good she was feeling, but part of her had to wonder why this good feeling was so late in coming.

"Callie, come on. It's his first night."

"No, she's right." Law straightened in the seat. "It's a fair question. Why not tonight?" He looked down at the can of pop in his hands. "From the moment I got Sue pregnant until only a few years ago, everything I did was because of two things. Guilt or the kids. Once the guilt was gone, it was all about the kids. I can't feel bad about that."

Callie swallowed. Guilt wasn't permanent. Eventually it had lost its hold on Lawson. That was good for AIF, but it made her think about Trevor.

"When wasn't guilt enough? I mean, when did you really decide to come back?" Callie wished she could eat her own words the minute they were out of her mouth, because they weren't about Lawson. They were about Trevor.

He shrugged. "When there was nothing left to feel guilty for, I guess. When I found out Sue was cheating on me any guilt evaporated. Then the divorce and all that, well, I was trying to keep the kids in one piece. Once I knew coming home wasn't just for me, once I knew it was for the boys too, then it was just a matter of getting Sue to agree. Which took way too fucking long, by the way."

"Damn right it did." Em patted Lawson's arm, nodding emphatically.

Callie couldn't focus on Lawson's drama. She was too busy thinking about her own. Every instinct told her no matter how Trevor talked or how sweetly he kissed her, there was no way she was going to let him stay in Pilot's Point. Because she wouldn't be enough to keep him, never had been.

Chapter Fifteen

It took less than a week for the new Baker additions to fold into the AIF goings on like they'd always been there. With each passing week of having her family in one place, of having three volunteers throw their all into AIF, Callie's mood improved. If that wasn't great on its own, there'd been enough flurry of activity to keep her from dwelling too much on Trevor.

Which was essential, because though Shelby's graduation party had been weeks ago, Callie could still remember that kiss with perfect clarity. Being legitimately busy and avoiding being alone with Trevor were about the only two things keeping her sane.

Today was different. She was beginning to realize she wasn't alone in putting up a wall; Trevor had been keeping his distance too. He'd been uncharacteristically quiet and introverted.

It made sense. He had a big decision to make. The right thing for him to do was head back to his normal life once September rolled around, but guilt was keeping him in limbo.

Callie wished she knew what to do to make it go away for him, but she didn't think even Shelby taking back whatever she'd said to him at graduation would ease Trevor's guilt. He always took on too much and took it too hard when he couldn't find the perfect plan to solve a problem.

For the past few weeks, Em had announced a mandatory Friday lunch for all AIF employees and volunteers. Everyone would squeeze onto the picnic tables outside the Canteen with sandwiches or barbecue, chat about the week behind and the week to come, and bond.

It was a wonderful tradition, one that seemed to cement everyone together in the common goal of keeping AIF afloat, but Callie had been making a distinct effort to keep from sitting next to Trevor on these Friday lunches. Today she couldn't muster the indifference. He was looking more and more miserable with each passing day, and she missed him.

If only there was a way to be his friend without all the other stuff getting in the way, but she was struggling with that line between friend and something more. In all her attempts not to lose him, she'd pushed them halfway there. He'd still be the first one in line if she needed help, but the day-to-day friendship that had bloomed since he'd been back was gone.

He might as well be in Seattle for as much time as they spent together.

She squeezed next to him on the picnic table and set a Mountain Dew in front of him. "You look like you need the caffeine."

He smiled and said thanks, and if she didn't know him so well she might have thought she was overreacting. But she knew him, and he wasn't himself.

Before Callie could come up with a joke or something light to say, Em slid next to Trevor on the other side. "Someone please come up with an excuse for me tonight."

"For what?"

"Billie's rehearsal dinner."

Callie immediately scowled. She hated that Em was in this damn wedding with Frank, but she'd been so wrapped up in all the other drama in her life she hadn't had time to worry over it. "Isn't Pete going with you?"

"He has to work, which means Frank and I get to be all nice

and cozy." Em grimaced. "I can't believe I let Billie talk me into walking down the aisle with him. He's so handsy. Blech."

"You shouldn't have let her." Trevor bit into his sandwich.

Em shrugged, plopped her chin onto her hand. "It's not my place. It's her wedding and her husband-to-be happens to be friends with..." Em trailed off, glancing at Callie and then the ten-year-old standing next to them. "A not so nice person."

"He hasn't turned over a new magical leaf and become a considerate pillar of society then?" Callie asked, earning a grin from Trevor.

"Not even a little. When the groomsmen were in town for the bachelor party Billie made the whole wedding party have dinner together, and Frank spent the entire time trying to convince me his divorce was days away from being final." Em shuddered. "Even though his mom is friends with my mom and, unless he's lying to his mother, he's not even separated from his wife. *And* I told him I was dating Pete. But he wouldn't back off. Ugh."

"You never told me about that." Callie didn't like it one bit. Frank should know better than to try and hit on *her* baby sister.

Em shrugged and avoided Callie's stare. "I didn't want you to get all angry about it and do something stupid, like come to the wedding."

"I am coming to the wedding."

"You can't be serious."

"I sent in my RSVP the minute I got the invite. You're crazy if you think I'm not going to keep my eye on that bastard when he's got his hands on you."

Em leaned closer to Callie, so that they were both squishing against Trevor in an effort to argue with each other. "We'll be in a church. There's not much Frank can do to me in

173

front of Pilot's Point and God. Pete will be there at the reception."

"Pete's a wuss," Callie replied with a disdainful snort.

"I hate to agree with Callie on this, but it's true. Pete isn't exactly the protector type."

Em scowled at Trevor. "I can take care of myself, guys."

"Of course you can." Callie smiled. "And I can take care of Frank."

"Oh no." Em groaned, smacked her forehead with her palm. "She's morphing into Bad Girl Baker. Somebody stop her."

Em wasn't far off. Part of it was anger that Frank had actually spent an evening try to sweet talk *her* sister, enough for Em to call him handsy—a protective instinct kicking in—but part of it was something a little more self-gratifying. Callie felt old emotions rushing in to fill empty spaces, and those old emotions whispered *revenge*. Maybe it had been thirteen years since Frank Winston had made her feel like dirt, but revenge sounded really, *really* good.

Callie smiled wider, flashing her teeth. "I don't know what you're talking about."

"You shouldn't go. You'll end up doing something stup—" When she glared at him, Trevor searched for a better word. "Er, ill advised."

Callie shrugged, practically giggled as her mind whirled with ideas of revenge. "It'll be fun."

"Trevor, you have to go with her and protect us all." Em nudged Trevor with her elbow. "You're the only one who can get through to her when she's in BGB mode."

Bad Girl Baker. Callie had missed her. The feelings of strength and purpose. New optimistic Callie was happier, but she missed this edge. This sharpness. "I don't need a babysitter."

"Yeah, you need an armed guard," Trevor muttered.

Callie's smile didn't dim, and she sipped her pop thinking about all the ways to enact revenge on Frank. If he so much as laid a hand on Em that wasn't expressly required by his groomsmen duties, well, he wouldn't be able to walk out of Pilot's Point.

"Who is this Frank guy, anyway?" Shelby asked.

"Just an old friend." Callie laughed at her own joke and Shelby's confused look.

Em cradled her chin in her hands. "Callie, you're scaring me."

"Oh, don't be scared," Callie replied. "I'm reformed, remember?"

"You don't look reformed," Trevor offered between bites of sandwich. He nudged her with his hip. "Go with me. It'll be fun. I'll keep you out of trouble." He smiled and looked better than he had in days.

"Sure." It would be nice to do something with Trevor again. Get away from AIF and spend some time together. Maybe it was a dangerous line to walk, but barely being a part of his life wasn't really any better than the risk.

If letting him think he'd keep her out of trouble made him happy, it was just another benefit. Maybe with BGB taking charge, she and Trevor would finally get all the weird stuff between them out of their systems.

After she crushed Frank Winston under her heel, of course.

Trevor pulled up to Em and Callie's cabin feeling oddly nervous. Like one might feel on a first date.

This wasn't a date, of course. It was two friends attending a wedding together. Not to mention, he was still kind of pissed at

Callie for talking to Shelby about his decision to stay or go. Added to that, she'd all but been avoiding him for weeks.

As he stepped out of the car, he wasn't thinking about being pissed. He was thinking about dancing with Callie at the wedding.

He knocked on the door, straightened his tie, and tried to remember he wasn't eighteen and this wasn't prom.

No answer. Frowning, Trevor tried to doorknob and it turned easily, so he let himself inside.

"Callie?"

"Sorry," her muffled voice called from deep inside the cabin. "I'll be out in a second."

"Okay." Damned if he could shake the teenage feeling of sick nerves. What was there to be nervous about? Other than the very real possibility Callie might throw a punch tonight or worse, but he'd gotten her out of tricky situations before.

A door creaked, and when Callie stepped into view, the words rushed out of Trevor's mouth before he had a chance to put any finesse on them.

"Holy shit."

She grinned, sauntered toward him. "You know, Trev, that was the *exact* reaction I was hoping for."

Trevor had to clear his throat, had to look somewhere other than the dangerous dip of her dress.

She cocked her head as she pulled some big, silvery bracelet over her hand. "You okay?"

"Fucking fantastic." He eyed a spot on the ceiling, refused to look away from it.

She laughed, a sound low and throaty, almost like she'd started smoking again. Oh, she had something up her sleeve. Except there was no sleeve on either nicely toned arm. "There's no chance in me convincing you BGB is a bad idea, is there?"

"It's just for the night. Enjoy her while she lasts. I'll shut her down in the morning." She walked past him, close enough he realized Callie Baker was wearing perfume. It had to be a first.

When she passed him, he couldn't keep his eyes on the ceiling. The dress was something black and lacy that clung to every angle and curve leaving very little to the imagination, especially the way she was sashaying around in black high heels. The neckline of her dress plunged low, and the skirt ended well above her knees. It showed off every last asset Callie had to offer, and Trevor was having a hard time hearing anything beyond the roaring in his ears.

Even her face was made up to look sexy. Her makeup was dark, smoky almost. Some time between yesterday and this evening she had gotten bangs. Long bangs that swept over her forehead, almost long enough to cover her eyes.

She looked like something on the cover of a dark, racy magazine. If he was going to make it through the night without having to hide behind things, he was going to have to stop looking at anything on her except the top of her head or maybe the points of her elbows.

She stood there, letting him drink it all in with an amused smile on her face. Trevor let out a long, slow breath.

"Ready?" she asked, feigning innocence.

"Not remotely."

That had her laughing. "Come on, now. Don't want to be late."

Trevor tried to focus his mind on something else, but he came up blank as he followed her out to his car. Twice his eyes wandered down to her ass, and twice he had to mentally slap himself. Not the time. They had a wedding and reception to sit through, and he didn't really want to spend the majority of that time trying to adjust himself.

Trevor started the car, gripped the steering wheel, and kept his eyes on the road. In fact, that would be his inner mantra for the drive. *Eyes on the road.*

"What exactly is all this trying to prove?" *Eyes on the road. Eyes on the road. Eyes on the road.*

"I'm not trying to prove anything." She crossed her legs and Trevor jerked the wheel when his tires hit the gravel shoulder.

"You okay to drive?"

"Yeah, just fine. You are very definitely up to something. Why don't you tell me so I can tell you how stupid you're being."

"I'm not being stupid." Some of the breezy casualness was out of her voice, which helped ease at least some of the tension in his shoulders.

"Is this all some sort of elaborate plan to get Frank back for what he did to you? Because this obviously isn't all about protecting Em. If you haven't noticed, she's a grown woman."

She crossed her arms under her chest, which pushed her breasts up against the skintight fabric. *Eyes on the road. Eyes on the road. You've seen plenty of breasts in your life. There are nothing special about those. Kind of.*

"Just because I want to look decent at a wedding in which many of my exes will be in attendance doesn't mean I have a plan. I'm going to keep an eye on my sister and have a free meal."

Trevor snorted. "You don't just look decent."

"I don't?"

"No, you look evil." Her smile spread slowly and Trevor had to jerk his eyes to the road again.

"I like that."

"It's been a long time since we were sixteen. Can't you cut the guy some sla—"

"I don't care how old we were. He talked me into having sex for my first time after my grandma dies, and then he breaks up with me about five minutes after it's over. Sorry, even sixteen isn't an excuse for being that big of an asshole."

"Maybe not, but I broke his nose over it."

"Yeah, you. *You*. Not me. I didn't do shit except let my friend stand up for me. Well, tonight it'll be me breaking his nose. Figuratively, of course."

Trevor sighed, momentarily sidetracked by her words enough to fight the distraction of her body. "Please do not get arrested for assault tonight. I don't have the pull I used to at county."

She leaned over, patted his cheek. "Oh, don't you worry. Frank's just going to get a taste of what he missed out on. Is that so wrong? And it'll keep his slimy paws away from Em."

"I don't know if it's wrong, but is it necessary? You're hot without the skimpy dress and all the shit on your face. You're happy, aren't you? Happiness is supposed to be the best revenge."

"I'll point out that you're pretty affected by the skimpy dress and the shit on my face. And, yes, I am happy, but it's really not enough unless I rub it in his face, is it?"

"It should be enough." Trevor pulled into the parking lot of the church, dread and arousal fighting for prominence.

"It's not." She stepped out of the car, and it was like stepping back in time. She was someone he didn't know what to do with, someone he desperately wanted to help, but didn't know how.

As the fighting gleam of BGB took over, Trevor had a very, very bad feeling.

Chapter Sixteen

Callie definitely underestimated the challenge of enacting revenge. Especially revenge she hadn't totally formulated in her head before she'd arrived at the reception. No matter how many times she'd tried to put together a fully thought out plan, nothing really gelled.

She powered forward. Looking really hot was the first step, and Frank approaching her had been the second. His eyes weren't on Em, and that was the important thing. Maybe Em *could* take care of herself, but she was too nice to be forceful about it. Callie didn't have that problem.

Now she was stuck standing around listening to Frank feign heartbreak over his recent divorce, which, according to most sources, was completely fictional.

She believed small town gossip way more than she believed Frank Winston.

Callie sighed and looked down at her drink. Now that they were in the midst of the reception and everyone around her was having fun, she felt foolish. If happiness was the best revenge, she was failing because she didn't feel happy. She felt sleazy.

She snuck a look at Trevor who was smiling and laughing with a small group of people from high school who'd left Pilot's Point. Figured. He would gravitate toward that crowd. Then there was Em on the dance floor with Pete, laughing at his awkward movements. Pete might be a wuss, but he was keeping Em occupied and out of Frank's line of sight.

Everyone was having fun, enjoying themselves, not worried

about high school hurts or slights. And she was standing here with some creep who kept staring at her chest while trying to drum up some sympathy from her.

He seemed to really think he had a shot of getting her to have sex with him again, and that was almost laughable enough to put a smile on her face. She looked at Trevor who was smiling at some blonde she didn't recognize. Any threat of a smile immediately vanished.

Frank was droning on about his job, how wonderful it was, all the while not-so-subtly inching closer. Callie forced a smile, but her eyes drifted to Trevor. This time, his eyes met hers. She tried to keep the smile in place, but it faltered.

God, she was an idiot.

Callie turned her attention to Frank and tried to get a word in edgewise so she could make her escape. This wasn't worth it. No matter what he'd done to her so many years ago, it didn't matter. He was a pretentious, blabbering idiot. Her life wasn't perfect, but it certainly didn't revolve around what Frank had done to her.

When he put a hand on her shoulder, let it slide down her arm, Callie had the very real sensation of wanting to gag.

"There you are, sweetheart." Trevor's arm came in, slid around her waist and pulled her close and away from Frank.

Callie tensed a little, but then smiled up at him. He always knew right when to swoop in, didn't he? Part of her wanted to be irritated by that, but he felt too good next to her to manage it. Besides, she'd been failing at making her own escape.

Frank's prominent nose wrinkled at Trevor's appearance.

"Heya, Frank," Trevor greeted cheerfully. "Your nose healed just right, didn't it? Can't tell it was ever broken." He tapped his own nose with a grin Callie had to match.

"Steele." Frank sneered his greeting. He obviously held a

grudge too.

"I'm going to have to steal my date away for a bit." Trevor aimed his smile down at Callie.

Frank studied Callie, Trevor's arm intimately linked around her waist. "Date?"

"Didn't you see us sitting together?" Callie leaned into Trevor, amused at Frank's irritation. Apparently he'd really thought he had his mojo working. Maybe there was a little sliver of revenge for the taking after all.

"I thought you two were just friends." Frank took a long drink from his glass, his eyes searching the room as if he was already planning his next conquest.

"Who could stay just friends with such an amazing woman?"

When Frank's attention was elsewhere, Callie pretended to gag, but Trevor kept grinning.

"Take care of that nose, Frank." Trevor began to pull her away, but Frank obviously wasn't done with the conversation. He stepped with them, his once charming smile morphing into a twisted scowl.

"Figures you two would finally end up together. After all, Callie wouldn't be satisfied until she slept with the whole town."

She could feel Trevor's body tense beside her, but before she let history repeat itself, she stepped between the two men and glared at Frank.

"You know what, Frank? You're a sorry son of a bitch. If I see you so much as touch another woman at this wedding, I will find your wife's number and let her know that you're running around pretending to be divorced." Maybe she had a little revenge in her after all.

He sputtered at that, surprised she seemed to know.

"You move away from small towns and you forget everyone

knows everything about you." Callie smiled. The shocked, outraged look on his face was almost as satisfying as throwing a punch. "Have a nice night."

She turned to face Trevor. "Let's dance."

"Revenge without punching somebody's lights out. Well, color me impressed." He allowed her to pull him onto the dance floor.

"You were far more in danger of throwing a punch than me." Trevor's hand rested on her hip, the other took her hand in his.

"I guess some people don't grow out of asshole." His expression slowly changed into a smile. "Man, was he pissed I brought up breaking his nose."

"And you were tempted to break it again, weren't you?"

"I guess it was a little residual FBI agent withdrawal."

"You miss it." Callie leaned her head onto his shoulder. She closed her eyes, breathed in the faint scent of his soap. She didn't want to think about the FBI or Seattle or anything beyond this moment.

"You're wearing perfume."

Callie couldn't fight a smile. He was changing the topic. "You like it?"

"Well, it's not quite as sexy as airplane grease, but it's not half bad."

His thumb brushed the inside of her wrist, his hand on her hip moving to the small of her back. Her pulse began to thump faster, a slow heat building from her core and waving outward.

This is what she'd been avoiding, but in the moment she couldn't remember why. The sensations were warm and nice, the feelings cozy and familiar. What was so wrong with this?

Callie sighed, pressed closer to Trevor. Whatever foolishness she'd felt before was gone. Leaning against Trevor, swaying to the rhythm of a slow song, she realized how much she'd missed him the past few weeks.

All the pushing away and avoiding, and what had she accomplished? Nothing. Because she was beginning to realize there was a bottom line here. Either she could push him away and lose him as a friend and whatever else was between them, or take her chances, temporarily, on what was between them and hope they could remain friends afterward.

Trevor inched his body away from hers, though he didn't loosen his grip. "You're going to have to back off a little bit."

"Why?" She pressed up against him, unable to fight the satisfied smile. She felt reckless tonight. She was tapping into some of that old Bad Girl Baker stuff, wasn't she? Why not take advantage, full advantage.

It couldn't be any worse than staying away.

He hissed out a breath. "Because I'd like to be able to get out of here without walking funny."

"What if I said I could take care of that for you?"

"Jesus, Callie."

"I'm BGB for the night, remember? Might as well have some fun. But only for tonight."

"Just tonight?" His hand traveled the curve of her spine all the way up and back down again, sending sparks of heat down her entire backside. She pulled back so she could look up at him, and she rolled her eyes at the cocky grin on his face.

"Well, maybe not only tonight." Surely they could tear up the sheets a few times before it got too complicated. "But it has to be temporary. I'm not starting something permanent with you."

"Even if I decide to stay?" His breath whispered across her ear; the hand on her back moved upward and toyed with the ends of her hair.

Callie thought about Lawson's words, dampening some of her good mood. "If you decide to stay, you'll eventually leave."

"Callie."

Tomorrow she'd worry about the ramifications. For tonight, she wanted to let herself go, cut the string of this damn yoyo. "Do you want to take me home, Trevor?"

"Hell yes."

"Then let's go. We can argue about this later." She squeezed his hand, began pulling him off the dance floor.

"Later?"

She looked at him, smirked. "After."

He grinned. "After what?"

Callie quirked an eyebrow. "Play dumb and we might not play at all."

"Yes, ma'am." He followed her out of the crowded reception into the lobby of Pilot Point's only hotel. He dropped her hand and slid his arm around her waist. "You sure you want to do this?"

Callie stepped into the cool night and took a moment to study his face illuminated by the parking lights. "Yeah. I do. It would be pretty shitty to spend the rest of my life pushing you away because I can't seem to keep my hands off of you. Might as well find out what it's like, and then I don't have to push you away anymore. As long as you understand it's—"

"Temporary." He frowned. "I get it. But—"

She slapped a hand on his chest, pressed herself against him. "Stop." She pressed her lips to his, a hard, promising kiss. "Arguing."

He cleared his throat. "Uh huh. Let's go."

They both hurried to the car and slid in fast. Trevor started the car, pulled out of the parking lot. Callie was in some kind of alternate universe. She tried to focus on the physical stuff. The way his hands felt on her back, the hard length of him pressed against her, his mouth on hers.

Thinking about all that had a flutter of panic surfacing. "Remember, this is temporary."

"I think I get the fucking picture," he muttered. But when she looked over at him, he flashed a grin. "What if I'm pretty confident I can change your mind?"

Callie rolled her eyes, focused on the strong feelings instead of the panicky ones. "Trust me. No one is *that* good."

"That sounds like a challenge."

"Shut up and drive, huh?" Callie stared at the road ahead, tried to calm the rapid and erratic beating of her heart. It was just sex. No biggie. She'd certainly slept with plenty of guys in her life.

The thought had her frowning. None meant anything near as much as Trevor did, and that was kind of pathetic.

Closing her eyes, Callie shook her head. She was giving herself one night to do something reckless and stupid. She'd worry about all these feelings later.

Chapter Seventeen

If he wanted to freak himself out, and he did not have any interest in doing that, he'd let his brain wrap around the fact that he was about to have sex with Calloway Baker.

Since he didn't want to freak himself out, he focused on the menial things he had to do to get there. Pull up the gravel drive to the cabin. Turn off car. Undo seatbelt.

They were all mechanical, careful movements. Callie didn't speak, and he didn't look at her. He got out of the car and followed her to the porch of the cabin trying desperately not to think about, well, what he'd pretty much been thinking about for two months.

They reached the door, but Callie paused. She stood there, her back to him. The night was dark around them, but he could make out her shape in the dim light of the moon. Around them insects buzzed their nightly tune, but over the sound of nature he could hear her carefully inhaled breath.

The darkness, the moment, it all worked together to have thoughts drifting away into action. Trevor swept the hair off her neck, placed his lips on the soft skin. She let out a gust of breath, and he planted another kiss farther to the side, then one just under her earlobe.

She turned to face him, her hand on his chest. He couldn't make out her expression, just the shadowy outline of her face. "So we're clear—"

"If you say temporary one more Goddamned time, I'll turn around and go."

She cocked her head to the side. "Really?"

"Okay, maybe not turn around and go, but I am definitely going to shut you up."

She moved closer, her hand on his chest sliding up to his shoulder. "Why don't you do that then?"

His lips curved upward as they bent to touch hers. In her heels, she almost reached his height, so it didn't take long. He took it slow at first, wanting the moment, the night to last. He had a feeling the minute it was over Callie would be babbling about temporary again.

One hand brushed through the silky strands of her hair, letting the other roam the small of her lower back.

Temporary? He didn't think so. Maybe he hadn't made any firm decisions on staying, but that didn't mean this had to be a one-time deal.

And it was definitely going on his happy list.

Her kiss became more insistent, her tongue more demanding. She leaned against him enough so he had to push her against the door for balance. For a few minutes, the urgent need took over and he forgot about slow. She pulled off his suit jacket; he pressed her hard against the door.

His mouth roamed her neck, his hands moved from her back, up her ribcage, and then rested over small, round breasts. She arched against them, rubbing center to center until he had to bite back a groan.

He tugged on the low neckline of her dress revealing one rounded peak and the fact she hadn't been wearing a bra all night about did him in. His mouth traveled down, tasted the warm flesh of her breast. She tangled her fingers into his hair, held him there. Hands now free, he cupped her ass and pulled her closer.

She wrapped one leg around him, moved her hips up and

down. He had a fleeting thought of pulling up her skirt, dropping his pants, and going at it right there, but it didn't feel right. Things were moving too fast.

"Stop."

"Are you fucking kidding me?"

He had to laugh at the outrage in her voice. "I meant, momentarily. Not stop altogether."

She let out a breath that fluttered her bangs. "Good, because I was going to have to kill you otherwise."

"Give me your keys."

"Why?"

"Because we're going to go inside."

She pressed up against him and a groan escaped his mouth. Her lips grazed his chin. "Why?"

"Because we're going to do this right the first time. In a bed. We can do it up against your front door some other time. Now, keys."

He held out his hand and tried not to chuckle at her pout, but she fished the keys out of her purse and handed them over.

Callie frowned at Trevor while he punched the key into the front door and opened it. She would have been just as happy getting it over with right then and there. At least temporary would seem a lot more plausible.

Then he turned to her, a light from inside spilling out and illuminating his face. He smiled, and she kind of forgot all about temporary. He took her by the shoulders, leading her backward inside and through the kitchen and down the short hallway to her room. He backed her against the door, his eyes never leaving hers.

"Open the door, Callie."

It was continually surprising how much Trevor bossing her around was a turn on. She groped for the doorknob behind her and twisted. When the door moved open, Trevor continued to push her inside until they were in the center of her room.

Then his hands moved to her face, his blue eyes staring straight into hers for a few humming moments before he kissed her. Soft, slow, seductive. All demands disappeared as his tongue lazily mingled with hers.

The kiss lingered, but his hands moved down her neck, to her back, where he slowly unzipped her dress, his thumb brushing the bare skin below as he went down. She shivered at the light touch.

Things had slowed, some of the demands melting into sensations Callie didn't know what to do with or how to fight. A mix of jittery nerves under the warm pull of everything he was doing to her. A part of her brain was urging her to do something, to move forward, to *hurry*, but the thoughts never became action. She was drugged into Trevor's agonizingly slow, sweet pace.

Trevor inched the dress off her until it fell at her feet. She wasn't the most well-endowed woman in the world and she hadn't been able to find a bra that didn't show under her dress, so she'd gone without. Now she stood in front of Trevor in nothing but panties and she would have felt self-conscious if he didn't look like he was about to start panting in appreciation.

Though her hands shook, she kept her eyes level with his. Part of her might be freaking out right now, but that didn't mean she'd give up all control. She stepped out of the dress and toward Trevor.

Slowly, keeping her eyes on his, she unbuttoned his shirt. He undid the buttons on his wrists and then she pulled the shirt off his arms in a long, fluid movement, and then she let her hands travel down the hard line of muscle from shoulder to wrist, and then over to his abs and up his chest.

He hissed in a breath and Callie's mouth curved into a smile as his hands secured on to her hips and pulled her to him.

Still in her heels, it only took him bending his head for his mouth to fasten onto her breast. She threaded her fingers through his hair, holding him there as the liquid warm pull of excitement waved to her core.

She moaned as he switched breasts, his hand moving up to massage the one he'd abandoned. Everything else disappeared. Where they were. All those jumpy nerves. Why this was a bad idea or temporary or anything. All she could focus on was the here and now, the sensations coursing through her body.

Callie reached for his belt, quickly undid it and the button and zipper. She took his pants and boxers and pushed them all the way down to his ankles, slowly brushing against him as she stood back up.

"For the love of God, please tell me you have condoms somewhere in this place."

She arched a brow, pushed him toward the bed. He toed off his shoes and stepped out of his clothes. "You didn't come prepared?"

"No, I didn't come prepared. Are you—"

She clucked her tongue and shook her head, then gave him a little push onto the bed. She wiggled out of her panties and stepped out of her shoes. The way he watched her as she grabbed a condom from the nightstand had her whole body humming with electric need. She moved over to him, slid onto his lap, and ignored the way her hand wanted to shake as she rolled the condom on.

Her heart stuttered as she moved close enough to guide him inside of her. This was it. Point of no return.

191

Slowly, she slid all the way down, him filling her completely. When she finally stopped, Trevor's hands dug into her hips, holding her still, his head pressed against her shoulder as he took an audible deep breath.

It was everything and nothing she had expected. So much more than she could have ever imagined. Everything she'd been afraid of for so long, but in the moment the fear was gone. A culmination of all the years they'd skirted around this very moment.

"You're so soft, Callie," he murmured into her skin. "Not so tough."

Callie squeezed her eyes shut, refusing to let the tears that threatened win. She leaned her cheek against his forehead and let the moment sit. She wanted to remember this. No matter what happened after. This was the perfect moment.

He kissed her shoulder and moved tantalizingly down to her nipple, taking it into his mouth, teasing it with his tongue. Callie began to move, riding him slowly, taking an agonizingly long time as her climax built. Trevor's fingers on her hips urged her on as he began to meet each thrust.

As she got closer, she quickened the pace, her hands moving from his shoulders to wrap around his neck. He moved from one breast to the valley between. He kissed the soft skin there and then moved to her other breast, taking the other nipple into his mouth, using his teeth lightly.

She called out as the action had the climax rushing over her quick and hard. He held on to her almost as tightly as she held on to him, breathing in the same, hard rhythm.

"Roll over, Callie." His turn to be in charge. She was more than okay with that.

On her back, he leveraged his body over hers. His hand roamed her calf, her thigh, teased and brushed over her sweat-slicked skin. His mouth moved like his hands without pattern so she never knew what to expect next. Before the aftershocks of her first climax were over, he entered her, had a second building all over again.

This time as they moved together, his eyes held hers and she couldn't look away. Couldn't ignore all that *feeling* inside of her. The second wave washed over her, as powerful as the first.

"Callie." He said her name like a sigh, and then his own release took over and he pushed deep inside and held her close. Callie held on, afraid to lose the moment, afraid of what she might feel when it was over.

Trevor kissed her shoulder, her neck, then her lips. When he smiled down at her she managed to smile back.

"Well, hell. Why'd we wait so long to do that?"

She chuckled, the humor lightening up all the dark pooling emotions inside of her. "Who knows?" She framed his face and kissed him before he rolled onto his back, pulling her into his side.

Not that he had a choice; on her full-sized bed if he didn't hold on to her she was liable to fall off.

"You need a bigger bed."

"I don't generally share."

He nuzzled into her hair. "Sharing is good for you."

A little squirt of panic sliced through the warm afterglow. "Trevor, I meant it when I said this was—"

He clamped a hand over her mouth. "I don't want to talk about that right now."

"Trevor," she protested into his hand.

He got off the bed, disappeared into the bathroom for a second. When he returned, he squeezed right back onto the bed.

"We should—"

He leveraged himself over her, shook his head. His blue eyes were serious even if his tone was light. "We can talk about it all you want tomorrow. For tonight, shut up."

"Fine." No use arguing with him now. Later, but not now. "That's really not the most romantic way to talk to a woman you've just had sex with."

"Well, trying to tell the guy you just made love to this is all a one-time thing isn't exactly whispering sweet nothings, is it?"

"But—"

"Keep talking and I'll leave and then we won't get to have sex against the front door."

It was ridiculous, and yet she found herself laughing. His laughter mixed with hers and there was a wholeness, a rightness to this moment. It reminded of her of how she'd felt with her family.

But this one couldn't last, and she couldn't forget that.

Chapter Eighteen

Trevor woke up to a sharp pain underneath his shoulder blade. Still hazy with sleep, he couldn't muster the energy to open his eyes; instead, he merely grimaced and stretched out his arm hoping to alleviate the pain.

Then he noticed the faint smell of coconut from the pillow his head was buried in. He would have smiled, except he realized he was in Callie's too small bed all by himself.

He sat up and tried to rub the sore spot on his back. If this happened again, and Trevor was determined it would, they were going to have to find some better sleeping arrangements.

Trevor slid out of the bed, rubbed bleary eyes and headed for the door to find Callie, but he was sidetracked by a mirror lined with pictures in the corner of the room. Considering the rest of her room was so sparse, the collection of photographs seemed odd and out of place.

Trevor stepped closer, studied the conglomeration of photos, colors faded with age. There was a picture of a couple he was pretty sure were Callie's parents holding a baby, which he imagined was Callie. Then there were a few Polaroids of her grandparents both at their house and at AIF. There was another Polaroid of Callie, Em, and Lawson when they were kids, posing outside of the AIF office building with their arms around one another's waists, grinning hugely. Trevor had to smile at that one.

The one that had him stopping short was a picture of him and Callie from high school graduation. His mom had taken a bunch of pictures at graduation, but none had Callie in them. Trevor tried to think to the moments after graduation and who would have taken this picture.

Fred Baker wasn't the camera-carrying sort, and Callie's grandma had been gone. He supposed Em must have put it upon herself to play photographer even though she would have only been fourteen.

Trevor studied the picture. Two eighteen-year-olds ready to start their lives in hideously ugly bright red and white graduation gowns. Or at least, he had been ready to start his life. Ready to escape, to leave behind the pressure of Pilot's Point and his parents. His smile reflected that, an excited eagerness.

Callie was smiling too, but it was different. Her screw-the-world smile, one hand on a cocked hip and the other around his shoulders. She'd still been fighting her way out of a life that had been too hard on her.

Ironic that nearing thirty she was the one settled into the life she'd always wanted—down to having all three Baker grandchildren at the helm of AIF, and his plan to get out had been screwed six ways to Sunday. Hell, he didn't have a plan anymore.

Which kind of explained why he'd given into years of temptation last night. Without a plan, how was he supposed to be sensible and navigate away from Callie and everything she offered? Avoiding her the past few weeks when she'd been within reach had been akin to torture. And avoiding her had put him no closer to knowing what to do.

He pulled on his discarded pants and shirt from the night before on the off chance Em had returned. He really hoped not. As much as he was all for ignoring their issues last night, they definitely needed to discuss them this morning.

When he stepped out into the small interior of the cabin, there was no evidence of Em. Callie was sitting on the window bench, her knees pulled up to her chin and her eyes glued to the window. She was in baggy sweats, her hair was a mess, and though she'd obviously washed her face, there were still traces of the makeup she'd worn last night.

She wasn't exactly looking beautiful, and yet his heart squeezed as he looked at her.

She turned to look at him, rested her cheek on her knees, and offered a really weak smile. "Hey."

"Hey."

"There's coffee." She gestured toward the kitchen.

As much as a cup of coffee might be nice, he crossed over to her instead. He sat next to her on the bench, then picked up her legs and put them over his lap.

The morning outside the window was a misty gray and fog rolled around the low-lying areas of trees surrounding them.

"This is weird."

He smiled, because it didn't feel all that weird to him. "Weird how?"

"Well, for starters I know what you look like naked now."

Trevor slid his hand up the inside of her sweats along her calf up to her knee. "I can refresh your memory if the details are a little fuzzy already."

She snorted, kicked his hand off her leg, but she was smiling and it wasn't that weak smile she'd managed when he'd walked into the room.

"We need to talk about this. Set some ground rules."

"Ooh, ground rules. You really know how to get a guy hot."

Her smile upended into a frown. "You said we could talk about this all I wanted this morning."

"Yeah, yeah, yeah." Trevor leaned against the cool glass of the window. "Talk away."

"Temporary." She said it as if it explained everything, as if it was the one word that would solve all their deep-seated issues.

"I'm getting to be less and less a fan of that word."

"It's important." Adamant didn't begin to describe the way she said it. Desperate was closer. A panicked holding on to something even if that something was fading away.

"I don't think it's as important as you seem to think it is."

"We've been over this a million different ways, and yet we haven't gotten anywhere. Maybe that's because we were so busy trying to keep our hands off of each other. Well, that's done. Now it's time to come to a conclusion. That conclusion has to be you going back to Seattle. The choice that will make *you* happy."

"I understand where you're coming from, but you're hitting this same note over and over again and I've moved on. Things are different. Staying here wouldn't be... It's not as bad as it used to be."

She shook her head and Trevor wanted to smack his own head against the glass until he could figure out a way to explain it so she'd understand.

"Guilt won't keep you here forever. Look at Lawson."

She frustrated him, challenged him, but now she was downright confusing him. "What the hell does this have to do with Lawson?"

"He married Sue because he felt guilty about getting her pregnant. Then he went to L.A. with Sue because he felt guilty about messing up her plans. That worked for a while. Long enough for them to have another kid and make each other completely miserable and get a nasty divorce, but it didn't change the fact Lawson belonged here. No amount of guilt could keep him there."

"First of all, that's completely different."

"No, it's not."

"Being sixteen and pregnant is a lot different kind of guilt than being my sister's *only* family. We're all different people, at different stages in our lives, with different circumstances and motivations."

"But guilt is at the center."

It had been a long time since they'd argued—really argued over an important point. He'd forgotten how impossible she could be when she had an idea stuck in her head. It would take an act of God to get through to her. He'd start praying for one tonight.

"Let's pretend for a second that you stay and you decide this is what you want. You promise to stay forever, but then ten years down the line Shelby's off in some big city being whatever she wants to be with a family of her own. And you're stuck here, missing the FBI so bad it hurts." She fisted her hand at her heart, and she looked at him so earnestly he could tell she could imagine it, picture it.

Strange he couldn't. "Where are you in this scenario?"

"It doesn't matter."

"It matters."

"Bottom line is you'd want to leave. Promises you made ten years ago wouldn't seem so important. I know you, Trevor. You'd stick to a promise if it killed you, but who would want to be around you if it was killing you?"

Frustration bubbled up enough he was sorry her legs were trapping him on the bench, because he wanted to pace, move.

"Promises can't be kept."

Irritation started to poke through understanding. "Come

on."

"Life gets in the way. Even if you're living that life, desperately trying to keep that promise, something happens." She took his hand and squeezed, and he saw the desperation in the gesture, in her expression. "You can't plan the future. You should know that. Anything can happen to break that promise. Maybe you wouldn't *want* to break the promise, but circumstances make it so. I don't want there to be any promises, anything like that. Because I've lost too much to be able to forgive you if you leave."

Trevor tried to wrap his mind around her logic. She seemed so certain, and he wished he could share in that certainty, but he couldn't make it add up in his head.

She was shoveling on, determined and focused on temporary. "If we agree this ends in September, if there's a plan set in motion, there's no threat hanging over our heads."

"Or I could stay. Or..." He pulled his wallet out of the pocket of his pants and unfolded Shelby's list. "Shelby gave me this the day she helped you out with Dana and you said something to her to make her feel guilty, I guess."

Callie took the list, smoothed it out and read over the cities and mileages.

"I don't get it."

"I could transfer to a field office closer. I guess she'd feel better if I was somewhere within driving distance, and I get that."

Callie's whole face brightened as she looked at the piece of paper. "It's brilliant."

"You're joking, right?"

"You'd still be in the FBI and Shelby would feel better. No guilt. It's not perfect, but I have to admit Shelby's got something here. It's a great compromise. You should do it." She looked up and smiled.

It caused a stabbing pain in his heart to think she could be so happy with him far away, even if it was closer than Seattle. "What if I want to be here?"

Her smile died. "Why are you holding on to that?"

"Because I'm not convinced it's a terrible idea anymore." Why was she so convinced it was?

"There will be women in every one of these towns willing to sleep with you."

"Don't do that. You know as well as I do that sex with you isn't like sex with anyone else."

She blinked down at the paper, then carefully folded it back up.

He took the outstretched paper, tried to keep the snap out of his voice and failed. "You know what? It's my decision. You're not interested in past September, so your opinion doesn't matter."

"Right."

He was a little rewarded by the frown on her face. Arguing with her wasn't going to get him anywhere. He had to prove to her she was wrong, and it would take a lot of time and a lot of effort and some covert manipulations, but he'd get her there.

He maneuvered one of her legs behind him and then crawled over, gently nudging her down into a prone position. He watched her mouth try to fight against the upward curve, but eventually she gave in to the smile.

"What are you doing?"

"Ending this conversation on a high note." He let his lips cover hers, his body cover hers.

The front door swung open. "From Trevor's car in the drive and his coat on the porch, I imagine I know what happened here last night, but I'm keeping my eyes shut until you can assure me all private parts are covered."

Callie worked her way into a sitting position. "Nah, we're having crazed sex in the middle of the living room as we speak."

"Oh, well then." Em grinned, dropped her hands off her eyes. She tossed Trevor his suit coat. "If this is going to be a regular thing, we're going to have to set some ground rules."

"What is it with you women and ground rules?" Trevor flung his suit jacket over his shoulder. "I have to get home. Not sure how long my 'won't be home tonight' text is going to hold Shelby over." He leaned down and kissed Callie. He could have forgotten all about Em seconds later.

"Ugh. Rule number one. No PDA."

Trevor chuckled but before he could escape, Callie pinched his ass. Hard. "Hey!"

"Sorry, couldn't help it. I don't have a lot of opportunities to make Em gag."

Because she was smiling, because despite all they'd talked about she looked happy, Trevor left feeling happy too. Callie had never been easy, and this wouldn't be any different.

But he wasn't walking away come September. And neither was she.

"So?"

Callie slid off the window seat and moved into the kitchen, avoiding Em's dopey grin. "So, what?"

Em threw her arms around Callie's shoulders, gave a squeeze. "So, you finally did it. Yay!"

Yay? Well, actually, it was quite a yay. A really yummy yay. "You didn't exactly make it home yourself."

Em grinned and snatched the mug of coffee from Callie's

hands. "Nope, had a little yay of my own. He might not look it, but Pete is pretty smooth."

Callie gave a baffled laugh. "Congratulations."

"Please tell me Trevor is everything he looks like he'd be."

Callie stared at Em. Though they both knew each other's relationship histories, they'd never really shared stories. Not like this. Callie had been too embarrassed of most of her stories and jealous of Em's serial monogamous relationships.

But here they were, talking about sex with men who mattered. Maybe her relationship was temporary, but it still mattered. Callie poured herself a cup of coffee, smiled. "Yeah, he's everything he looks like he'd be."

Em sighed dreamily. "Lucky us."

Callie looked down at the black liquid in her mug. "Yeah. Lucky us." Well, she would be lucky for a month or two more anyway. Her smile faded at the thought.

"Uh oh."

"What?"

"Second thoughts already?"

"I'm not having second thoughts." Callie scowled over at Em who was stretched out on the window seat, gracefully sipping her coffee in the pastel blue bridesmaid's dress she'd worn last night.

How Em could make the morning after look so put together was downright unfair. "Last night was great. Really, really great." But her own buzzword haunted her. *Temporary.*

"Then do me a favor, Cal?"

"What?"

Em sat up, fixed Callie with a stern stare. "Enjoy the hell out of it."

Callie laughed, plopped next to Em. "I'll see what I can do."

Chapter Nineteen

"Hey."

Callie bobbled on the stepladder but managed to catch herself. She shoved bangs out of her face and tried not to look like such a fucking spaz.

"Hey."

Trevor grinned, causing her to scowl. She had to act normal. Nothing had changed between them. They were still friends. Friends that, for the next two months, could have sex whenever they had an inclination.

Man, did she have an inclination. Especially now that she knew every inch of what was under the baggy gym shorts and grimy T-shirt.

Swallowing, Callie moved unsteadily down the ladder and pushed the bangs out of her face again. She'd only had them for two days and she already regretted letting Em talk her into cutting them.

Callie stepped off the ladder, but she kept it between her and Trevor, though not sure why. Maybe because everything in her body screamed at her to cross the floor to him. Luckily, her brain was functioning. For now.

"What's up?" She tried to look normal, but she no longer had any idea what that looked like, so she fiddled with the irritating hair hanging over her eyes instead.

"I finished up for the day, thought I'd stop by make sure you didn't have anything you needed me to do."

Oh, she could think of something he could do. "No, I'm

good out here."

"Stearman completely finished?" He nodded toward the plane visible through the door to the hangar.

"Yeah, all polished up and ready for the fly-in." Ready to sell. But she didn't say that out loud, because she didn't want to think about it.

"Okay, can we cut the bullshit now?"

"Huh?"

"Go out with me."

"Trev-"

"Dinner, a movie, go to the park and make out like we should have done in high school."

"I can't."

"Why not?"

Why not? Because spending extra time with him made her nervous. Because every time she was around him she had to repeat to herself over and over again that the only safe way to deal with Trevor was to be sure he was heading away from Pilot's Point in September.

An irrational part of her had thought maybe finally having sex would make that easier. Thinking about the "will we won't we" all the time had made it this all-encompassing thing. Now she realized it had been easier when she'd been so focused on avoiding getting physically wrapped up with Trevor. Crossing that line opened up her mind to think about far more dangerous things.

In weak moments, really, *really* weak moments she thought about what it might be like for him to stay, and it all but crushed her heart. Because no matter how many short-term scenarios were perfectly cozy and enticing, inevitably her imagination cracked it in two with the long-term reality.

She'd never be enough to keep him. Callie scowled at that

thought. No, that wasn't right. Pilot's Point would never be enough to keep him. This wasn't about her.

"How long am I supposed to wait while you come up with some fake excuse?"

"I wasn't coming up with a fake excuse. I was just..." Thinking. Pining. "Fine. But just dinner. We'd never agree on a movie in a million years."

"What about the making out at the park?"

Callie rolled her eyes, feeling exactly like a teenager. Or what she imagined a normal teenager would feel like. She never had been normal. "Negotiable."

"I'm fairly confident in my negotiating skills."

"Go home. Wash up. I'll meet you at your house at seven, okay?"

"Yes, as long as you promise to wear appropriate date attire."

"This is not a date."

"Oh yes, it is."

Hands on her hips, she gave him a disapproving scowl. "Trevor."

He mocked her stance and tone. "Callie."

"I really don't know what I could possibly see in you."

He let his hands fall off his hips and grinned. "Do you want me to make you a list?" And then he was stepping toward her and the small stepladder between them wasn't enough of a barrier.

"You go ahead and make your list. On your way home."

He stepped around the ladder and there was a part of her that wanted to retreat, that was afraid if he touched her enough times the voice of reason in her head would completely disappear.

His hands moved around her waist, gently pulling her to him. "It's not particularly easy working all day out there knowing you're banging away on your airplanes in here."

He didn't need to touch her, sometimes his words could kill that voice of reason too. Instead, the voice of reason morphed into a very naughty voice. *Why should I be banging on airplanes when you could be banging on me instead?*

Yikes. "We shouldn't... We should have a line here, you know? Not mix work with other stuff."

His head bent toward hers, but he slid his lips against her cheek rather than her mouth. "Why? You afraid I'll talk you into having sex in an airplane?"

She couldn't help laughing because the image was absurd. "Yup, that's exactly it."

He pulled his head back, his hands moving from her waist to her face. She was such a sucker when he did that, looking at her with those intense blue eyes. And then his mouth met hers, a lazy, seductive kiss full of promise.

He pulled away so quickly her head spun. "I'll see you soon." He strutted to the door with a stupid cocky grin on his face.

She waved him off only breathing a sigh of relief once he'd left the shop and she could take a full breath again.

There was no reason to rush home and get ready. It wasn't a date, just a get together. Hanging out. She didn't need to put on makeup or wear anything besides her normal jeans and T-shirt.

Half an hour later, she found herself in a short black skirt and a borrowed top from Em. Since Em was a little bit rounder, the shirt was a little baggy, but that was okay. Callie wasn't trying to look super sexy.

Just casually sexy.

Nicole Helm

Callie gathered her purse and keys while Em sat on the couch curled up in the corner with a book.

"Where are you two going on your date?" Em placed the book in her lap, smiled dreamily.

Em's obvious romanticism of the situation had Callie bristling. "It's not a date."

Em's nose wrinkled. "Then what is it?"

"I don't know. It's just..."

"You're sleeping together, and you're going to go out to dinner together. I'd call that a date."

"Look, don't get your romantic hopes and dreams pinned on this, okay? Trevor and I are just..."

"You keep saying just. Just what?"

That was the problem. Callie didn't know. The more she tried to come up with the right terminology for what they were, the more she regretted letting this whole thing happen.

"It's not permanent. Trevor and I agreed whatever happens between us beyond friendship is just a..." There was that just word again. "A temporary thing."

Em rolled her eyes before sticking her nose back in the book. "I know whose idea that was."

"Don't start."

"I wouldn't dream of it." Em discarded the book again and slid off the couch, all graceful hurt. "My talk about letting down your guard and letting people in obviously fell on deaf ears when it came to Trevor. Well, I give up." She sauntered off to her room in an unusual huff.

Which only served to make Callie more unsure and antsy. She should call and cancel. She should tell Trevor this whole thing was a mistake and they never should have slept together and maybe they would be better off meaning nothing to each other at all.

Middle ground was slipping through her fingers. It seemed no matter what happened between them, it was too little or too much. Too little would be the smart thing, the right thing.

Callie stood at the door and stared at it. In the end, she couldn't do the right thing.

Meaning nothing to each other was the worst-case scenario, and she wasn't ready to go down that road. Surely there was a middle ground road hiding around somewhere. She just had to find it before things got too sticky.

Callie drove away from AIF and into the heart of Pilot's Point. She pulled up to the Steele house the same time another car did, and when Dan got out of the driver's side, Callie felt even more like a foolish teen. On a sigh, she stepped out of the car and pulled at the hem of her skirt a little.

"Well, hey, Dan."

Dan smiled in cheerful greeting. "Hey, Callie. What are you doing here?"

Callie had to fight to keep a pleasant smile on her face. "Oh, Trevor and I are going to, um, hang out a bit."

He looked down at her skirt, looked away quickly, and then blushed. "Oh. Cool."

Callie rolled her eyes. If she couldn't fool Dan, there wasn't much hope in fooling anybody.

"I want to thank you for letting me help out at AIF. It's been really awesome, and we never would have done it if you hadn't tricked us into it. But it's practically been the best part of my summer."

Callie knew what that meant. Shelby had been the best part of his summer. Callie fought off the grimace and kept her lips curved upward. Foolish, hopeful teen love was enough to make anyone a little sick to their stomach.

"I'm glad. You're welcome to volunteer any time. We'll

always need help. Breaks. Next summer. Whatever."

"Thanks!" His exuberance and excitement were infectious and Callie didn't have to fake her smile anymore as they stepped up onto the porch. "Man, I can't believe we'll be leaving in three and a half weeks. Everything has gone by so fast."

Three and a half weeks. Mid-August. Shelby would be gone and Trevor would be free to focus on his choices. Seattle. A Midwest field office. Pilot's Point.

Then in September he'd make his choice. He'd either ruin everything by staying, or he'd rip her heart out by leaving. Maybe sometimes, against her will, thoughts popped into her head like Trevor staying and things going on as they were. Winter when things at AIF were slower and they'd be able to curl up by the fireplace and...

She sighed and pressed a finger to the doorbell. Her heart would be ripped out either way. Picturing things that would only make it harder was a bad move. It was absolutely best to know when so she could prepare for the heart ripping instead of getting lost in some fantasy and then having the rug pulled out from under her.

Dan hit the nail on the head. Everything had gone by so fast. So fast Callie didn't know which way was up anymore.

Everything seemed to right when Trevor answered the door and half of the worries in her head got drowned out by the eagerness in his smile and the fact that, for right now, he wanted to be with her every bit as much as she wanted to be with him.

Didn't she used to be good at ignoring things? At putting up walls? Why not put up a wall around the end result and enjoy the here and now? She'd done that once, and maybe it hadn't always been the best way of dealing with life, but it seemed like a hell of a good idea tonight.

"Isn't this special, Shelby? Both our dates are here."

Shelby appeared next to Trevor, and she didn't gag or insult Callie. Instead, she seemed pleased Trevor had called Callie his date.

Must be some weird trick of lighting.

"We'll get out of your way," Shelby said in a sing-songy voice as she pushed past Trevor. "Don't wait up. We won't be home until late."

"Midnight."

"One-thirty."

"You're not home by one I get one of the guys at county to send a patrol car after you."

"Whatever." She flounced away on Dan's arm, but Dan looked back at Trevor with a look of panic.

"One," he mouthed.

Callie bit back a chuckle until the teens were in the car. "That's sweet."

"What?"

"That little protective moment you just had, and the fact Dan is still such a wimp that he's scared of you. You realize once they go off to college you won't be able to dictate what time she gets home?"

Trevor grimaced. "You're mean."

"Yes, I am. Remember that."

"If I was afraid of a little meanness I would have kicked you to the curb a long time ago, Calloway."

"Do not use my full name." She poked him in the ribs, but he grabbed her hand and held it so any irritation immediately petered out as his warm hand closed over hers.

"Any ideas on where you want to go to dinner?" He pulled her inside the entryway. "We could drive out farther if nothing in Pilot's Point sounds good. Anything in Heartland or Gwenview?"

"We don't need to go to Heartland or Gwenview. Hunan Wok here is good." She laughed when, as expected, his whole face twisted with disgust.

Trevor closed the door and stood in front of it with his arms folded across his chest. "Chinese is not food. It's disgusting slimy noodles and vegetables."

"You asked where I wanted to go."

"I get to veto."

"That hardly seems fair."

"Let's skip dinner." She was in his arms before she had a chance to react. "We'll order in."

Callie smiled against his lips. "Hunan Wok delivers."

"That's it. I'm taking you upstairs." Despite her shocked screech, he swept his arms under her legs and carried her toward the stairs.

"You're not seriously carrying me right now."

"I seriously am. It's a romantic gesture. Feel free to swoon."

Callie held on to his neck, fought the flutters in her chest. "I'm not much of a swooner." She sighed and rested her head on his shoulder as he huffed up the stairs. "But maybe this once."

Chapter Twenty

Trevor sat on the couch staring at his Happy List. He'd added enough items to Pilot's Point that it was now tied with Seattle. The additions weren't even all about Callie, which was kind of surprising. He'd resorted to adding little things. Shelby's cookies, Friday lunches at AIF, Evan's incessant questions on how many guys he'd shot.

He just needed one more happy item to tip things the way he wanted.

Which was idiotic when he really thought about it. If he wanted to stay, why didn't he just stay? What did this damn list matter in the grand scheme of things?

It would matter to Callie. She'd been bringing up September more and more each day. Over the past week he was pretty sure he'd heard the word September about a hundred times.

Almost as many times as he'd heard Callie complain about Em. He didn't know how the two were related, but there was a correlation.

Em and Callie were in some kind of fight that had been escalating with every day, and as much as Callie tried to pretend she was unaffected by it, she had been sullen and broody.

Trevor stared at the list. He had to stay. Even if the list didn't reflect it, a life without Callie, a life without AIF, a life different than the one he'd been leading for the past few weeks made Seattle or the FBI anywhere pale in comparison.

He was needed in Pilot's Point. Callie needed someone to calm her down when she flew off the handle. Even with Lawson and the boys back, AIF needed an occasional hand. Shelby needed him to be in a place she could call home.

He always thought being needed felt like being choked, but it didn't. Not when the people who needed him just wanted him to be Trevor. Not better or smarter or more successful. Exactly as he already was.

As much as it made him feel guilty, with his parents gone, Pilot's Point didn't demand any more of him than that.

The doorbell rang and Trevor folded up the list and put it in his pocket. He'd find that one last thing for the list. Maybe a few more for good measure, and then he'd tell Callie he was staying for good and he'd find a way to convince her he wasn't going to leave.

When Trevor opened the door, Callie looked more sullen and broody than she had all week. That was a scary thing.

Trevor tried out a dazzling smile. "Hi, gorgeous."

She rolled her eyes and pushed past him. "Make me vomit, why don't you?"

So much for compliments. He should have known better. "I see you're just as cheery as you've been all week."

She shot him a killing look over her shoulder. "I'm fine."

"Yeah, fantastic." Trevor closed the door and followed her inside. "You want to go catch the movie or you want to stay here and tell me what crawled up your ass? It is your turn to choose, remember?"

Callie turned to face him, arms across her chest, lips in a firm, angry line. He hadn't seen her like this in a while. In fact, it was a look he associated more with old Callie.

She opened her mouth, shut it, and frowned. "I don't know who she thinks she is," Callie muttered, sinking into the couch.

Ah, so they were going to talk about Em. Trevor hoped Callie was going to vent about the real issue so she would get it out of her system and finally talk to Em about whatever it was they were arguing over.

"Telling me what I think or feel. Pretty sure I'm the only resident of my brain." Callie hopped up and stalked the length of floor in front of the couch, back and forth.

In between her pacing, Trevor moved onto the couch and made himself comfortable. He had a feeling this was going to take a while.

"Like she has any room to talk about this stuff." Callie kicked at the floor. She paced, she stopped, she paced again. "She's still pining after Luke and it's been seven fucking years. She is not the world's expert on relationships." Her voice got louder with each word like she was hoping Em could hear them all the way back at the cabin.

"I really don't think this is about Luke." Not that he had any earthly clue what it was about, but he liked the word relationship peppered in there. Progress.

Callie crossed arms over her chest, blew a breath out that fluttered her bangs. "She says I'm reverting."

"Reverting?"

"Yeah, walls up and all that other bullshit." She threw her hands up into the air and then pointed a finger at him. "I am not reverting."

He held up his hands. "On any other occasion I might be inclined to agree with you, but this, uh, outburst is a little old school Callie."

She scowled at him. "You want to be on my fight list too?"

He reached out and took her hand, pulled her closer to the couch. "No. I want you to be happy."

She sighed and let herself be led until she folded next to

him. He moved his arms around her and she didn't fight him. He tried not to grin. Em was wrong. Callie wasn't reverting. She was giving in. Inch by little inch. A reverting Callie never would have leaned into him, never would have accepted comfort. Hell, she wouldn't have told him what she and Em were fighting about.

Things were going exactly right. Callie was softening, leaning on him. He was winning, just by being there. Pretty soon, he'd tell her he was staying and she wouldn't freak out.

He just had to find a way to help her overcome those last little pockets of fear.

"You want to go back and work things out with Em?"

She pushed him away. "I do not have anything to work out with her." Callie shot to her feet. "Let's go. You were going to buy me popcorn at the movie, remember?"

Trevor pushed himself off the couch, Callie already at the door. So much for getting lucky tonight.

By the end of the movie and a walk around town, Callie had calmed down and eased up a little. She wasn't totally present, but she wasn't brooding every second either. Trevor would have to give himself a pat on the back.

They pulled into the Steele driveway a few hours later and Callie looked almost peaceful.

"The lights are off. Shelby must not be home yet." Trevor glanced at the clock on the dash. "And an hour before curfew. You know what that means?"

Callie rolled her eyes, but her lips curved upward. "Well, considering you have a very one-track mind these days, I have a pretty good idea of what you're getting at." Though her tone was disdainful, she stepped out of the car.

Trevor hurried to get out himself. When he met up with her on the walk, he slipped an arm around her shoulders. "You're coming in?"

"Certainly don't want to go home," she muttered.

Trevor stifled a sigh. "You two really need to make up. Sulky Callie is not my favorite version of you." Trevor shoved his key into the lock, but when Callie didn't say anything he turned back before opening the door.

She had stopped on the porch and was pouting up at him. Though he knew it would make her mad, he couldn't fight a smile. He brushed his thumb across her protruding bottom lip. "Although the pout is pretty cute."

Her lips flattened into a scowl. "Maybe I do want to go home."

He slid his arms around her waist, pulled her to him. "Don't do that." His lips brushed hers, once and then a few more times until the scowl softened and she relaxed in his arms.

It should have been getting old, all the feelings rushing inside of him. But nothing had dulled since the first time. Everything stayed at that same, scorching intensity. Maybe it had only been a few weeks, but he couldn't imagine this ever getting old.

"What if Shelby comes home?" Callie's words fluttered against his neck as her lips trailed across the line of his jaw.

"We'll be upstairs in my room with the door locked. And we'll be very, very quiet. If you think you can manage it." He groped behind him to open the door, his other hand running over the curve of her ass.

As the door opened, he was distracted by the fact that despite the darkness, the TV was on. He flipped the lights on and two figures popped up into a sitting position on the couch.

It only took a second and a glimpse of rumpled clothes to realize what had been happening.

"What the hell is going on here?" Trevor demanded, getting a déjà vu flash of his dad yelling the exact same thing when Trevor had been in a very similar situation. The reminder of his dad didn't ease any of the anger coursing through his veins, making his hands clench into fists as he detangled himself from Callie.

"You said you wouldn't be home for another hour," Shelby squeaked, trying to fix her shirt without calling attention to it. Dan's face had paled considerably, but he wasn't piping up with any kind of explanation.

"That doesn't answer my question." Trevor realized he'd seriously neglected his basic guardian duties by thinking Dan was harmless. No teenage boy was harmless. Not with his sister who, knowing Mom, probably didn't even know what a condom was let alone that she should use one.

God knows he'd only known because Dad had thrown a box of condoms on his bed and said, "Use these."

Shelby's guilty surprise morphed into irritation quickly. "It's none of your business what we were doing."

"Are you out of your fucking—"

"Trev, come on." Callie tugged on his hand. "Leave them alone."

"Like hell." Trevor jerked his arm away, but Callie clamped back on a lot stronger the second time. This time when she tugged on his arm, he couldn't fight her off.

She had him halfway out the door before he realized what was happening.

"Dan, you better disappear. Got it?" he yelled, still trying to pull away from Callie's strong pull. Damn it, how the hell was she so strong?

"Don't you dare turn those lights back—" Before he could finish, Callie had him outside. She gave him a hard push and he stumbled backward before she slammed the door and blocked it with her body so he couldn't get in.

"What the hell? Did you see what they were doing?"

Callie's head tipped to one side in disdain. "They were just making out."

"How do you know that's all they were doing?" he demanded. "On my mother's couch!"

She shrugged. "Their pants were still on. Mostly."

"Jesus. What am I supposed to do? If Mom and Dad were here, she'd be dead."

Callie's face softened, but she didn't let him move any closer to the door. "But you're not your mom or your dad and she is eighteen. It's kind of hypocritical to go in there and tell her she can't be making out with her boyfriend when you would have been doing the same thing at her age. *And* you were trying to do the exact same thing before you opened that door."

He shoved his hands into his pockets. "I don't give a damn if it's hypocritical. I'm responsible for her, and if she gets herself... Look, I don't know what kind of stuff Mom talked to her about. What if she doesn't know about..." Trevor grimaced. He couldn't force out the words.

"She's smart. I don't think you need to worry about it. And Dan, the guy is harmless."

"Yeah, your cousin wasn't exactly a Romeo bad ass when he got a girl knocked up at sixteen." He wanted to kick something, punch something. Preferably Dan, square in the thick, black glasses.

"You have to trust Shelby. She'll be at college in a week. That means no big brothers barging in on her make out session."

"Gee, thanks for that thought." He shoved fingers through his hair as his stomach pitched. "You have to talk to her." It

219

was a desperate plea.

Her practiced calm disappeared into wide-eyed shock. "I have to what?"

"You're a woman. You can talk about all that girl stuff. Birth control and self-respect and..." Trevor shuddered. "Whatever it is girls need to hear before they go around letting guys talk them into this sort of thing."

"Get a grip, Trevor."

"You have to do this for me. I can't do it. Knowing Mom she just told Shelby not to have..." He could say the word. Sure he could. "S-sex until she was married. And Dan's dad isn't around. Who knows what that kid knows."

"They're not Amish. I think they probably have a pretty good idea about birth control."

"If something happens, I'm responsible for it. Me. I don't get to pawn it off on Mom or Dad. There's no way in hell I'm going to let her make some kind of mistake."

Callie stepped toward him, patted his cheek. "Honey, you've lost it. Seriously."

"You have to talk to her." He grabbed her hands, desperately hopeful. He couldn't do this alone.

"Trev, I love you and all, but there's no way in hell I'm going to talk to your sister about sex."

Every angry thought flew out of his head. Every thought about Dan, Shelby, and his parents vanished. It all melted away as the words entered and rattled around in his brain. "What did you say?"

She shook her head, looking stricken as she dropped his hands. "That's not what I meant."

"It's not?"

"No, it's a saying. It wasn't... I wasn't... I don't..." She took a step away from him.

"Say it again, Callie." For every step she took away, he matched it with two toward her.

"You are crazy." She swallowed, looked around the front yard. "I do not... love you, Trevor." But she didn't look at him when she said it, and that had him smiling wider.

"Your sister is in there right now probably having sex." She pointed at the house, a last ditch effort to throw him off. Except, he didn't care at the moment. This trumped everything else.

"Say it again."

"I do not love you."

All that panic, if only he could find the source of it, the real reasons behind it. Then he might be able to get through to her. Because she did love him. He knew she did.

She had run out of space, so he had her trapped against the front door. Trevor reached out and touched her cheek. "Yeah, I do not love you either." When he pressed his mouth to hers, gently, sweetly, she didn't kiss him back at first.

Eventually she acquiesced and her arms came around his neck. Yeah, she loved him. He just had to find a way to make her really admit it.

"What about Shelby?" she murmured against his lips.

Trevor sighed and leaned his forehead to hers. For a long, humming moment he simply looked at Callie. Really looked at her. She was everything he wanted. If only he could get rid of her fear.

"I guess maybe I overreacted. A little. But she could have done it in a more private place."

"All those teenage hormones don't always allow you to think. Sometimes you do things you shouldn't."

Even though she was talking about teenage hormones, Trevor wondered if she was talking about Shelby and Dan.

"What am I supposed to do?"

"Give them some time to cool off. Then you go in and apologize. To both of them."

Trevor grimaced. He'd almost rather give Shelby a lecture about safe sex. "You sure you won't talk to her?"

"Positive. You really don't want to do it, throw some condoms in her room or something."

That sounded all too familiar. "I'm going to be sick."

"She's leaving soon. You don't have much of a choice if you're really this worried about it."

He moved onto the bench on the porch and sank onto it. "I officially hate this." It wasn't so bad when he could make jokes to Dan about his guns or argue with Shelby about curfews, but this big stuff? He was lost in it. A floundering idiot. A floundering idiot who missed his parents' guidance.

Callie sat next to him, but toward the edge so there was a space between them. "It sucks. But, that's life."

"That's the best you can do?" Even though it wasn't comforting, having her there was. How could he articulate that on to a list?

She smiled. "Sorry, pep talks aren't my specialty." She was quiet for a moment, then looked over at him. "Speaking of Shelby leaving. You haven't mentioned whether you're going back to Seattle or if you applied for a transfer."

Trevor shrugged. "Still thinking about it." Now wasn't the time to tell her he was staying. She was too unsure, unsteady. He still had some work to do. Call his boss in Seattle, call Sheriff Burns and see if he could get his old job back. Settle things before he told her, then she would know and understand he wasn't going anywhere.

"Don't you think you should make a decision? I'd think a transfer would take time if that's what you decided on."

Trevor looked at her, couldn't read all the emotions ranging across her face. There were too many and they were too complex to figure out. He took her hand in his, brushed his thumb across her knuckles. Maybe now wasn't such a bad time to tell her. Maybe in the midst of all this chaos would be the perfect moment to try and create an anchor.

"Callie—"

Dan burst out the door, Shelby on his heels.

"You don't have to go!"

"Bye, Shel. I'll call you tomorrow." Dan scurried away without looking anywhere near Trevor.

"You are such an ass," Shelby yelled, flinging her arms toward Trevor before storming in the house.

Callie patted his knee. "Go talk to her. I'm going to head home. I'll see you tomorrow, huh?"

"Yeah, leave me here to suffer."

She smiled, but it didn't reach her eyes. She didn't even bend down to kiss him before she was walking to her car.

When her car disappeared, Trevor felt like he was floating in an ocean all alone with only the hope somehow he could get through to the two crazy women in his life.

Chapter Twenty-One

Callie sat in her grandfather's office—actually now it was Lawson's office. Except, Lawson wasn't here right now so she was pretending nothing had changed, even though many of the piles had been cleared out and organized and the smell of cigars was so faint she really had to sniff to bring it to life.

Em and Law and the boys had all gone home for the evening, but Callie stayed. Desperate for some peace. Desperate for some answers.

She was coming up empty. Feelings drowned out thought, drowned out action. It was like the time after her grandmother's death when she'd been so overwhelmed with everything but hadn't figured out a way to channel it.

Booze and boys weren't an appropriate answer this time, and even throwing herself into her work didn't help as it had after Gramps's death. Now, wrapped up in her work were memories of Trevor and all he'd done to help over the summer.

Callie pulled her knees up to her chin and stared out the window at the black night. Black. It suited her mood.

Trevor had all but said he loved her. The "all but" being imperative to remember. Except of course he'd meant he loved her. And he did. That was the scary part. It wasn't something Trevor would lie about.

Even though in some distant part of her heart the knowledge warmed, her brain was on overdrive swimming through fear and panic and so many feelings she couldn't identify.

How could he love her? She was such a mess. Sure, a better mess than she had been years ago, but still. She'd never been in a real relationship before, and she was scared to death of losing anyone who meant anything to her because she knew over and over how hard it was to deal. She was scraping the bottom of the barrel of coping mechanisms. There wasn't much left to give.

Trevor was good and strong and perfect. He was smart. He was successful. He knew how to be around people and comfort and save. Maybe he made mistakes occasionally, but in her current mood she was having trouble giving those any play.

She'd never saved anyone or anything. At her best, she could listen to a person's problems. At her worst, she told them to go to hell. She was rude and cranky and not overly feminine. What was there to love?

That was the true source of the fear. It had been so easy to blame it on all the other factors and ignore this sharp pain, this sad, bleak truth.

She didn't think she was good enough.

That sounded pathetic. She was being pathetic. She couldn't crawl out of that self-pitying hole, and what she really wanted to do was talk to Em. No. Scratch that. Em would say exactly what Callie had no interest in hearing.

He loves you. You love him. Ask him to stay.

Hell no. The thought had the contents of her stomach threatening to revolt. How could she put her heart on the line when she knew it wasn't good enough?

"Callie?"

Her whole body jerked at the sound of Trevor's voice. When he appeared at the top of the stairs, she couldn't find her voice.

"Where the hell have you been? You were supposed to meet me in the shop a half hour ago."

She'd forgotten. Or last track of time or she didn't know. She hadn't been able to go down there and face him. Not with all the doubts and fears and insecurities plaguing her mind.

"Sorry."

He crossed over to the window seat, worry lines etched on his face. He wouldn't be angry. No, that wouldn't fit Trevor the Protector. Trevor had to be worried and sympathetic. "What's wrong?"

Callie shook her head, fought to find her voice. "Sorry. I was just thinking."

He slid next to her on the seat, and when he pulled her legs over his lap she nearly cried. Instead, she pulled her legs back and moved into a standing position. "We need to talk."

He frowned up at her. "I guess we do. I'd also guess whatever you want to talk about isn't something we're going to agree on."

"We can't do this anymore."

His frown deepened and he got to his feet. "Do *what* anymore?"

Callie swallowed, not daring to meet his intent gaze. Though panic seized her mind, urged her to get it all out, a piece of her heart jumped to her throat, blocked the words. She swallowed, croaked out one word. "This." She gestured between the two of them.

He was silent, completely silent. He stood there, staring at her. Callie turned away and hugged herself, but she couldn't stand the silence. "It's not working. It was a bad idea. It's... It's just..." Callie squeezed her eyes shut. It had been more than a week since she'd tried to explain things to Em and she never could get any further than that damn just word. "It's just not."

"It's just not?"

"Yeah."

"That's all you've got?" Worry was gone, and there was the anger she'd been looking for minutes earlier. It didn't make her feel any better. It didn't make her feel anything except less in control, less sure. She had to be sure.

"I don't know what you want me to say. I've told you all along that this was going to be temporary. It needs to be a little more temporary than we thought. Things got too..." Too what? Too good. Too comforting. Too scary and threatening and complicated.

"I love you, Callie."

She shook her head, dug her nails into her arms. "Don't." Her voice broke, but he was continuing anyway before she could beg him not to say it.

"And you love me."

Panic mixed with the sick feelings inside of her and she whirled to face him. "I never said that." When he narrowed his eyes, she turned around so her back was to him. "Not really."

"Bullshit." She couldn't remember a time she'd ever heard Trevor so angry, and she didn't know what to do about it. He wasn't supposed to be angry. Maybe hurt, maybe upset, but then he was supposed to understand and walk away. Not argue.

"You do love me, even if you're too chickenshit to really say it. You do even if you're being a total and utter moron right now."

Insult had her bristling through all the darkness inside her mind. She turned to face him again and mustered her best disdainful old Callie look. "Are you done?"

"Hell no, I'm not done." It exploded from his lips with such force Callie almost winced. "I won't be done until you get it through your head that this..." He gestured at the space between them. "This is it. This is what should be."

Callie tried to push past him to the stairs. She had to

escape, had to get away from his words and *him* and everything she felt, but his hand clamped on to her arm.

"Let me go."

"Let me *in.*"

She wrenched her arm away, barely resisted the urge to punch and pummel him. She resisted only because she was afraid of the tears and emotion that would come with the physical outburst.

She couldn't let her guard down.

"Trevor, I can't make this work. I'm sorry. It's not that big of a deal."

"Not that big of a deal." He looked at her like she was speaking a foreign language he didn't understand. Maybe she was. He looked at the world through his normal, rational mind. What could he possibly understand about all the flaws inside of her? "Have you lost your fucking mind?"

"You promised we could end this in September and still be friends." Callie was disgusted with herself when it came out sounding like she was begging. "I'm moving up the expiration date a little bit."

"I never promised a damned thing. What would it matter if I did?" He threw his arms into the air. "You don't believe in promises anyway."

"No, I don't." She clenched her hands into fists and gritted her teeth.

"Fine." He whirled away from her and headed for the stairs. He was halfway down them before her brain caught up.

"Fine? That's it?"

He stopped, turned to face her, and she'd never, ever seen him look so cold or emotionless before. "Yeah. Fine. You don't want to do this? Okay. You don't want to believe one fucking word that comes out of my mouth. Just fucking great. You think I'm going to beg? Screw you."

And then he stomped down the remaining steps and disappeared. Callie sank onto the floor. It took a few minutes for the tears to form, but once they did, there was no stopping them.

Rage was not an emotion Trevor was used to. It took a lot to get him going. It had made him a good cop, an excellent FBI agent. He'd been good at it because few things got under his skin.

So, the rage that had him stomping to his car, wrenching the driver's side door open, wasn't something he knew how to handle.

He knew Callie loved him. *Knew* it. That's why her trying to break things off was so damn infuriating. She was scared and panicked and if he could keep his cool he could talk her out of this whole stupid thing.

But he couldn't keep his cool. He couldn't hold on to his normal calm. What more did he have to do to prove to Callie that this was it? If she didn't feel it now, trust it now, believe it now, what the hell could he do to make that change?

Trevor sat in the driver's seat with the door still open and looked helplessly at the sky. It was black. No stars, no moon, just an eerie endless black. He knew he should shut the door and drive home, but when he went to dig his keys out of his pocket his hands were shaking.

What the fuck was happening to him? What was he letting her do to him? And why, damn it, why couldn't he just walk away and cut his losses?

"Trevor?"

He jumped a foot, swore, and thanked God he didn't carry

a weapon anymore because his finger would have been on the trigger at the surprise interruption.

"Sorry," Lawson offered, just barely illuminated by the interior light of Trevor's car. "Thought you heard me come up."

"No. I'm headed home."

"Right." Lawson stepped back. "See you later, man." He began to walk toward the office buildings, but before Trevor could put his key in the ignition, Lawson turned around and started talking.

"I don't like to stick my nose into other people's business," Lawson began, hesitantly walking toward the car. "But, I'm guessing by the fact that you looked like you could have killed me with your bare hands, you and Callie aren't exactly seeing eye to eye, and Em will kill me if she finds out I saw you here and didn't say anything."

"Why don't you go talk to Callie instead?"

Lawson snorted. "I know I was gone a long time, but I'm not stupid."

If Trevor wasn't still so pissed he would have laughed. Trying to get through to Callie *was* stupid. Why bother?

"Um, just, cut her some slack." At Trevor's muttered oath, Lawson rocked back on his heels. "You know as well as I do what she's been through. Shit like this is hard for her."

Trevor shook his head. "Life's been hard, but you know what? I'm not exactly sitting around with a full family table either. You don't see me running for the hills."

"Right, but..." Lawson let out a loud breath. "Jeez, I don't get why people like butting into other people's business. Look, it's not just losing her parents and Gramps and Grandma. It's not just about the death stuff. People walk away from her all the time."

"Lawson—"

"I know, maybe it's not an excuse, but I left. My parents moved away. Hell, she had a stepmother for four years and lost her too, although that was her own choice. The point is, aside from Em, no one's ever stuck for her, you know? Don't give up on her quite yet."

Trevor sighed. "I don't think I could if I wanted to, but she's got to let me in." That was all he wanted. He didn't want to walk away, didn't want to join the ranks that had deserted her, but a man could only do so much.

"Yeah, man. Just stick. She'll come around eventually."

The sound of a door opening and closing interrupted the sound of bugs and hoots of owls. He couldn't see through the dark that far, but he imagined Callie was on her way home.

Trevor shook his head. "I gotta go."

Lawson stepped back. "Yeah. See you around."

Trevor turned the key in the ignition. He was still mad, but the rage had weakened into something bearable. Could he stick with a woman who pushed him away at every damned turn?

Well, he'd come this far.

Callie stood in the dark. Even though she couldn't hear what they were saying she could see Trevor in his car and Lawson talking to him. She figured he'd be gone. She'd given him time to leave, hadn't she? Now he was just sitting there talking to Lawson like nothing had happened.

Callie sniffed, wiped her wet cheeks with the back of her hand. Finally, Lawson stepped back and Trevor drove away. She should walk home, leave it at that, but there was a whole hell of a lot of anger inside of her and nowhere to throw it.

"What did you talk to him about?" Callie called into the darkness.

"You, unfortunately."

"Stay out of my business. You have no right."

"I know I don't, but Em-"

"She doesn't have a right either." The tears were threatening again. Damn it. How was it possible there were more tears to shed?

"She's probably the only one that does. You know I don't like to meddle-"

"Then don't. You don't know a damn thing about my life." Em wanted her to break down walls? Em wanted her to *express* what she felt. Well, here was some damn expression for everyone.

"No, and I'll take partial responsibility for that." He sounded almost sad, almost apologetic, but then his voice hardened. "Partial."

"Fuck off, Lawson."

"You're the one who called me over here."

Callie shook her head, started to walk away. She wanted to be alone. She deserved to be alone. Where no one would care what she did or how badly she screwed up.

"I told him to cut you some slack." Law's voice rose over the distance. "And I told him he should stick."

More tears. Why didn't anyone understand? Why did everyone refuse to listen? Sticking wasn't possible. Not with her, not for her.

Chapter Twenty-Two

Shelby stood in front of the joint gravestone not sure what she should be feeling. She was leaving for college tomorrow. She was happy and excited and nervous and ready.

Why was she standing here in the midst of all this death? Even though their names were etched onto the stone with birth dates and death dates, her parents weren't here. Not really. She didn't feel them. Standing here, she felt empty and alone.

"Great minds think alike."

Shelby turned to see Trevor standing a few feet behind her. He looked like hell. Which suited the mood he'd been in the past few days. All dark and cranky and mopey. She'd finally figured out why on Friday during the AIF lunch. Em had made a big deal about having a kind of going away lunch for her and Dan, even though they'd likely be back for part of the fly-in. Shelby had been excited about it, until she'd noticed the current of tension running under everything.

Now it wasn't just Callie and Em ignoring each other, but Callie and Trevor had kept their distance too. The anger emanating off the pair had been like a physical being in the air. No one had known what to do about it except pretend everything was normal.

"Hey." She moved over so Trevor had some room in front of their parents' grave. "I guess I wanted to say goodbye." She looked at the gravestone. "That sounds stupid, doesn't it?"

He approached, rested his arm across her shoulders. "No, not at all."

Shelby studied Trevor out of the corner of her eye. They hadn't talked about his long-range plans after she left. Once he and Callie had gotten together, she'd been sure he'd be staying, but now? Now she wasn't so sure. "Are you saying goodbye?"

"No." His arm squeezed her shoulders. "I'm staying. For good."

"Even though you and Callie are fighting?"

"I'm not staying because of Callie. I'm staying because I want to." He fished something out of his pocket. "Here. Look. Someone might as well see this."

She took the piece of paper that had been folded over and over again so the creases were worn. Carefully, Shelby unfolded and studied it. In Trevor's messy scrawl, there were two lists. One with the positive points of Seattle/FBI life and the other with Pilot's Point.

Seattle had lots of things. Things Shelby could understand wanting. *Restaurants open 24 hours. Movies come out the week they're supposed to.* But they weren't important things. Not compared to what Trevor had for Pilot's Point. *Callie. Friday lunches at AIF. Shelby's cookies. Messing with Dan.* This list was about people, not things.

Shelby didn't have any words. She stared at the list, her eyes filling with tears. Trevor's arm squeezed around her shoulders again.

"I owe you a thank you because I'm not sure I would have really thought about what it would mean to stay if you hadn't asked me to after graduation. It's hard to believe I'm saying this, but I think I'll be happier here."

Strange those pathetic words were the moment that had turned the tides for him when she'd spent so much time and effort trying to trick him into staying.

Shelby blinked back the threat of tears, cleared her throat

so she could speak. "Only if you and Callie get back together."

"No. No, I could still be happy here."

"Look at this list." Shelby held it out to him. "Yeah, you've got a lot of great stuff that isn't Callie, but there's very little she hasn't touched."

He stared down at it, let out an unsteady breath. "Maybe. Look, you're leaving tomorrow. I don't want to think about Callie and all her drama right now."

"You love her, don't you?" She had seen it, hadn't she? The way they looked at each other, the way they were together. Like a unit. Even when they argued, a clear thread tied them together. It reminded Shelby of their parents. They had had that.

One day she hoped to have it too. Maybe even with Dan.

Trevor frowned, obviously not happy she wasn't letting this go. "Yeah."

Feeling a little sorry for him and how miserable he looked, Shelby turned to look at her mother's grave. "God, Mom would hate that."

It produced a little bit of a laugh, so it was a start. "She really would."

Shelby leaned her head into Trevor's side. "She would have been wrong though. Really wrong. I was wrong for a long time about her. You fit."

"Thanks, Shelby." His arm squeezed around her shoulders. "That means a lot."

They stood there, arm in arm for a few minutes. Shelby was lost in the past eighteen years, and dreams of what her future held. The fact her parents wouldn't be there to support her all the way.

But Trevor's arm was on her shoulders and he was staying. He'd found his link to Pilot's Point. More than guilt, more than her.

Shelby took a deep breath. It sucked and she would always, *always* miss her parents, but she was doing all right. She would keep doing better.

"Let's go home, order some pizza, pack up the car. We've got an early start tomorrow."

Shelby nodded and let Trevor lead her to the parking lot. Trevor moved toward his car, but stopped before he got in. "Got any grand ideas on how to convince the crazy woman I'm in love with to be with me?" He smiled when he said it, but anyone could tell he was hurting.

"Be you, Trevor. You stick and you're always there. Eventually, you'll get through to Callie. You just unfortunately picked an incredibly stubborn person to fall in love with."

"Stick, huh? I've been hearing that a lot lately." He frowned, stared at the ground. "I wasn't always there for you."

Shelby thought about that. She'd accused him of such in as many words, but she didn't feel that anger she once had. "Maybe you weren't supposed to be. Anyway, you've more than made up for it."

Before she could move toward her car, he pulled her into a hug. "I'm going to miss you."

Tears threatened again, but she didn't let them fall. "I'm going to miss you too." She smiled into his chest. "But you'll see a lot of me. And next summer? You'll be wishing you moved far away."

He chuckled and gave her one last squeeze. "Yeah right. If you're still with Dan, I'll barely see you."

Shelby smiled at the thought of still being with Dan a year from now. She sure hoped so.

"Look, uh, you know, in college there are certain temptations."

She pushed him away. "Oh my God. Stop trying to talk to me about sex. You're terrible at it and I'm not an idiot. I won't do anything stupid."

"Promise?"

The genuine worry on his face made her smile. "I promise. As long as you promise to never, *ever* bring it up again."

"Gladly."

Shelby stepped away from Trevor and to her car. Tomorrow she'd be stepping away in a very big, very real way. It was scary, horribly nerve-wracking, but she was ready for it. She was ready to take that big step toward adulthood, because Trevor, and a whole bunch of other people would be there to help her when she stumbled.

She wasn't alone.

Chapter Twenty-Three

Callie sat on the porch staring into the sunset. Before Grandma died, they used to sit on the same exact swinging loveseat and rock gently together watching the sky bloom in color. Callie couldn't remember the last time she'd wished for Grandma's presence so much, so painfully.

She needed advice, guidance, and someone to tell her everything would be okay. Callie squeezed her eyes shut. That was stupid. No one could tell her that, and even when someone did, she didn't listen.

She was two parts angry, three parts sad, and four parts who knew what. Her mind was in a fog and she didn't know what to do. Especially with the fly-in starting tomorrow when there'd be hard work, long days, and little sleep.

Something had to give before the first visitors showed up.

Callie opened her eyes when she heard the door squeak. Em stepped out onto the porch. Instead of the disdainful frown she'd been getting from Em the past few weeks, Em offered a smile.

"Hey."

Callie swallowed. "Hey." She didn't have Grandma anymore. Or Gramps or Dad, or maybe even Trevor, but she had Em. Even when they fought, even when Callie had been a screw up of epic proportions, Em had never let her down. It was high time Callie remembered that.

Em glided over to the loveseat and slid next to Callie. She looked out at the sun, pressed her foot against the floorboards to send the swing rocking. "How's it going?"

Callie shook her head. "How do you do that?"

"Do what?"

"We've been pissed at each other for weeks now, and you can just come out here and ask how I'm doing because I'm a wreck."

Em turned to face her, their father's blue eyes staring at Callie. "You're my sister. I love you. I can only stand so much of you being a wreck before I start to feel sorry enough for you to ignore the pissed off part."

Callie's throat tightened, so she looked away, back out at the colorful clouds. She tried not to let that make her feel like less. "I'm glad one of us can do that, because I never would in your position."

"That's not true," Em said gently. "You're too hard on yourself."

Callie frowned. It wasn't something she was used to hearing. After all, she'd spent most of her life being too easy on herself. "I'm not."

Em waved her off. "Do you really think the past two years hasn't changed you?"

"No, I've changed but—"

"Don't but it. You've changed. You've grown, matured, and become a better person. Sometimes I get the feeling you still think of yourself as that person who couldn't control herself, who was so lost in her own hurt she couldn't deal with anyone else's. That's not you anymore."

Callie leaned back in the chair and let out a whoosh of breath. She'd known that. Hadn't she? It felt like such a revelation. Such a weight off her shoulders. Maybe she had known it, but it hadn't quite reached that inner part of realization yet.

Well, shit.

They sat in silence for a long time. The world around them got darker, the trees first, and then the ponds in the distance, until darkness closed in. The scent of clover hung on the air, insects hummed, a few birds called to each other.

It was the kind of moment Callie always loved as a kid. There was something centering and calming about the sounds, the smells, the way the whole world felt, and she so rarely felt that calm or centeredness.

Callie stared into the darkness in the distance. "I guess you were right."

"I usually am."

"I don't know." Callie shook her head and swallowed. "It's stupid, isn't it, that I'm sitting here miserable when I could go over there and fix things?"

"Very."

Callie put a hand to her stomach. "But the thought of it makes me want to vomit."

"It must be love, then."

"But, what if—"

Em stopped rocking the seat and faced Callie. "Don't start that. It won't help anything, not the way you play what if. You play negative what if where you imagine all the horrible things that could happen, all the ways you could hurt each other or be miserable. Well, you're doing both right now so what's the point? Maybe you should try a positive what if."

"A positive what if?"

"Yeah, like what if you go make things right with Trevor and he forgives you and you end up building a relationship that lasts. *The* relationship. The big old till death do you part."

Callie pressed the hand to her stomach harder. "I really am going to throw up."

"Suck it up. You know if you go over there right now, Trevor isn't going to slam the door in your face. Look at everything he's done because of you. He's changed his *whole* life."

"But I don't want him to!"

"Screw what you want. That's what he did. Because he wanted to be with you. You haven't done a whole lot to show him you want to be with him. Your turn."

"But—"

Em put her arms around Callie and squeezed. "That ends my advice, sis. The rest is up to you."

Em stood, walked toward the door. "I love you, Callie. You're better than you think you are or give yourself credit for. I wish you could see that. Trevor and I do."

Em disappeared into the cabin, and though Callie still felt parts angry and sad and unsure, there was a little seed of light blooming in her chest. A warmth, a sureness, a belief.

A positive what if. What if she could be stronger than she had been? What if all the changes she'd made in the past two years were enough or, if they weren't, they were good enough that with the right support she would get there?

Negative what ifs threatened. What if she did all that and it still wasn't enough? What if Trevor changed his mind?

Callie shoved to her feet, her hands curling into fists as if she could physically fight the negative what ifs.

One last what if, neither positive nor negative just a plain old what if. What if she went to talk to Trevor and they figured it out? Together.

Trevor sat on the couch in the darkened room. He knew he should turn on the TV, but he couldn't quite muster the effort.

The house was like a tomb. Dark and stark and empty. It wasn't really empty, but without anyone else living there with him it felt empty. His mother's white, ruthless style haunted him.

He scowled. This was his house now. It didn't have to feel that way. He didn't have to keep it as some sort of shrine to his parents' lives. No, if he was living here, and he was, it needed to be his.

He didn't think Shelby would mind. It would still be the home she'd always lived in, it just wouldn't look exactly the same inside. It would be warmer, cozier. Probably a hell of a lot messier.

Trevor stood up, determined to start immediately. Only, he didn't have any idea where to start. He couldn't rip up the white carpet or paint the white walls at nine o'clock on a Wednesday night. It would be stupid to get rid of furniture when he didn't have any to replace it.

Feeling impotent and angry, Trevor clenched his hands into fists. This was not supposed to be what staying felt like. It was supposed to be good, and he supposed once he got back to work it would be, but he had to wait until October to get a spot at county.

He wished he could be excited about the fly-in. It had been years since he'd been to one, and he'd never been on the other side, working, helping out. He'd always been a bystander. Now, he'd be in the thick of things, and he'd be miserable because somehow he'd let Callie make him that way.

No more. Nope. She wasn't ready to get over all her insecurities, well, he'd done all he could. He'd stuck, and she just... It didn't matter. Not anymore.

Before he could sit down and settle in with a baseball game, a knock sounded on the door.

Every other time this week a knock had sounded, he'd been so sure it was Callie. Each and every time he had been disappointed. Mail lady, salesperson, neighbor kid. It never was the one person he wanted to see.

It seemed appropriate the one time he didn't expect Callie on the other side of the door, that's exactly who would be standing there.

She held up a hand in an awkward wave. "Hi."

Though hope was the first emotion, it was quickly tempered by anger and irritation. "Hi." She didn't say anything else. He didn't say anything else. They stood staring at each other.

"Can I come in?"

Trevor crossed his arms over his chest, leaned against the side of the door, blocking entrance. "Depends."

"On?" There was no snap or spark to her response, which was a little unsettling.

"What you want to talk about when you come in."

She looked down at her tennis shoes. "Um, well, the fly-in starts tomorrow."

"Wrong answer." He stepped back and slammed the door in her face. Maybe it was childish to feel some satisfaction in the action, but after everything that had happened between them she didn't have the right to come in and pretend she wanted to talk about the damned fly-in.

Satisfaction quickly melted into doubt, because she didn't knock again. He stood staring at the door as seconds ticked by in a dark, oppressive silence. Trevor shoved his hands into his pockets, hoping the physical action would prevent him from giving into the impulse to open the damn door back up.

He didn't believe she would walk away. He didn't believe she had really come to talk about the fly-in either. There was no way one slammed door in her face would make her turn around, give up, and walk away. The Callie he knew was a hell of a lot stronger than that.

Except she hadn't looked it, standing on the porch all unsure and uncomfortable. There'd been no battle light in her expression, no glimpse of what core strength she relied on.

He was not going to give in to guilt. Not over this. He had nothing to feel guilty about. If Callie was messed up, that was not his fault. He'd fought, he'd pushed, he'd put it all out on the line, and she'd thrown it in his face. No way he'd crumble now.

Except he hadn't put it *all* out on the line. He hadn't told her he'd quit the FBI or talked to Sheriff Burns. He hadn't told her no matter what happened between them, Pilot's Point was his home again.

She'd find out soon enough. It really didn't have any bearing on what they were fighting about anyway.

Trevor's fingers tapped in his pockets. Maybe he should open the door to see if she'd left. If she hadn't, he could just close it again. Or yell at her to leave. Or pull her into his arms and—

Nope. No safe way to go down that road. He was going to walk right over to the couch and watch the ballgame and ignore she'd ever showed up on his doorstep.

Except before he could manage the action of moving away from the door, a knock sounded on it. No, not a knock. An insistent, hard banging that practically shook the front of the house.

He reached out, opened the door, working up his best look of detached calm. "What?"

"Slamming the door in my face was completely unnecessary and a dick move to boot." Her hands were clenched into fists, and her eyes squinted in frustrated anger. There was the battle light, the core strength.

The image warmed his heart. "Yeah, well, maybe I feel like getting in a few dick moves."

Without hesitation, she pushed past him into the house. "I'm coming in and we're going to talk."

Trevor slammed the door, this time with Callie on the inside. "Oh, we're going to talk?"

"Yes."

"About what? AIF? The weather? Maybe you'd like to discuss politics."

"I... We..." She stopped, flustered enough some of the anger left her face and confusion took over. "It's..." She shook her head, straightened, lifted her chin and looked him directly in the eye. "I'm sorry."

Like hell she was getting off that easy. "For what?"

She kept eye contact, but he noticed that her hands shook briefly before she clasped them together.

"For the other night."

"I'm afraid you'll have to be more specific."

She took a deep breath, but her eyebrows slanted farther down, her frown slashing deeper lines in her face. "When I broke things off. When I told you I couldn't do this." She shook her head, looked miserable. "I was wrong."

Even though sympathy was threatening to take over, Trevor held on to the icy calm. "Why were you wrong?"

"Because..." This time her voice shook along with her hands, and she dropped her eyes to the floor. "Because I love you." She looked up at him, brown eyes reflecting both fear and hope, and a part of him nearly gave into the need to cross over to her, kiss her, and tell her he loved her too.

Not yet. There was still work to be done, things to be sorted out. "I already knew that."

It obviously wasn't the answer she was expecting because

her brows bunched together and she looked down at her clutching hands. "Okay."

"Give me something more."

She nodded and met his gaze again. Even though tears shone in her eyes, she didn't shed them. Instead, she squared her shoulders, clutched her hands hard, and stared right at him. "I want you to stay."

That wasn't the response he'd been expecting. After all the time she'd spent talking about how he belonged in Seattle, about how he couldn't be happy in Pilot's Point, even now in the midst of her apology he hadn't expected such simple powerful words. He didn't have a comment, negative or otherwise. He simply stared.

"You probably already made your decision, and I'll support any of them." Her voice cracked a little, but she didn't look away and the tears didn't fall. "But, if you want to know what I want. I *want* you to stay. Even though it scares the hell out of me."

There it was, the words he'd wanted to hear. The words that would soothe every last doubt in the corners of his mind. She wanted him to stay. *Wanted* it. "I am staying. I made all the arrangements. Quit the FBI, got my stuff in Seattle settled away. I start back at county in October." Though he said it mechanically, the emotion was there in his face.

She nodded, blinked a few times. "Okay. That's good."

Trevor had to laugh, even if it felt a little hollow. "You sound less than enthusiastic."

"I." She bit down on her lip, looked to the ceiling. "Did it ever occur to you I couldn't be what you want me to be? That I'm not capable of doing this, this us thing?"

"No." Never. No matter how many times she'd hinted around that idea, he'd never been able to really believe it.

Maybe he should have known her well enough to know underneath all that strength was a crushing sense of self-doubt, and even if it hadn't occurred to him, it had occurred to her. "You're stronger than you give yourself credit for. You seem to focus only on where you falter, but there are a million ways you don't."

He stepped forward. "You were there for Shelby's graduation, even when I fell apart. That day you made me take a nap in Fred's office. A million ways, Callie, where you've been the strength I needed and couldn't muster on my own."

She swallowed again. "Em said basically the same thing." She cleared her throat. "Without the specific examples."

"At what point are you going to start listening to us?"

"I'm trying." The first tear fell and it about broke his heart, but he didn't move. If he touched her now, he'd have to kiss her. And he wouldn't want to stop.

"It's just you," she said in a squeaky voice. "There's a part of me that always wanted this, and I don't know how to make that any less scary. In my life, I very rarely have gotten what I truly wanted. I'm sorry it's so hard to believe it when it's right in front of me."

The last remains of bitterness fell away. When he took the last step toward her, more tears began to fall onto her cheeks. He reached out, brushed them away, framed her face with his hands.

"Believe me, Callie. Believe in us." He pressed his mouth to hers, tried to make it a promise she could believe in. "I love you."

Her hands clung to his arms and she met his eyes. "I love you too."

She buried her face into his shoulder, wrapped her arms around him and held on. "I'm still going to be scared sometimes," she said into his shirt. "You'll have to bear with me and not get pissed when I do."

"Then you'll have to trust me enough to tell me you're scared. And not try to push me away so I have to get pissed at you."

She sniffled. "I guess that's fair."

"And you have to believe in promises." He pulled her back, studied her tear-streaked face. "And a future."

"Okay, but then you have to..." She trailed off, frowning. "Damn it, I can't come up with anything else."

He laughed, a real, happy laugh, and then captured her mouth with his, losing himself in the kiss.

Epilogue

Callie had never been so ready for a fly-in to end. Between the normal sleep deprivation that came with putting on a weeklong annual event and spending a little too much time in Trevor's bed, Trevor's shower, and maybe they'd finally managed it up against the cabin front door, she was bone-deep exhausted.

When she went to check on the Stearman only to find the For Sale sign missing again, what she really wanted to do was crawl into the plane and sleep and worry about selling the damn thing another day.

Until she saw Trevor standing on the other side of the plane, deep in conversation with one of AIF's longtime members. Something that resembled a For Sale sign folded in half was shoved into his back pocket.

She might love the man, but he was about to get in some very deep shit if he didn't have a decent explanation.

She marched toward the pair, and the minute Trevor saw her he angled his body so his back was out of sight. *Yeah, too late buddy.*

Callie sidled next to Trevor and gave a bright smile to George. "How's it going, George? You have a good fly-in this year?"

"I tell ya' what, you should have brought Lawson home years ago. This is the best fly-in you guys have put on since Fred passed."

She fought to keep her smile in place and ignore the slight.

A lot of the old guard seemed to think AIF had needed a man at the helm for it to get back on track. That was great for donations and all, but it meant Callie had spent a lot of the fly-in biting her tongue.

Trevor's arm came around her waist. "Lawson's a great addition to AIF, but Callie and Em did most of the work this year. Lawson couldn't get away from California until mid-summer."

George nodded, but his attention was already elsewhere.

"Well, it's a shame you're not selling the Stearman, Callie. You do good work and I sure wouldn't mind getting my hands on this one." George looked at the plane wistfully, and just as Callie was about to open her mouth and say that it *was* for sale, Trevor's hand clamped on her shoulder and began leading her away.

"We'll see you later, George," he offered, turning her around.

"Trevor, am I going to have to kill you? I'd hate to have it end that way, but you seem to be messing with my livelihood here."

"Your livelihood is fine. Em told me that the fly-in will put you even and AIF doesn't need the money from selling it this year. She admitted it might be nice to do some expanding, but it's not necessary."

She stopped in her tracks and shrugged Trevor's hand off her shoulder. "Are you nuts? What business is it of yours to go behind my back and talk to Em about this?"

"Well." Trevor rubbed the back of his neck sheepishly. "It's just, I've been thinking."

She had to remind herself that she loved the guy or she was going to give him a black eye. "You better start making some sense."

"I want to have kids with you."

"You *what?*" She wasn't sure he could have said anything else more confusing and more out of the blue.

"Hold on a sec." He dashed away, and Callie thought maybe the exhaustion was finally getting to her. This was some kind of waking dream, a hallucination. Trevor went over to where Shelby and Dan were working a drink stand and consulted with the pair.

Across the short distance Callie couldn't hear their conversation, but she could see Shelby break out in a wide grin and dash off around the building toward the parking lot.

Trevor walked back, but he did so slowly. Callie tried to remember she was pretty sure she was hallucinating, or she was going to scream.

"I'm about seventy-five percent sure I can fight you off, but I'd rather not take the chance. Please don't try to beat me up."

"What the hell is going on?" Callie demanded through gritted teeth.

"I've been thinking. A lot these past few days. I got to thinking that we might as well go ahead and get married."

Callie reached out for something to hold on to for balance. All this hallucinating was about to make her faint. Except there was nothing to hold, until Trevor took her hand.

"If we get married, we'll have kids. If we have kids, one, if not all of them, are going to inherit the psychotic part of your brain that thinks riding around in a tiny contraption thousands of feet above the ground is a good idea. So, you're not selling the Stearman."

"I'm not?"

"Er, okay, let me rephrase. It wouldn't be the best idea for you to sell the Stearman. It means a lot to you and it would be nice if it was around for those inevitably crazy children." He

251

flashed his best charming smile. "Please."

Shelby scurried up to him and dropped a velvet box in Trevor's hand. Callie blinked a few times, gave in and sank onto the grass, letting Trevor's hand slip through her fingers. "This is a dream, right? I'm losing my mind."

He crouched next to her and opened the box to a simple silver band dotted with white sparkling gems. "Afraid not."

"Okay." Callie took a deep breath, let it out. "This isn't too fast?"

"I've known you my whole life. I wouldn't say it's too fast."

"Okay." The word kept repeating in her head and she tried to focus over all the feelings roaring through her mind.

"Going to let me put it on?" He just kept *smiling* like this was the most normal thing to be doing.

"Okay." He took her hand in his and slid the silver band onto her finger. She stared down at it, tried to come up with a joke so she didn't give in to the impulse to cry. "Not much of a rock, is it?"

Trevor chuckled. "Figured that wasn't your style."

"No. No, it isn't." Finally she managed the courage to look up at Trevor. He looked so sure, that stupid cocky grin on his face. If he was sure, maybe she could be too.

She reached up and touched his face. "Getting married as in wedding, white dress, tux, the whole bit?"

"Kind of what I had in mind. And then, the best part."

"What's that?"

"The rest of our lives, together." He pulled her onto her feet, and then into the circle of his arms. "I love you."

She leaned against his warm strength, felt it melt away much of the panic. And the panic that was left was manageable. "I love you."

No matter what happened, she'd believe in this amazing promise.

About the Author

Nicole Helm grew up with her nose in a book and a dream of becoming a writer. Luckily, after a few failed career choices, a husband, and two kids, she gets to pursue that dream. There is nothing Nicole enjoys more than writing about strong women and the handsome men who win their hearts.

Nicole lives in Missouri with her husband and two sons, and writes her novels one baby's nap at a time. She's slightly (okay, totally) addicted to Twitter (@nicolethelm), loves watching the St. Louis Cardinals, and, much to her husband's dismay, just about any reality competition show.

You can contact her via email: NicoleTHelm@gmail or visit her website: nicolehelm.wordpress.com.

She'd be the perfect catch if he could take his eye off the ball.

Pitch Perfect
© *2013 Sierra Dean*
Boys of Summer, Book 1

Emmy Kasper knows exactly how lucky she is. In a sport with few opportunities for women at the pro level, she's just landed her dream job as head athletic trainer for the San Francisco Felons baseball team. Screwing up is not an option.

She's lost in thought as she pedals to the spring training facility, her mind abuzz with excitement as she rounds a corner—and plows head-on into two runners. The end of her career dances before her eyes when she realizes she's almost run over the star pitcher.

As Tucker Lloyd watches the flustered Emmy escape with his bandana tied around her skinned knee, the view is a pleasant change from worrying about his flagging fastball. At thirty-six, the tail end of his career is glimmering on the horizon. If he can't pull something extraordinary out of his ball cap, the new crop of rookies could make this season his last.

The last thing either of them needs is a distraction.

The last thing either of them expects is love.

Warning: Contains a down-on-his-luck pitcher, a good-girl athletic therapist, chemistry that's out of the park and sexy times that'll make them round all the bases.

Available now in ebook from Samhain Publishing.

PUBLISHING

It's all about the story...

Romance

HORROR

www.samhainpublishing.com

CPSIA information can be obtained at www.ICGtesting.com
Printed in the USA
LVOW11s1121030814

397294LV00006B/697/P